CW01638491

**The CULLEN books by Mark Farrer (in chronological order):**

Dirty Barry

Where Seagulls Dare

Bronchial Billy

A Fistful Of Collars

Pale Ale Rider

The Good The Bad & The Rugby

# BASE COWBOYS

mark farrer

funny business press

BASE COWBOYS



ISBN: 978-1-9164892-2-6

Published by Funny Business Press

*To Karen*
*For flying to the rescue.*

*This is a work of fiction.*
*Names, characters, places and incidents either are products of the author's imagination or are used fictitiously.*
*Any resemblance to actual events or locales or persons, living or dead, is entirely coincidental.*
*Except for Big Paul.*

## CONTENTS

# FOREWORD

This is a new book that is a collection of old books.

I know. Sorry.

But I thought if I put it right up front, I won't get complaints about mis-selling or fraudulently passing off old material as new material. So, if you have read the following three novellas: *Dirty Barry, Bronchial Billy* and *Pale Ale Rider* then there is nothing new for you here.

Apart from this foreword. This is all new.

So, what's the deal?

Well, I get asked questions all the time. Questions, questions, questions. So many damned questions. The most popular question is usually why? Why am I writing, why have I written another one, why a novella? On and on with the questions. Now, usually, I let them wash over me. Leave them guessing; be enigmatic. Smile. Like that.

But, for once, I thought I'd answer them. So here goes:

### *What's a novella and why have you done three?*

A novella is a posh word for a book that is too long to be a short story and not long enough to qualify as a novel. My novels are typically in the 90-100,000 words range; a short story, for me, would be less than 10,000 words. So a novella is something in between these two.

The three novellas contained in this volume are all around the 25,000 word mark and take me roughly two months to write - this compares favourably with the eight or nine months it takes me to complete a novel. So, the first answer to this question is that novellas are a whole lot easier and quicker to write.

Second answer is that they started out as an experiment. *Dirty Barry*, my first novella, was originally written to be given away free – to entice readers into Cullen's world. I didn't want to spend 7-8 months of my life writing a novel only to give it away for nothing, but I was prepared to invest a couple of months.

And I enjoyed it.

And the third answer is I wondered if novellas could act as "filler" stories which fitted in between the novels. So I wrote two more and, now, I am considering continuing this pattern for every novel I write.

True, they haven't worked out as I expected: I thought they would bridge a gap between the end of one novel and the start of the next. But they don't.

All the same, they have allowed me to flesh the character of Cullen out more, reveal more of his backstory and let some of the minor characters from the novels breathe again.

So, in short: they're fun! They are also a pain in a way which novels aren't. But you don't need to bother yourselves with that. I am thinking of doing more and will continue to publish them as I have with these three: individually as E-books only, and then collected together in three's as a paperback.

***So, where do all these stories fit in the Cullen canon?***

Ooh, get you. Canon!

Well the novels were written first and form the

backbone of the series, so they are numbered #1 to #3, starting with *Where Seagulls Dare.*

But *Dirty Barry* is an origin story (even though it doesn't tell Cullen's backstory but Paul's, and how the pair first met). So, that makes it book #0.5 in the series!

Then comes *Where Seagulls Dare.* (#1)

Then there is a short story called *Woof Justice* which picks up right after *Where Seagulls Dare* ends, and is only available if you join the Cullen & Big Paul Fan Club, at **http://download.markfarrer.com/seagulls**.

Then *Bronchial Billy* comes next (#1.5), before *A Fistful Of Collars* (#2) - although the only indication of this chronology is that Paul hasn't met Shirley yet.

*Pale Ale Rider* (#2.5) comes after that and takes place almost immediately before the events in *The Good, The Bad & The Rugby* (#3).

Next will be *Lay Misty For Me* (#4) and then there will be another novella, currently untitled, which occurs between novels #3 and #4, so it will be #3.5!

No, it's not confusing.

But Amazon won't let me number my books with decimal places, so this numbering scheme is just between you and me. And, you know, the chronology detail is minor and I think there is just as much fun to be had reading them in the order they were written.

Of course, YMMV.

### *Why the title 'Base Cowboys'?*

Well, one definition of the word *base* refers to immoral, low or dishonest behaviour – and the bad guys in each of these novellas show one, two or all three of those things. And because they are also reckless, careless or aggressive – qualities associated with the modern-day usage of cowboy in such phrases as *cowboy builders*.

*Dirty Barry* is an immoral dentist who blackmails married women; *Bronchial Billy* is a choleric pensioner, a miserable husband and a slum landlord; and Tyler, the baddie in *Pale Ale Rider*, is an amoral teenage thief with the eyes of a serial killer.

But, all that said, let's face it - it's just a great pun on another Clint Eastwood film title.

***Ok. So why are all your book titles puns on Clint Eastwood films?***

Because Cullen, is a lone anti-hero. A former Police Detective with a strict moral code who sleeps rough in the bothies, abandoned buildings and barns across the Scottish Borders. He is self-contained and content with a solitary existence, living and remaining off-the-grid. Unfortunately, the world he is hiding from seems unwilling to leave him alone and he keeps finding himself embroiled in immoral or unjust events.

So, he is the archetypal loner: resourceful and capable, able to take on injustice, deal with it calmly and effectively, and then disappear without fuss. He is a kind of Scottish man-with-no-name (as in the Clint Eastwood westerns) - albeit without a horse - who rides into town, rights a wrong and then rides off into the sunset.

That's why.

***Gotcha. So, why are these novellas all named after the bad guys?***

Well, firstly because they are the most interesting and enjoyable characters to write! I have heard many actors say similar things about playing bad guys – it allows them let their hair down and they can relish those roles like no other. So, maybe it's something like that.

Or maybe it's just because I had some spare Eastwood movie title's going unused and I hate waste.

Yeah, maybe that.

***Ok. Final question: will I learn more about Cullen by reading these stories?***

Actually, yes. Quite a lot more than I originally intended, in fact.

*Dirty Barry* is not so much an origin story – there's an origin story of Cullen to be told, one day, but Dirty Barry isn't it - but it does tell you probably all you need to know (and maybe more than you want to know!) about Big Paul.

*Bronchial Billy* hints at the traumatic events in Cullen's past which go some way to explaining why he is the way he is, and give a few clues as to what those events might be.

*Pale Ale Rider* does the same but also touches on Cullen's frailties. He is only human after all, and things don't always go the way he plans.

Anyway. That's enough questions! Read the bloody book why don't you? And, if you enjoy it, leave a review on Amazon or, better yet, join the Cullen & Big Paul Fan Club so you can read the *Woof Justice* freebie, and get first drop on new Cullen stories in future.

mjf
2.7.2019

# DIRTY BARRY

mark farrer

funny business press

Published by Funny Business Press

*To Paul*
*For putting up with it.*

*This is a work of fiction.*
*Names, characters, places and incidents either are products of the author's imagination or are used fictitiously.*
*Any resemblance to actual events or locales or persons, living or dead, is entirely coincidental.*
*Except for Big Paul.*

## CONTENTS

# PART ONE

## THE TOOTH

# ONE

The man in the cowboy hat stood in the shop doorway trying not to stand on the cheese.

"Come in! Shut the door." Archie fussed. "Not quite open yet." Cullen closed the door behind him and slid into the shop, surveying the interior: shelves still being stocked, half-unpacked cardboard boxes scattered across the floor. Cheeses, large and small, everywhere.

"Mind!" Archie warned as Cullen dripped onto the newly-laid wooden flooring. He was wearing a battered leather cowboy hat, currently dark brown, saturated as it was with heavy rain donated gratis by the Scottish Borders weather. His waterproof was a dirty lime green, with a rip in one shoulder and heavy stain below the right pocket; similarly rain-soaked camo pants clung to his legs and dripped onto the tops of brown leather walking boots that had seen better days. He stood there, staring into the middle-distance - like a horse taking a long piss - while Archie weighed him up.

Cullen stood a smidge over six foot with a relaxed, muscular ease and a detached bearing. The clothes might have said shambolic but the stance and gait told a different story. His grey eyes were alert and sparkled in the thin overhead lighting and, as he turned his head to scan the shop, Archie could see a broken nose, clean jawline and strong forehead, creased and lined; few laughter lines around the eyes. Wisps of salt-and-pepper hair curled untidily beneath the brim of his hat which was jammed onto his head rather unceremoniously, forcing his ears outward so that they stuck out rudely.

"Come through, come through!" Archie waved Cullen into the back room, peering out through the window nervously. On the counter was a large wodge of paper carrier bags, still wrapped in cellophane, which bore the legend: *A B Cheese Ltd* and underneath, in a different font, *Goodness Graters Me.*

The two men passed into a narrow corridor which turned sharply left then right and opened out into a dark, cold space with walls of bare brick and stone. Archie threw the switch which jolted four strip-lights high above them into stuttering life. They illuminated a large storeroom containing several rows of slatted wooden racks, tiered from floor to ceiling, some fifteen feet high. The racks were arranged down the room like shelves in a library, with space to move between each one and a ladder at each end to allow access to the top two or three sets of shelves. Each shelf was full of rounds, wheels, cubes, slabs and enormous portions of cheese.

Cullen scanned the setup and wrinkled his nose at the rank mixture of aromas infiltrating his nostrils.

"What do you think, hmm?" Archie gestured proudly, surveying his stock. "Best selection of cheeses North of the border by a mile. Thousands of pounds' worth here in the room. Thousands!"

"Huh." Cullen said.

Archie scowled and busied himself with the loose ends of a string which had been holding a set of Jarlsberg wheels together in a pile. He was a small, delicate man, with narrow face and dark-brown eyes, and a shock of grey hair which almost stood on end. This, combined with his rapid movements, made him look a bit like a Great Crested Grebe. He looked around at Cullen, curious.

"Where's your... weapon?"

"Don't do weapons." Cullen shrugged, scanning the storeroom. "What's here?"

Archie's face fell and a sudden panic gripped him. "You never said that!" He looked Cullen up and down, worried. "Hand-to-hand combat, is that it?"

"Last resort." Cullen huffed, pulling himself up onto one of the ladders and testing the sturdiness of the ceiling-height rack.

"Great." Archie put his hands on his hips. "Mr Resourceful then, is it? This is my livelihood we're talking about here!"

"Be fine." Cullen answered, eyes creased in thought. "Any other exits?"

"Be fine? Listen, if you can't catch this bloke, I may as well not open for business at all! No, the one we've just come in through and that back door there, all there is." Archie pointed to a black wooden door bearing a large Fire Exit sign. "That's the way he must be getting in and out. Got an alarm out front. Fitter's coming back Tuesday to do this back one."

"Hmm." Cullen looked down from his perch onto Archie. "Should have got 'em done the other way round."

"Yeah. Thanks, Mister Hindsight. Look, none of this is... my area of expertise. My area of expertise is cheese!"

"Hmm." Cullen repeated, absently, sucking his teeth in thought. "Maybe we can use your expertise then."

"What, you gonna do? Kill him with a cheese?"

"No-one said anything about killing anyone." Cullen, his face now five shelves up off the floor, prodded a large cheese wheel in front of him. "How heavy are these things?"

"If you did - it'd be a cheese topping! Geddit?" Archie looked up to see if Cullen had caught his joke and then howled in protest. "Hey, don't do that! That's Cornish Yarg. You damage the nettle covering and people won't buy it."

"How heavy?"

"Depends." Archie sighed. "These here..." he waved at a rack beside him. "Smaller ones: four, five kilos for the Goudas or Bries, up to maybe nine or ten for the large ones like the Lancashire or Stilton."

"What's that in old money?"

"Anywhere from ten to twenty pounds. Weight." Archie added.

"What about this one?" Cullen picked up a large grey cylinder and gave it some thoughtful heft.

"That's a soft cheese. Not sure you could kill someone with soft cheese, could you?"

"I told you - there's no killing here. What's your biggest one?"

"Ooh, that'll be the Cheddars down the back there. Forty, forty-five kilos I think. Ninety-odd pounds." Archie converted helpfully.

"Christ!" Cullen grimaced. "Not sure I could lift that."

"You don't have to lift it, do you? Can't you just push it off the shelf?"

Cullen had stopped listening and moved over to another rack.

"This one?"

"Parmigiano-Reggiano. Beautifully complex. Nearly forty kilos. You can't use that! Sell that in small portions, it's worth nearly a grand. You'll put me out of business!"

"Thought that was this other guy's job." Cullen moved

along the shelves, poking and prodding the mouldy rinds of cheeses, while Archie winced below.

When the handle on the back door first twitched, Cullen was lying on the top tier of shelving in the dark, his chin resting on his arms crossed in front of him. Archie was hunkered down behind a stack of empty packing crates in the far corner with a perfect view of the door.

There was a scratching and ratcheting sound and then the lock gave suddenly. A balaclava'd head appeared around the door, silhouetted in the lights from the alley outside. The head waited half a minute, cocked slightly, before quickly glancing back and then ducking inside and closing the door behind it. The light in the room shrank further and the figure paused once again, perhaps waiting for his eyes to adjust.

Archie crouched motionless, holding his breath. He looked up to Cullen's perch but found he was no longer there. His eyes scoured the room, ears pricked for the slightest sound. All was still and quiet.

The intruder stepped lightly forward two paces and turned his head to the side, as if looking straight into Archie's eyes. He turned his head away again and took one more step forward, before being flattened by forty-five kilos of Cheddar. Extra Mature.

Cullen jumped down from nowhere and stood over the fallen figure. He reached out with his right boot to nudge the body on the floor and Archie unfolded himself from his hiding place and reached for the light switch.

"Yay! Nice work. Though was hoping you'd have gone for the Double Gloucester. Cheaper." He screwed his eyes up as the strip-lights blinked on, just as the figure on the floor lashed out with one leg. Cullen collapsed on his coccyx, yelling out in pain and surprise.

"Shit!" As the figure in the balaclava struggled to his knees, rubbing its shoulder, Archie reached to his left for anything he could grab. His hand found half a wheel of his finest Gorgonzola Piccante, £16 per kilo, and he reluctantly launched it at the head of the intruder. The cheese sailed past the man and splattered against the far wall, leaving blue-veined chunks stuck to the painted breeze-block.

Cullen was now back on his feet and he leapt at the figure in black, knocking them both to the ground. They wrestled briefly until Archie's fingers found a ball of eighteen-month old Gouda, pristine in black and gold foil. He closed his eyes, unable to accept he was throwing good money and fantastic cheese at a stranger, before gritting his teeth and hurling the missile at the tussling pair.

The cheese smacked Cullen squarely on the jaw, knocking his hat off with the impact

"Ow, fuck!" Cullen lost his grip on the intruder who squirmed back to his feet and lurched for the door. "Help me out, Archie! Fuck sake!"

Archie flicked the lights off again and tried as stealthily as he could to make his way round to the back door and cut off the intruder's escape. Cullen flailed blindly for the stranger and caught his heel, sending him skittering off-balance and slamming hard into the shelving to his right.

It started to rain small pieces of cheese.

Cullen hurled himself into the stomach of the man, now defending himself from an attack of Danish Blues, Babybels and smaller Edams that hailed down on him from above. The pair grappled and bounced along the shelving unit, like paired ball-bearings in some demented pinball machine, each impact showering more discs of Camembert, Cambozola and Brie down to earth.

Cullen had a clear height and strength advantage over the chubbier compact figure in the balaclava who skidded on a Blue D'Auvergne and fell to his knees. Cullen reached for the nearest cheese he could grasp and round-housed it into the man's face, delivering the *coup de gras*. The intruder slumped unconscious to the floor and Archie threw the lights back on and hurried over to Cullen. On his knees, panting raggedly, Cullen dropped the bloody, mashed cheese weapon to the floor.

Archie let out a plaintive cry. "My Stinking Bishop!"

Cullen looked up at him, testing his lower jaw. "You're welcome." He got to his feet and retrieved his hat, planting it roughly back on his sweat-soaked head. "Who is it then?"

"Hmm?" Archie was surveying the carnage that had been his cheese storeroom, his face etched with sadness and dismay. "Look at it! Just... look at it."

"I'll do the honours then, shall I?" Cullen strode over to the figure on the floor, bent down and peeled back the balaclava.

"Simpson!" Exclaimed Archie, looking at the unconscious man's swollen face.

"You know him, then?"

"Runs the deli down the High Street." Archie spat. "Bastard! So that's his game, is it? Damaging and stealing my stock, trying to put me out of business before I even open. Huh, business must be bad." He cast his eyes glumly over the floor. It was littered with several smashed wheels of cheese, some stamped on, one flattened. Cheese shrapnel everywhere. "Guess he was scared of competition. Going to struggle myself now, all this damaged stock." He strode over to the unconscious figure and aimed a sharp kick in the man's ribs. "Take that, you bastard! I hope your business goes down the toilet, where it belongs."

"Steady." Cullen said, raising his eyebrows.

"Don't steady me. That's who you've got to blame for a sore mouth."

"Well, no. Technically, that was you."

"Fine. Whatever."

"And it hurts." Cullen cradled his mouth and tentatively waggled his jaw.

"Well, that's all very well and good but what about my shop? I'm opening in two days." Archie held himself close with both arms and frowned at Cullen. "What about all this?"

Cullen ignored the damage in the room, nursing his mouth. "Still hurts."

"Are you serious?" Archie glared at him. "Look at it! I'll be able to salvage these hard cheeses. I guess. Cut off the dinged and dirty sections and leave the clean stuff for sale. But this softer stuff - it's flattened. Or ruined. Who's going to want to eat any of this?"

Cullen shrugged. "I will."

"Well you're fucking welcome to it." Archie snapped. "Here."

He scooped up the mashed wheel of Stinking Bishop, shoved it into Cullen's hands, and then bent to the task of picking all the salvageable pieces off the floor. Cullen watched Archie go about his business for a while, then stuffed the cheese into his rucksack and slunk out of the room, head down.

# PART TWO

## THE BLUETOOTH

# TWO

Barry Sullivan's dental surgery in Peebles was a modern, brightly-lit affair with blonde wood, pastel carpets and not a tropical fish in sight. On the ground floor of a modern office block, the front door opened onto a large reception area, seats along three sides of a rectangle with a wall and inset glass screens along the fourth, behind which sat the receptionists: gatekeepers to hallowed pain relief.

From here, a long corridor led down the central spine of the surgery with three separate rooms leading from it, each the dedicated nest of one of the resident dentists: Michael Willingham, Sally Richards and Barry himself. The whole surgery reeked of the hushed tones of the church - ironic, really, Barry always considered, since what a dentists actually needed was some significant background noise to drown out the sounds of whining drills, grinding sanders or the intermittent cries of pain from protesting patients. A respectful hush hung over proceedings - from the customers themselves, silently supplicating in the waiting area, through the soothing plainsong of the novice receptionists on the phones, to the whispering chapel of uniformed dental assistants quietly shuffling like a choir of Clarins-clad nuns.

Novices and nuns. Always women. Barry made sure of that.

He watched Alison rule front of house like an angry

tamarind monkey protecting her fruit from a marauding chimp, but insisted that he personally vet new receptionists or dental assistants as the final step in the recruitment process. She may have excelled at placing adverts, perusing CVs, arranging and conducting interviews - but that counted for nothing if a candidate had a small chest, thin lips or was likely to refuse him a quick feel at the end of a hard day.

And days were hard. Or at least, that's how it felt when you were staring into the stinking abyss of bad dental work seven hours a day. The mask helped, of course, but the constant reminder of poor oral care, and the probing and tutting over past scars of repairs done in the dark, barbaric ages of 20th century dentistry - they all took their mental toll. Come 5pm, what Barry needed most of all was a damn good shag. Or blowjob at least. Something that would cleanse his mind and clear the custard.

He had started this dental practice from the ground up five years ago, having moved from an over-crowded practice on the other side of town, and brought many of his patients with him. The upside of taking on NHS patients had been a quick growth to capacity in terms of patient numbers; the downside had been the quality and opportunity for custard-clearing available to him. So he had applied himself with a steady focus and changed it.

Because Barry was nothing if not focussed. And his goal was now extra-marital sex.

In fact, it was extra-marital on both sides. Not for him, the pursuit and capture of innocent single women whose cavities he could probe. He wanted the thrill of more mature women - married, sexually accomplished and, not to put too fine a point on it, more at ease with the idea that a man might press and demand so that a woman would acquiesce and comply. Not for him these modern women who would cry harassment the minute you looked them up and down admiringly; he had no time for innocents who had had fewer partners than they had untrimmed pubic hairs.

When Julia McInnes initially walked into his surgery, Barry's eyes bulged noticeably. *Jesus suffering fuck*, she was gorgeous! He mentally reviewed her file that he'd seen for the first time that morning:

39 years old, married (natch). Perfect dental health record, no allergies. X-rays on file from her previous dentist showed a good set of top and bottom teeth. Hygienist records showed good alignment, no discolouration or gum issues, and evidence of excellent personal hygiene and oral care.

Barry's own ideas of Julia's oral care gave him a momentary throb in his pants. He watched her as she entered the room and manoeuvred herself into his leather dentist chair. She was tall and slim, long legs and shapely calves showing beneath a fairly demure knee-length skirt and navy blue woollen coat, which she had shed and sloped carefully on the guest chair by the door. Her legs were bare, smooth and wore the remains of a tan. She had a mole by her right ankle.

Her hands were slender with long fingers, nails polished expertly in a glittering blue. She wore a small diamond engagement ring, a simple gold wedding band and no other jewellery. On her left wrist was a thin silver-strapped watch with an analog face; on her right was a pale blue Fitbit.

Her hair was an auburn bob, short and thick with a

feathered edge which framed her oval face. Her brown eyes sparkled with good humour and warmth and her eyebrows looked like she had had them recently plucked. She wore pale pink lip gloss above a pixie chin, but the laugh-lines around her eyes gave her a more wearisome expression when up-close.

As he reclined the chair and moved the lamp over her face, he watched as her blouse shifted and the slight swelling of her breasts was revealed as the chair reached the horizontal. When she opened her mouth he could see beautiful healthy teeth, moist pinkness and a small tongue.

With a stud in it. Barry's pants throbbed again.

"Any issues or concerns about your teeth, Mrs McInnes?" He ran his tongue over his front teeth and smiled encouragement. He thought he could detect her eyes widening.

"No. I'm good." Julia replied confidently.

"Yes. Yes, you are." Breathed Barry, and fumbled awkwardly for his dental pick.

"So, I think that back tooth there perhaps needs some further investigation. Other than that everything looks fine. Better than fine, in fact. Excellent!" Barry pulled back his stool on castors and raised Julia slowly back up to a sitting position in the chair. "I'm a bit pushed for time right now. But I do have free slots later in the week - if you could pop in for an x-ray and a closer look."

Julia looked doubtful. "Well, I'm only five minutes away but I do have an awful lot on this week."

"Well it would probably only take five minutes." Barry breezed. "Tell you what. Ask reception on the way out for a 5pm appointment. I always have a bit of free time then and they'll know it's ok to squeeze you in if you tell them that."

"Right. Ok." Julia swung her legs beautifully over and stood up, heels clicking on the tiled floor as she put on her coat.

"Super. Well, it's a date then!" Barry gave a broad grin and Julia smiled shyly in return. She picked up her handbag and tottered wonderingly out of the surgery.

Paul McInnes was known to everyone, even his wife, as Big Paul. She alone had an intimate knowledge of "little Paul" as well - and even that was big. Big Paul was often shortened to B.P which was itself, again, shortened to Beep. A nickname which, ironically, measured up poorly against the scale of the man it described. Paul was a man mountain. Six foot five and eighteen stone, broad and wide, heavyset and muscular, with a bull's neck, an ox's chest and forearms like Popeye's bench-press nemesis.

Paul and Julia lived in a 3-bedroom semi on a new-build estate on the south-eastern edge of Peebles. Built on land that used to be part of a farm - until the farmer realised he could retire from rearing meagre livestock grazing on crap soil and exchange it for the simple pleasures of tarmac, driveways and money in the bank.

In some aspects of life, Paul was a master. He was, for instance, an excellent carpenter and a practical hands-on sort who could fix or knock up a solution to anything if it involved wood, screws or nails. Or glue. Paul was big on glue. Some things may be beyond him: literature, physics, tact. Others came naturally to him: heft, strength, practical ingenuity. Today, though, had seemed to involve Paul in an almighty helping of something he was appalling at - and always had been: punctuality.

When he was a boy, being on time had been uncool. Profoundly uncool. Coolness was denoted by a swaggering insouciance and don't-care attitude in the face of foolish teachers and their hysterical demands for homework. Paul withstood them all. And if it involved getting six of the best, trousers down, so be it. All that would do would ratchet up the cool factor. Plus liking school - I mean, actually liking it? Major minus coolness points for that alone. Not giving a shit, made major league sense. So that is what he did.

To many of his classmates, Paul seemed to have it all. Alas, once adulthood and the world of work beckoned, the pinnacle of cool swiftly melted into a puddle of mediocrity. Paul, with his natural Panglossian outlook, tried to swan serenely through it, brow unfurrowed by worry, uncreased by doubt. Bish-bash-bosh, job done and on to the next one. Next week would take care of itself once it became this week. You could worry about it, or not worry about it - made no odds. So, the easiest approach seemed to be to not worry about it. So Paul didn't.

And this lack of concern for earthly things, things that other mortals fretted over, could have - in other cultures, perhaps - made him something of a holy man. A sadhu, hermit, guru or seer. Someone who could sense beyond the material and value what was truly important and inescapable about life: its sheer brevity and glory. Revel in the now, worry not about whether your windows needed cleaning or your toilet was blocked. This was great wisdom - until you needed new front tyres and you had no money to pay for them, or you got a puncture on the M8 at midnight in a downpour.

So, time for Paul had a relativistic quality that Einstein

had identified but few others had genuinely grasped. Dilation it was not, but it certainly felt different for each participant. Paul would be there when he got there. For the waiting person, it was infuriating. And the fury was compounded when, in any attempt to explain to him why punctuality might be a good idea, Paul looked kindly at you as though you were clearly failing to grasp the larger, cosmic picture and say *Right, cool.*

And today, Paul was late. Relatively. With or without the nod to Einstein. Julia had told him, many times, that they were due at a dinner party at 8pm. And that, furthermore, a shower and change of clothes would be required of him as a minimum after he had been sanding solid oak flooring for eight hours straight. The invite had been extended to them by Stephen, Julia's boss, who owned the wholefoods distribution business she worked for. Julia, ever-ambitious, was angling for a promotion and this unexpected invitation had delighted her. This could be the break she needed and all Paul had to do was not fuck it up.

"Consider it done, my sweet." Paul's very words. "Which Steven was this again?" They knew a few Stevens.

"Stephen! You know! He always bangs on about it, Stephen with a 'ph'?"

"Phteven?"

Julia had clamped her jaw tight and glared at him. "Just. Don't. Be. Late".

It was 8:14pm when Paul's van pulled into the drive.

# THREE

Julia loved Paul.

Or used to. Or still did? She asked herself this question daily and, daily, the answer changed.

Julia was bold and brassy, with a grin like Julia Roberts on acid and a laugh like a freshly unblocked drain. She could, and would, be the life and soul of the party at the drop of an ice cube in a Gin and Malibu - a Limbo Lady cocktail, her favourite. There was something just a little off-kilter about her features but her brown eyes glinted with a wickedness which was accentuated when she smiled, which she did a lot. She was tall, 5'10", and had spent a lifetime affecting a stoop for shorter boyfriends so that she never seemed to appear her full height, even in heels (which she had tended to avoid for the same reasons). Meeting Paul, a more than healthy 6'5" had meant for the first time she could hold her chin up, put on those heels, and not feel like some freak from Ringling Brothers Circus.

She hailed from the Isle of Sheppey, her father had worked at the Pool of London, before it had all been torn down and replaced with millionaire pads and Arab investment apartments. Her mother had been a translator in the Foreign Office, pouring over faxes and telexes day after day and translating communiques into diplomatic French in the days before the EU had accepted the universality of the English language with bad grace. Her father had loved her mother and Julia both - but left them anyway when she was barely into her teens. Having a wife who earned more than him, and had a higher social standing, ate away much of his pride and self-esteem. Dock closures and drinking away his redundancy pay took the rest. Julia clung to her mother and grew up reluctant to accept inferiority in male company, whilst eternally afraid that this very attitude would put paid to any chance of a long-term relationship. This, and her height, resigned her to singledom more often than she liked. So, as each year rolled by her standards lowered another notch.

Julia pretended to her girlfriends that she was more than delighted with her bachelor-career-girl status. She was a thrusting business-woman with deals to do and people to meet - she had no time for romance or children. Those could wait.

In the end, they waited far too long.

Eventually, and purely by accident, she had found herself migrating northwards to Edinburgh where she found a lover and boyfriend who happened to be the son of a wealthy farmer in the Scottish Borders. They had been planning a life together until one day she found him in the hay barn, *in flagrante* with one of his father's prize-winning ewes. Lowering standards or not, Julia had bolted from that relationship like a CEO with a plane to catch. On her last night at the Peebles Hydro, where she was attending a conference, she had been drowning her sorrows at the gin bar when she met Paul.

Paul was tall and olive-skinned, always wearing a beaming smile, with jet black hair cropped neatly to his large head and a short goatee which shone silkily. He was ubiquitous in the many pubs, bars and chippies that Peebles had to offer - it was even rumoured that he had black card membership of Greggs. And he was often to be found there in his working outfit of tatty old T-shirt, baggy grey jogging bottoms, and sweat-stained trainers. This despite the fact that work seemed to be something which often eluded him.

Or rather he eluded it.

Paul's attitude to work was one of benign tolerance. He enjoyed his job - he was a joiner by trade, and a very good one at that - but placed himself very much in the "work to live" camp, as opposed to the "live to work" one. His modus operandi for life was to coast along until money ran short - or out - and then rely upon the world to provide a job which would bring in some cash to allow this cycle to be repeated. And, truth be told, this worked out for him quite well. What might have infuriated and stressed many was, to Paul, a marvellous facet of life which he now took for granted. To any who would ever remark on the serenity and serendipity of his day-to-day existence, Paul would smile his broad smile, exposing glistening white teeth, tap the side of his nose theatrically and say "Trust the soup, mate. Trust the soup."

What he meant by this was, actually, known only to himself. But he said it with such confidence and conviction that everyone he said it to would just smile, think it was just Paul being Paul, and then ask about his dogs. And these three things - the soup and his two dogs - were the triumvirate of permanence on which Paul's existence rested.

His trusty Jack Russell terriers were called Penn and Teller. He had acquired them together as puppies when an old mate he had been doing a job for was short of readies to pay him and had suggested instead payment in kind - to whit, two cute puppies and a large dog basket. Charmed by their fluff and helplessness, Paul had agreed - knowing that the electricity would get paid some other way - and he had taken them home. Turn the clock forwards a few years and here they were, always by his side, as faithful, playful and fun-loving as Paul himself. Teller was the quiet one - large black and brown patches scattered over a mottled white coat with one ear that was constantly pricked and one which was not. Penn was a bouncy, yapping scoundrel who would steal your last sausage and then wag his tail at you, barking animatedly, whilst weighing you up with adoring eyes as if to say *Ok, so I nicked your last sausage, but I'm cute right?* He too had a mottled white coat with a single black patch which covered his front legs and chest.

And so it was, that Julia had seen Paul across the crowded bar. Mystically halo'ed somehow amidst the crush, like a prize ram being presented at auction. She had sized him up, assessing him for suitability in terms of size, smartness and looks. With only days to go before a friend's wedding she was due to attend with a plus-one she now didn't have, her quality benchmark was at an all-time low; Paul hurdled it with scant inches to spare. With the benefit of several gins under her belt, Julia had approached him and mercenarily extended her wedding invitation and the deal was quickly struck - almost as if Paul had no actual say in the matter - which was actually a state of affairs that suited him quite well.

The following weekend, at the end of the wedding reception, Julia and Paul had retired to the room she had booked for the night and they had balled each other's brains out 'til morning. There were complaints made at reception about the noise but when Julia had checked out later, with the shadowy hulking figure of Paul nuzzling her neck from behind, the manager had decided that discretion was the better part of valour and let the whole thing lie.

Alcohol may have had a large role to play in their successful date but, boy, was Paul sensational in the sack. Sure, her standards were temporarily low (and Prosecco seldom raised them) but he had strength, stamina, girth and heft where it counted. In fact, Julia had taken it upon herself to carefully scrutinise his girth and heft, once at close quarters with her eyes and hands, and twice with her mouth.

She had later compared notes with the no-longer blushing bride and discovered that their respective night-time experiences had been chalk and cheese, and that Julia had got by far the better of it. With the blindness that is lust, Julia became infatuated with Paul and the sexual delight he gave her. Weeks and months passed in a blur and they spent every second in each other's company that they could manage, sharing delight in each other's passions. And a wee personal mantra was born, one that Julia had recalled from an old childhood TV programme and which Paul too remembered when it first sprung, out of nowhere, to her lips:

*Me and You, You and Me*
*Lots and lots for us to see*
*You and Me, Me and You*
*Lots and lots for us to do.*

But as these things sometimes do, their romance blossomed only until the ardent nature of their coupling began to inevitably fade.

When Paul moved into Julia's flat, the practicalities, irritations and mundanities of life started to shape their lives more than their desires. And here it became apparent that for each and every facet of his magnificence in the bedroom department, Paul overcompensated by one or more corresponding failures in most other departments in the IKEA store of life. Grunting heavily, he would whistle aimlessly past the kitchen area, clog up the wardrobe and storage sections, ignoring home furnishings entirely before grinding to a complete halt at the checkout where actual money had to be exchanged.

Julia may have been an ambitious career woman, but her earnings were relatively small. She got by and was able to splash out now and then but it suddenly appeared as if she was now spending for two - on food, heating, petrol and so on - and not getting anything in the way of contributions other than the girth and heft that constituted Paul's payment in kind. He made a payment towards her rent but it was not always - scratch that, was never - on time and this was the start of Julia's frequent brushes with the maddening soup-trustiness that was Paul's stock-in-trade.

Within months, the grinding of teeth and gears in their relationship had started to bellow above the din of their intercourse. Which was when, entirely coincidentally, Paul had knocked her for six, charmed the socks off her and completely won her over when he asked her to marry him.

They say love is blind, and Julia had already decided that she was unsure whether she loved Paul or whether he was just so bloody loveable that it seemed that she did. He was fantastic and maddening in equal proportions and she realised that, since all individuals are flawed and none perfect, she should perhaps check the beam in her own eye before complaining about the mote in his. But above and beyond everything else - the lack of care with money, the vagueness, the undetectable work ethic - towering above all these, like some giant minaret in silver and gold, was his punctuality. Or lack of it.

It drove her completely nuts.

She tried to analyse it, reluctantly concluding that the sparks from *his* trait too often spat onto the scruffy hearthrug of *her* hang-up: being late. The result was never pretty.

It didn't matter whether it was business or pleasure - a meeting with a prospective customer or a dentist appointment - she became physically hot and sweaty, angry and ashamed, whenever she ran the risk of being late for anything. If she sat at the lights and calculated that she would be a few minutes late by the time she arrived, on came the hot flushes and the anxiety. And to the fore came her subconscious looking hungrily for someone or something to blame, that wasn't her: the weather, the traffic, the post, the prior appointment that had overrun. All would stand as she rolled them around in her mind's eye to see if they could justifiably be used as reasons for a possible late arrival, when all along she knew the basic truth was that she should take responsibility for her lateness by not cutting it so fine. She was a frustrated idealist - wanting the world to be perfect, making plans on the basis that it was, then becoming inevitably angry and disappointed when it turned out not to be and her plans collapsed in ruins. Rinse and repeat.

So Paul's approach to punctuality pushed all the wrong buttons for her and made her life intolerable whilst she sat there of an evening desperately trying to convince her inner voice that it was her, not him. But coming to the

nightly conclusion that it was him and something must be done.

But what?

Julia loved Paul. Like a slug hates salt.

Paul loved Julia. Like a dog loves his master, like a child loves ice-cream, like a lawn loves the rain. As a sailor loves the sea, Paul relished life as it rose and fell beneath his feet, the breeze in his face and the horizon on the, erm, horizon. Nothing between here and there, so let's ride the tide to there and see what's there when we get there. Usually it was just more *there* that was there - but what the hell.

But just like a sailor needed shore leave to avoid going crazy, so Paul felt the deep draw of satisfaction when he found himself in a steady relationship. And found was a keyword here, as these things seemed to happen around him and he would wake up one morning and realise he was now part of a couple and was really quite delighted by his good fortune.

The stability and routine offered a steadiness and familiarity, cosiness and warmth like a wooden bowl of soup on a cold winter's day. It reinforced his view that life was good and the soup was to be trusted. Here was Julia: an attractive, shapely woman with a dirty laugh, smiling eyes and an excellent cook. She was resourceful, financially independent, enthusiastic and diligent and completely in love with his dick. Genuinely infatuated with it, it seemed. She sought it out whenever she could, sometimes looking to physically devour it as soon as it hove into view. There were many times when he actually wished she'd leave the bloody thing alone - and how many men would be able to say that? Or would be delighted to be in a similar position?

But there were a few times, he couldn't help but notice, when she grumped and moaned at him. Folded her arms and her mouth grew hard. He'd let her down, he guessed, but she wouldn't say why out loud and he didn't want to ask. So they steered a course from one bout of great sex to the next, by tacking into the wind: a repetitive, tiring practice of steering windward and feeling the boat and sails grow taut; straining under the tightness, until you needed to swing around and, in that moment of adjustment, everything grows slack and you have to smartly wrestle to regain that tautness to keep your momentum. Zig-zagging to a destination you couldn't reach in a straight line because that would require you to do the impossible: sail into the wind.

And that was their relationship - an uncharted journey to a hopeful destination which required them to constantly sail into the wind. For the five years of their marriage, each had tacked their own way, grew exhausted, only to reignite their energy in bed to give them the fight to tack once again the next day. While sharing a common goal and keeping their relationship on course, they nevertheless found the process exhausting and knew, deep down, that they couldn't maintain this effort indefinitely.

Something would have to give.

"Where have you been?" Julia, hands on hips, had been pacing and phoning, pacing and texting, pacing and calling Paul fit to burn at the top of her voice. She didn't want to sit down and crease her new frock. The frock that Paul hadn't noticed - no change there then.

Paul wondered what was wrong, saw his wife all dolled

up and mentally started to rappel back through the rickety rolodex in his mind for an engagement of some kind which might require dressing up. He came up empty. "Where're you off to?"

"What?" She instantly held up an angry hand to stifle the inevitable repetition of the question she knew Paul would utter. "Rhetorical. This-" she swept her hand down her outfit, ending with a blue nail-polished flourish. "Is what is called being ready for a dinner date. OUR dinner date. The dinner date with Stephen and Olivia I have been reminding you about over and over recently."

The fridge-door light in Paul's head winked on. "Um, yeah. Phteven?"

"The very same." She fumed. "Well?"

Paul looked at her, brows creasing. "Um."

"Where the fuck have you been? Why didn't you call to tell me you'd be late? And why aren't you fucking racing to the fucking shower this very fucking minute?"

"Is it now?"

"Get in the fucking shower you... arsehole!" Julia launched a failed kick at his backside as he slunk away towards the stairs.

"I'm going! I'm going!"

"I swear to God..." Julia picked up her phone and dialled Olivia, swallowing hard for a suitable apology.

When Paul came back downstairs he had a towel round his waist and was rubbing his hair dry with another. "What the fuck are you doing down here? Get back up those fucking stairs and get shaved and dressed pronto! No. Wait. Fuck the shave. Just get dressed. I've gained a thirty minute reprieve from Olivia, let's see if we can astonish her by getting there early, shall we?"

Paul, turned seamlessly on the stair and padded back

up, shaking his head slowly.

"I've left clothes out for you. On the bed!" Julia shouted at his back. "Don't touch anything else, just put those on and get back down here. Quickly!"

On the short walk home at the end of the night, Julia needled and jabbed at Paul trying to understand what had happened to cause him to be late. She knew it was pointless. Either he had forgotten all about it, never remembered in the first place, or didn't care. Either way, it was all too evident after years of marriage that Paul clearly could not be relied upon to turn up when needed. Inherently unreliable - her mother's words when she had first met him. Actually, no, her first words had described Paul as being something like a cross between a hoover and a head injury. Whatever.

Julia wasn't sure how her mother had been able to come to that conclusion so rapidly, and back in those days when her head had been turned by this magnificent specimen of masculinity, Julia had defended Paul proudly. These few years later, as her heels clacked on the frosty paving stones, she realised bitterly that her mother had been right, and Paul was never going to change. Her choice was to accept that and love him. Or not.

And after tonight's debacle she was sliding inexorably into the *not* camp. It was all too late for recriminations, she was just going through the motions: the tediously inevitable marital game where the arguments changed each time but the underlying issue remained constant. The evening had been a disaster and it was all she could do to stop herself from getting into a brawl with him right there, in the freezing night air. There was to be no promotion.

Probably not ever now. The anger and betrayal roiled within her, stoked by a feeling of utter powerlessness over her own future.

Paul slouched along in silence beside her, bent beneath a silent barrage of outrage and bitter disappointment. At the end of their driveway, Julia stopped and let Paul shuffle to the door and open it. He looked back and held the door open, quizzically for a second or two and then, seeing she was not moving, gently left it ajar and disappeared upstairs. Julia looked up at the stars for a few moments, saw their bedroom light come on and then hung her head and let the tears finally come.

# FOUR

Barry "Beaver" Sullivan had a stiff neck and a dead arm. He woke, bleary-eyed and thick-headed, lying on the carpet in front of a looping Blu-ray menu on a large TV screen with the sound off.

It was Monday, 5.30am.

In a few hours' time he had to be at work, and this evening he had a room booked at his usual hotel in Edinburgh where he would be entertaining his latest Stepford Wife. Dealing with the hurt pride of his own wife, Melinda, could wait. It wasn't the first time, and it wouldn't be the last. Maybe it could wait forever. He, on the other hand, noticing a budding morning glory rising in his trousers, could not.

His weeks didn't usually start like this. Sometimes, but not usually. Last night had not been unusual in that he had had a row with his wife, and let her stomp upstairs to bed while he finished off the bottle of Pinot Grigio. They hadn't even got to the end of the film before the argument broke out. That wasn't unusual either.

Neither was the fact that the row had been about money. Because it was always about money. His money. Melinda spending his money. He had had too much to drink, and the film had been shitty, and he couldn't resist having a pop at her about her weight while he was on a roll. She was an easy target, too large to miss. And she was a champion bitch - in the super-heavyweight division.

She had fled upstairs, sobbing quietly. He had turned back to the movie and poured himself another glass of wine.

The "Beaver" in Barry "Beaver" Sullivan was not a self-honorary title. He had been given it at High School when he had been a buffed Adonis with thick luscious hair, an athlete's physique and a libido like any other teenage boy stuck in a boys' school next to a girls' school. Separated only by a hole-ridden chain-link fence between the sports pitches, and a rickety gate behind the bin area where the smokers and graffiti artists gathered.

And the shaggers.

Male and female.

It had always intrigued Barry that many people - many boys anyway - saw girls as conquests, targets to be acquired; primary, yet passive, objects in the pursuit of finding a repository for teenage ejaculate. Barry's starting assumption - which had proved presciently bang-on - was that it took two to tango and hormones did not discriminate on the grounds of gender. There was as much oestrogen wafting across the hockey field as there was testosterone raging on the rugby pitch.

With this in mind he had confidently preened and posed along the fence whenever any sporting occasion allowed and, as a result, secured the admiration of many of the senior girls (and some not so senior) and found himself with his hands often sticky and his cock often fondled. Home runs with the senior hockey eleven had been numerous and Beaver became *numero fucking uno* in the poundtown stakes.

His studies in female anatomy led him to muse on the idea of joining the medical profession but he was promptly cured of his disillusion when he saw the extent of the studies and years of dedication required to reach even junior Doctor status. Inborn bone-idleness and a piercing intelligence did the rest. He realised he need only rip out the few chapters on teeth from the burgeoning shelf of medical textbooks in order to specialise in dentistry. The only consideration had then been whether he would be able to stomach the idea of spending each day peering into the halitosis'ed caverns of rotting gums that yawned beneath the hairy noses and spotty complexions of unhealthy Scottish patients. When he had the good fortune to connect with a busty blonde dental technician who took a shine to him, dentistry had a new convert and his name was Barry Sullivan.

Throughout his twenties and into his thirties, Barry hit on anything in a skirt. Persistent and methodical - with practised ease - he smoothly screwed his way through the young and healthy female population of southern Scotland.

But his dentistry started to suffer.

And, possibly worse than this, he started to harbour something which he had never encountered before.

Doubt.

A very unusual state of affairs which troubled him deeply and would have given him sleepless nights - if he'd had any nights alone in which to catch some sleep. But he had pondered on it, long and hard, and came to the astonishing conclusion that what he needed, what he was sensing, what he was missing, was stability. He needed to settle down. Get married.

An amazing conclusion, but there it was. Without realising it, he had been searching for happiness - albeit in the skimpy underwear of many, many women - but searching nonetheless. And not finding it. This insatiable thirst for new conquests had become a treadmill from which he could not escape.

Except by stepping off.

The conviction had struck him forcibly and clearly and he was in absolutely no doubt that marriage was his solution.

But, boy, had he been wrong.

Melinda Forrest had been a gorgeous, vivacious brunette when he first saw her. Iridescent in a nightclub under the black light, she had shimmered and shone and given him a blowjob while he fingered her in the end cubicle. They had dated, moved in together, got engaged and then married in a whirlwind three months and she was pregnant with their first child before their first year together was up.

Barry couldn't have been happier.

At first.

Two more kids later he was wondering what had hit him.

Melinda had ballooned from a voluptuous size twelve to a gargantuan twenty-two, with stretch marks that looked like a contour map of the Cairngorms and a pussy like a wizard's sleeve. Barry had stared into a future offering eternal stability, security and the warmth of a family environment and realised that what stared back at him was an endless hell of sameness, familiarity and soul-crushing routine.

Divorce would ruin him; fidelity would kill him. Something inside Barry fell on its side and he realised that he had made a massive - *massive* - mistake. As quickly as he had persuaded himself that marriage was the solution he had had a Damascene conversion and now reverted to his original life-affirming philosophy of skirt-chasing.

He had just omitted to tell Melinda.

But while she might have been fat, she wasn't stupid. Barry had not exactly been subtle. Melinda didn't have the energy or self-confidence to do anything other than accept it for what it was. For now. Her life was her three young children and all her focus was devoted to them. But she would get around to disentangling herself from his wretched womanising when she had regained her energy and vitality. Meanwhile she could enjoy herself, and his money, distracting herself from his infidelity by excessive consumption.

Barry took this air of detachment as tacit approval. She no longer had any sexual interest in him. Well, *right back at you, fatso.* Life was short.

And he had an old nickname to live up to.

"Hello. Janine, is it?" The thin, pallid woman had an *I-want-to-see-the-manager* haircut. She was wearing white crocs and a pale blue tunic, buttoned to the neck, over dark blue slacks. Janine guessed they were elasticated at the waist. The woman held out her hand. "I'm Alison. Welcome to our little world."

*Oh. My. God.* Janine wanted to barf. So lame. Our little world!?! WTF? And crocs? She hoped against hope that what Alison was wearing was not a uniform she would be required to adopt. Ugh. White plastic clogs with strategically placed holes in them? Those holes - that was where your dignity leaked out. And those trousers made from fun-repellent material? Janine wasn't having any of that. She did not intend to start filling her basket in the *I've-given-up-caring* shop just yet, thank you very much.

Alison led her through to a small office off to one side

and closed the oak-veneered door. The stillness was soggy, squatting heavily over everything. Whilst Janine had been sitting in reception waiting, she had noticed this odd sensation - unable to quite locate it. Now, in this little cubbyhole of a room, it revealed itself to her. The whole place was hushed but loud at the same time. As if the very silence converted the slightest sound into a massive echo resonating around a vast dental cathedral.

"I thought I'd spend some time taking you through basic information and general rules, stuff like that. Then, once we've got that out of the way, I've got a few forms I need you to fill in - Health & Safety, Personnel, Payroll, Next of Kin - and then I'll give you a tour of the place. Won't take long." She smiled an apologetic crease of her lips, showing no teeth, dipping her head down to the left as she did so, like a poorly-coordinated Disneyworld animatronic. "Would you like a cup of tea?"

"Do you have any Doctor Pepper?"

"No." That smile again. "Tea. Coffee. Or water."

"I'm fine, thanks." Janine fiddled with the handbag in her lap and wished she had bought a bottle of something fizzy on her walk from the bus stop. This might be a long day.

"Okay. Well..." Alison smoothed her hands down her tunic, picked up a clipboard from the desk and clicked a ballpoint smoothly with her right hand. "Let's get started shall we?"

Janine sat silently as her induction into the particulars and peculiarities of Peebles Dental Surgery began. She rapidly tuned out and watched in a disembodied fashion as Alison pattered on about core working hours, annual leave, calling in sick, out of hours cover, yada yada. It was just like being back in Mr Jeffries' English class when he was banging on about Othello's anguish or something. As the droning continued, Janine belatedly realised there would be no bell to end the period today. That was last week. Last week she had been a student in High School. A young adult, as the Rector kept calling her and the other kids. This - *this* - was the world of work.

Oh God, what had she done? Maybe her pastoral teacher had been right about studying hard after all. This was looking grim. She screwed her eyes up slightly and examined Alison's face with a coroner's scrutiny. She was honest and straight, no doubt, but she also seemed somewhat efficient and cold. Maybe butter wouldn't melt in her mouth, but it probably wouldn't melt anywhere else on her either.

She let the talk wash over her and waited for the blessed relief of her first working lunch-hour when she could escape the looming suffocation by wall-to-wall carpet.

Julia pulled open a drawer and ran her eyes over the selection of underwear she had to choose from. Her mind wandered helplessly. Barry had a suavity and sophistication which her husband lacked. It aroused her simply by its novelty. And his sheer attention to her - just little things: brushing her arm here, stroking a stray tendril of hair off her face there - were a world away from the seeming indifference and casual slobbiness of her husband. Barry had subtlety and he was erudite. Paul had all the subtlety of a water cannon and probably thought erudite was a type of glue.

Barry had chatted admiringly, fawned almost. And made it quite clear that he desired her. Wanted her. Found her irresistible. Her ego had blossomed under his gaze and she found herself feeling newly sexy. When he had proposed dinner at a hotel she had known exactly what it meant. Felt the lack of passion from Paul like a raw wound. And wounds won't heal if they are neglected.

Barry wouldn't neglect her. He would bathe and stroke and attend. He had a magic touch. She smiled inwardly as she picked out a pair of briefs and placed them gently in her overnight bag.

*Scantio removum.*

Magic indeed.

# FIVE

Barry's father had been an on-course bookmaker all his life until he had a heart attack at 61, during the 3:15pm at Kempton. All bets taken were declared null and void.

Throughout his formative years, from the time he was able to add up and scribble numbers down, Barry's father had dragooned him into the family firm and, until puberty and girls had intervened, Barry had loved it. The thrill, the excitement, even the downmarket smells of greasy food and unwashed punters, stale fivers and oily coins couldn't detract from the feeling that, when you were at a racecourse, you were at the centre of a maelstrom of wonder and power, galloping beasts making the ground tremble so that a handful of men (his father, hopefully, included) could put dinner on the table every night.

This hunger for the thrill and the chase had never left him and since segueing into the world of dentistry, he had used his familiarity and experience of horse-racing as a guide to help him structure and manage his off-course activities with the fillies.

So, Barry's process worked like this:

***1. Studying the form:*** As any keen race-goer would know, the form-book was all. You can only judge a horse by the races it's won and Barry believed in research and attention to detail. He checked all new patients registered and perused his appointment list daily with a keen eye. When a new name showed up, he made sure he had some time spare to review the patient's file.

***2. In the paddock:*** this was really the only random part of the process and was truly organic as far as Barry was concerned. He was a dentist and he saw 20-odd patients each day. All it took was one of them to be an attractive married women, in her twenties or thirties or forties, and the gleam in his eye lit up like an overhead examination light. He watched them move, watched them smile, saw how they engaged with him and how comfortable they were in his environment. Like being led around the ring by stable hands, their legs and their backsides, their sashays and their swaying, all gave clues as to their flexibility and suitability in the sack. When he was confident he had a good bet, he moved in.

***3. Placing a bet:*** Smarm and charm offensive. Nothing too obvious at first, a light brush of an arm, compliments, a glint of a smile and a warm conversational interest in the woman herself. Very often they lit up at the slightest sign of flirtatiousness from him. Too many of these women seemed to be in loveless marriages themselves, with husbands who took them for granted and paid them no attention. Barry kept himself in shape. And he had lovely hair and teeth.

***4. Going down:*** This was the riskiest part of the venture because, until this had been accomplished, he was fully exposed as a potential sex pest. And he had to ensure that his partner was, above all, willing. He would propose a second appointment, one always scheduled at 5pm. The end of surgery. Normal appointments ran until 4.45pm so that, by 5pm, everything was finished and he could close down, go home, finish off or attend to non-clinical admin and the like. Professional development he liked to think of it. Setting himself up ready for 5pm gave him something to look forward to and, once the patient was back in the chair, he would move in unambiguously and assess the welcome that awaited him. Sometimes it was downright hostility but most times it was uncertainty and a coy reluctance followed by a tentative engagement and then full-blown enthusiasm. He rarely had full-on sex in his surgery - the lighting was far too harsh - but getting to first or second base was all that was needed to gain agreement to move to the next phase.

***5. Under starter's orders:*** He would meet them in the lobby bar, have a drink, put them at their ease before taking them to his room. Barry had a standard, recurring room booking at the Double Tree Hilton hotel, at Edinburgh airport which had served him well over the years. Airport hotels were used to one-night bookings, short notice, cancellations and delays, and frequent attendance by business travellers. To the uninitiated, Barry looked like all of these. If his partner was ill at ease about being detected she could even get the tram to the Park'n'Ride. Barry had thought of everything.

***6. They're off!*** His regular room was 107, chosen because it was a disabled room with an extra-large shower/wet room, with strategically placed handles and grip bars for extra acrobatic support (and a pull chain in emergency, just in case something got out of hand!). The bedroom was large and spacious without being ostentatious and the large TV positioned on the bureau opposite the end of the bed, had a black bevelled trim on which it was child's play to conceal a small video camera which, *in situ*, was essentially invisible if you weren't looking and, if you were, looked like an innocuous infra-red receiver or mini-smart box that hotels used to control TV access. Nothing out of the ordinary to the untrained eye. In fact, once Barry had forgotten it and left it in place by mistake until the following week's booking and it was still there, untouched, its recording still in place on the tiny memory card which lived inside. The video it recorded may not be cinema-quality but it was HD and, whilst it lacked decent sound, it was entirely sufficient for his purposes. The pictures were worth a thousand words.

***7. The winner's enclosure:*** The morning afterwards was usually an awkward time. His sexual prowess meant that his filly would certainly have enjoyed their time together - he'd never had a disappointed customer - but the cold light of day and sobriety often brought regret, lip-biting and nervousness about what had transpired plus how to get home. This was either the time when the wife realised her excuse had not been as carefully planned and prepared as she'd thought; or that the night had been so enjoyable - reminding a mature woman what good sex could be like outside a stale marital bed - that there were further shenanigans initiated upon waking. Barry would take a view at the end of the night and determine whether to rise early and disappear before she woke up, or risk an early morning quickie. If the latter, this would usually be followed by a stilted goodbye and a lift to some drop-off point. Barry always used swift checkout to minimise any awkward walk of shame through reception in the morning. He was, he thought, consideration itself.

***8. Out to pasture:*** As the number of his willing mounts grew, so he needed to pay closer attention to maintaining the best performers and retiring the also-rans. When the novelty wore off, for him, he needed to be ready to engineer a break-up. Smoothly. Breaking up successfully was like knocking over a Coke machine: you didn't do it with one push, you had to rock it back and forwards a few times. Build momentum. Barry was always alert, listening to his dick, prepared to start the process at the first sign of boredom. The has-beens were put out to pasture as efficiently as he could manage, while he scouted for newly registered patients to replace them.

***9. Managing his stable:*** More frequently, alas, it was fear, reticence, shame or guilt which caused his winners to want out. Just as he listened to his dick, he also listened to his gut. And sometimes he swore he could tell the end was coming. Maybe it was after just a one-night stand, or perhaps a two-or-three night affair, and there were some who kept it up for much longer. But inevitably a point would come where the lucky woman would say "Enough!". Because her husband was starting to suspect, or people were starting to talk, or she was feeling dirty and used, missing the reciprocity of love. This was where the video camera came in. Yes, he could use it for the purposes of his own entertainment - committing his best performances to the record for later, repeat viewing. And, yes, he did do this from time to time - no shame in revelling in your own excellence, Barry thought. But managing a stable meant using a little bit of carrot, a little bit of stick. And when the carrots no longer kept the fillies compliant, the stick came in handy. *Now, what would a husband say if he saw a video of his wife cavorting with another man? Surely, we don't want to get to that point, do we? Hmm? Precisely. So, how's Tuesday looking for you?*

Whatever the reason, whenever it arrived, Barry stood ready. No horse's head in the bed required. He had a much simpler offer the women couldn't refuse. And, after all these years of successful stable management, Barry wasn't at all sure whether this might not be the bit he actually enjoyed most.

The morning light filtered through the floor-length net curtains at the window and Julia woke blearily, momentarily confused as to where she was. Remembering with a jolt, she looked down at herself and rolled her eyes right to see if Barry was awake.

She was alone.

Appalled, confused and scared in equal measure she sat up in bed and looked around the room. Her clothes were scattered all around and she was still wearing a white suspender belt and one stocking. Nothing else. The champagne bottle was upended in the ice bucket. Slowly, she became aware that there was nothing in the room to indicate that Barry had ever been there. Her mind recoiled.

Was this, perhaps, intentional? To minimise any chance of her being found out? No trace of their assignation, no evidence that it had ever taken place? She wondered if she had dreamt the whole thing.

Or was it, perhaps, an indication that she had simply been used? Discarded, now that he had got what he wanted? Not even the human decency to go through the morning-after "Hello"s, "How was it for you?", "I'll call you"s and "It's not me, it's you".

She wasn't sure, and neither at this point would have surprised her. Relieved, nevertheless, she got up and walked round the room and the bathroom, checking. Truly, there was no mark of any kind to show she had not been alone the entire time. No wet towel, only one champagne flute, no used toiletries, abandoned cufflinks, or discarded condom wrappers. Wait! Had he used a condom? Disgusted with herself, now, she realised that not only could she not remember, she hadn't noticed because she hadn't cared. Her only thoughts had been her selfish pleasure and the feeling of getting some kind of bizarre revenge on Paul by engaging in this deceit.

She showered, turning the temperature as hot as she could bear, trying to sear the memories aware, slough away the skin that shamed her, and burn into her mind a plan as to what she should do now, how she should behave, what she should say to anyone about where she'd been, and what she'd done.

Sometime later, sitting on the hotel bed swathed in a white towelling robe, Julia dialled and tried to stay composed. Her thoughts were ricocheting but the only conclusion had been clear to her. She needed to speak to Barry and tell him she'd made a stupid, stupid mistake.

"Hello, dental surgery." The same sing-song tone as every other time Julia called.

"Hello, yes. I'd like to arrange an appointment please? With Mr Sullivan?"

"Can I take your name please?"

"Yes, it's Julia McInnes."

"Date of birth?"

"12.3.78"

"Right, Mrs McInnes. When were you thinking of?"

"Any day. This week. The sooner the better."

"Oh. Is it an emergency?"

"Yes. Yes, it is." Julia swallowed hard. "Do you have anything at 5pm?"

Somewhere near Cringletie farm, along what used to be the Cross Borders Drove Road and which was now little more than a muddy sheep-trodden path, Cullen sat on the wet grass with his back to a dry-stone wall.

His feet hurt and his mouth hurt and he was annoyed.

Annoyed because gone were the days when he could eat up twenty miles walking without noticing it. Age can do that to you. Whilst fifty wasn't exactly old, it's not exactly young either. He made a reluctant mental note to try and dial back his expectation of the miles he could manage in a day and moved on to the next annoyance: the damage Archie's cheese had wrought on his mouth.

He'd rooted through the medical kit in his rucksack and found nothing that suited. His nearest stash of tools, medicines or emergency supplies was even further away and, dammit, his feet hurt. He felt gingerly along his gum line with one grimy finger and, encountering tenderness, he winced. A line from an old movie sprang unbidden into his head - *A man's got to know his limitations* - and an image of his wife standing over him appeared suddenly out of nowhere and he wondered what she would say if she were still alive. *Stop being a big baby and get it sorted,* she'd have said. Of course she would. He smiled at the thought.

With a deep sigh, he pushed himself up from his sitting position and started walking along the Drove Road to Peebles.

"What delivery?"

"Flooring." Paul said, waving vaguely at an imaginary pallet full of wooden planks. Julia couldn't see them either, as she was on the other end of the phone.

"Flooring?"

"Yeah. Mitchell's delivering at 5.00. Or 5.30. Or something."

"Or something?" Julia was beyond exasperated. "What does that mean?"

"Last thing, s'what it means. They close at 5.30 and this is the last delivery off their lorry."

"So when will it be exactly?"

"Five-ish."

"Paul, I said exactly."

"Yeah, five-ish." This, for Paul, was just about as exact as anyone should reasonably require.

"I have a dental appointment at five."

"Right." Paul acknowledged this in a tone which indicated the information she was providing was interesting but ultimately irrelevant.

"What I mean is, I can't guarantee I'll be here for this delivery. Can't they just leave it on the drive?"

"Well yeah, they can. But I don't want six hundred quid's worth of oak flooring left out where any Ned can half-inch it. I should be back by then, touch wood."

"Touch wood? Is that some kind of joke?"

"No, just sayin' that with a following wind an' that, I'll be home in time. Just lettin' you know, is all."

"Paul, I have to go to the dentist. It's important!"

"Is it?"

"Yes."

"Why?"

Julia felt a cold sweat rising to meet a hot flush descending. Her stomach knotted and she blinked furiously. "Because... I have had to cancel and rearrange this bloody appointment so many times now, all because you can't be here when you're supposed to be!" She had started the sentence off flustered and panicked that she might be giving herself away, but ended it triumphantly with the tables turned and the pressure placed directly on him for his lack of punctuality and track record to prove it. Paul caved.

"Look, I'll be there alright? Just make sure that delivery doesn't take place unattended."

"You'll be here?" She knew he wouldn't.

"Promise." He definitely wouldn't.

"Great." Julia hung up.

Now she was stuck. She'd have to rearrange her appointment. Another day wouldn't hurt would it? Or perhaps the longer she left communications with Barry the worse this would get. What if he had notions of an affair, or romance? She took a deep breath. Calm yourself, woman. You don't want to confront Barry in his surgery anyway, do you? What sort of madness is that? Leave him a note. Arrange to meet somewhere discrete, away from Peebles. Not the hotel again, definitely not there. Somewhere else.

Think.

She rang the surgery to cancel her appointment and then went in search of a pen and paper.

## SIX

Janine put down her emery board with a sigh and answered the phone on her headset.

"Good afternoon, Dental Surgery."

It was half-past two and already she was losing her bright-and-breezy telephone manner. Whether the callers could detect her boredom she could neither say nor find it in herself to care. If her vocabulary had stretched to encompass the word *ennui* she would have recognised it at once, clasped it to her bosom, and vowed to use it daily hereafter. Only halfway through her first week and the awful emptiness of an afternoon's double geography stretching before her now seemed a lot more attractive than she had ever thought possible.

And hidden, below the desk, was the crowning insult to this ordeal. Worse than the boredom; worse than the petty rules and regulations; worse than the endless forms; worse than everything else. She wriggled her toes in the pair of white crocs Alison had given her and winced at the total and utter indignity.

She glanced over to the photocopier, half-hidden at the back of the admin office. Alison was there now, flapping at the touch-panel like an albino sea-lion typing an angry email, eyes only for the tiny screen on the machine currently telling her there was a paper jam.

Somewhere.

Janine sighed again and turned back to the PC showing

the telephone control panel. The Office Manager was a smart, prim, rail-thin woman with a face like haunted tupperware. Her dark brown hair was cropped close to her scalp and she had a tendency to move her head in snatches as she talked, her neck jerking out then back in, making her look like a startled bird, on the alert for the neighbour's cat, ready to fly at a moment's notice. Ever since her welcome on Monday, and her orientation and training, Alison had been hovering round Janine like a cloud of midges at a water treatment works.

And she was cold. Oh, so cold. Her pinched face was Tippex white, her eyes pregnancy-test blue, her lips the colour of an angry bruise. And to denote her seniority, inside the collar of her pale buttoned-up tunic she wore a chiffon scarf the colour of a DUI urine sample. Maths had never been Janine's strong point but she reckoned Alison was 50% puritan, 50% sergeant-major and 75% passive-aggressive control-freak.

"Above all else, Janine." Alison had reassured her. "Don't worry about making mistakes. It is your first week of your first ever job. We all make mistakes. Making mistakes is how we learn. And you will find I have no problem with mistakes, providing you learn from those mistakes and don't repeat them. It takes time to become familiar with a new role and develop the skills you need to do well in a job. And time needs patience. Fortunately, I have the patience of a saint."

Yes, thought Janine, if we're talking about Saint Fuck-Me-I'm-A-Hypocrite.

"One day, if you apply yourself determinedly, you could be a Senior Receptionist." Alison had smiled, intending encouragement - probably - but delivering menace. By the end of orientation, Janine had no more ambition of becoming a Senior Receptionist than she had of becoming a drugs mule. She put her right hand to her headset, pushing the speaker more firmly to her ear. The connection sounded like they were calling from a toaster on a submarine.

"Hello? Dental Surgery. Can I help you?"

Nothing but static and a decrepit whisper. Ha! Janine thought, it's the hoarse whisperer!

"Hello."

Janine jumped in her seat as a man's voice, rich and deep came not from the headset but from the other side of the glass screen in front of her. She looked up from the computer into the speckled grey eyes of a tall man wearing a damp leather cowboy hat, a dripping waterproof which had seen better days, and a lined and weatherbeaten face bearing a grimace. He had both hands splayed on the counter, nails short and trimmed, his fingers like those of an old man, wrinkled and hairy. She blinked, confused, and then hearing nothing more through the headset, cut the connection and flicked the sliding screen door open to talk directly to this old man.

"Can I help you?" She tried on a smile, hoping it would fit.

"I need to see a dentist."

"Which one?"

"Any one."

"Sorry, I mean which dentist are you registered with?"

"I'm not registered."

"Oh." Janine's face fell. Her first new registration and she had quite, quite, forgotten the procedure. Alison had led her through it on Monday but the information graft had failed to take and now, a whole day and a half later, all that was left was something about a form. She glanced over to the photocopier but the angry email was no nearer completion. Janine decided to take an executive decision. She pulled up the appointment diaries of the two dentists on duty today and scrolled briefly through them.

The dental intercom briefly buzzed into life, the sound suddenly filling reception: *Helen Masters, Surgery 3 please.*

"Name?"

"Cullen."

"Date of birth?"

"Look, I just want to see a dentist."

"Mr Cullen, I need your date of birth."

"Why?"

Janine blinked and sat back in her chair. She didn't know the answer to the man's question and now wondered what the answer actually was. She stalled for time.

"Address?"

"Look. Can I see a dentist today or not?"

"Mr Cullen..." Janine, finished scrolling through the diary and found nothing.

"It's an emergency." The man grimaced and ran his tongue over the teeth behind his top lip.

"I'm sorry, I-"

"Please?" His probing tongue struck tenderness and he winced.

Janine looked into his sad eyes and felt herself yield. She could see that there were no empty slots left this afternoon. All appointments, fifteen minutes apart, were showing solid blue - meaning each patient had been contacted earlier that day or the day before and had confirmed their attendance. She scrolled down to the white emptiness on the calendar which started at 5pm. Next to Barry Sullivan's name was a winking asterisk.

Janine hovered her mouse over it and a pop-up window appeared showing a 5pm slot with the name Julia McInnes in green italics with a strikethrough.

"All we have, Mr Cullen, is a 5pm with Mr Sullivan. Is that too late for you?"

"I'll wait." And, with that, the man withdrew from the desk, and sank down on a chair in the corner. Like some kind of electronic device, he appeared to freeze, his gaze locking on the middle distance and an invisible silence immediately surrounding him. Janine looked askance again at the clock and then back to the man, realising he was planning on sitting there for the next two hours.

She watched him for a short while but when he showed no sign of returning her look, she turned back to her screen and waited for the phone to ring once more.

Barry was closing his laptop lid when the door opened and a tall cowboy strode in. Barry's boner fell.

"Can I help you?"

"Cullen. 5 o'clock." The man surveyed the room and moved towards the dentist chair without prompting.

"I, er, wasn't expecting... I mean, I wasn't aware that I had any more appointments for today. Would you mind if I just check briefly?"

"They've gone."

"Who?"

"The girls at reception. The last one was putting her coat on when she asked me to come through."

"Ah, I see. Well, er, this is most irregular. Mr, ahm..?" Barry peered the the computer screen on the desk away to his right which his assistant used. She, too, had left early believing the diary was done for the day.

"Cullen."

"Yes, well you see Mr Cullen-"

"Just Cullen."

"What? Ok. Whatever." Barry didn't have the time or patience for this right now. Where the fuck was Julia? That's what the diary had said. He'd been looking forward to this all day. "You see, Cullen. My assistant has gone home and I am unable to perform any treatment single-handedly so if you could just make a new -"

"You're a dentist aren't you?"

"Well, yes, of course."

"Then dent!"

"Mr Cullen, I really-"

"It's just Cullen." The man was as calm as you like but there was steel in his eyes and the set of his jaw. His voice was quiet and soft but Barry found himself held by it, vice-like. "I have been in pain for 48 hours and I have been waiting outside all afternoon for my 5 o'clock appointment. It is now 5 o'clock - ten past actually. I am here, you are here. I have a pain in my mouth, you are a dentist. I see no reason why we can't just get this done, here and now."

"As I have tried to explain Mis-, ah, Cullen, my assistant has left for the day. It is she who prepares anaesthetic needles, sterilises my instruments, records my actions and notes, and so on and so forth. Without her, well, I'm afraid you might experience some pain which would be unnecessary and, well, painful." Barry gave a wan smile and ran his tongue over his front teeth as if to emphasise the issue at stake.

Cullen sat forward in the dentist chair and gazed into Barry's eyes, his face mere centimetres away. "I am experiencing pain now. If I have to experience a little more in order for this pain to go away, I will happily do so. That would be preferable than spending another 24 hours with this pain right now." He looked askance at Barry. "Do I need to sign some form? A waiver or something? Is that it?"

"No, no. That won't be necessary."

"Good. Ready when you are." Cullen leant back in the chair, raised his face towards the ceiling and threw open his mouth.

Barry, realising that this man was not going to shift and could well become agitated if pressed further, decided that discretion was the better part of valour. And besides, he thought, as he selected a clean pick, put on a new pair of surgical gloves and manoeuvred the light over his pliant patient's mouth, the man didn't want pain relief! This might actually be fun.

Alison Fairbright was patient. She could do patient exceedingly well. And efficient. Patient and efficient: these two strengths had served her so diligently over the years. Wherever would she be without them?

Patience was a virtue and she knew all about virtue, having kept hers intact for many, many years. Her dutiful approach to work had taken precedence over everything else for most of her life. She'd been busy working hard, doing her utmost for this company or that boss. Slaving away, ignoring idle distractions like personal relationships. Until one day she looked up and realised she had missed the "here, have a boyfriend" meeting and was staring lonely middle-age in the face.

Lonely middle-age had stared right back at her, and Alison had blinked first.

She had tried online dating and found it full of men who were awful, predatory or just unsanitary. From their photos alone, many of them looked the sort who would turn up at a sex trial just to bang on the van. So when she had taken the job at the Dental Practice, Barry had wafted into her life like a dream incarnate. A vision of class and style lacking all but the white charger.

And patience. Unlike herself, Barry normally had all the patience of a wounded wasp that had spent twenty minutes on hold. But she forgave him - because she understood. He had often taken time out of his busy day to talk to her, reveal his inner turmoil and the troubles with his marriage. With Melinda for a wife, why - he had shown the patience of a saint to put up with it for as long as he had!

So here was her golden opportunity. A marvellous man with talent, looks, money and prestige. And all that she needed was patience. His marriage couldn't last forever. Meanwhile she focussed on keeping the dental practice running like a well-oiled machine. How could he fail to value her, not notice her worth to the practice? To him?

She didn't bother herself with those mindless, squawking gossips on reception. What did they know? She knew her Barry. If he did have a roving eye - *if* - that was all it was. Harmless flirting, at best. She was his intended, perfect life partner and she could feel it in her bones.

And so, daily, she waited. Patiently.

# SEVEN

Barry leant back on the dental stool and watched the finished video with some satisfaction. And a sizeable erection. He'd read the note Julia had left at reception after the cowboy had gone, and his gut had twitched. It told him she wanted out and he found himself not entirely surprised. But she had been quite, quite spectacular in bed, and he wasn't about to let a little reticence stop him from enjoying many more sessions like that one. Oh no. Here was where the fun really started.

Stable management procedures: engaged.

An old hand at this, it had taken him less than an hour to edit down the raw footage into something usable which he could put on a cheap memory stick. He wasn't making a cinema feature here, just needed a few basic clips, each clearly showing Julia's face and body, while she engaged in obvious and unambiguous sexual activities with him. All he needed were the highlights, topped and tailed by a head-and-shoulders piece to camera which he would do now in his surgery.

He liked to see if he could get his videos to be exactly fifteen minutes long - he had long forgotten why that was; presumably because the first one he ever did had been exactly that long, by coincidence, and he liked the symmetry of them all being the same. As he pulled his stool closer to the counter and positioned his webcam ready to start recording his bit to camera, he looked across to the shelf containing all his previous blackmail tapes. Ever considerate of longevity he had copied them all to DVD in HD quality and filed them carefully on a CD rack on the shelf above his squash trophies and medical certificates. Cognisant of the need to keep them from prying eyes he had chosen to hide them in plain view, here in his surgery, rather than somewhere at home where his ever-expanding wife might accidentally stumble across them. To ensure no-one like Alison ever looked at them he had carefully labelled the spines of the jewel cases with stickers which read Tax Returns, Receipts & Invoices, and so on.

Smiling, he checked his reflection in the webcam image on his laptop screen and pressed record.

"Hello, Julia." He began.

The package dropped onto the doormat and Julia somehow sensed that, whatever it was, it wasn't good news. Something about the *pher-lap* sound it made. She put down her handbag, picked up the padded envelope and ripped it open. There was no return address, no note inside. Just a small USB stick. Nothing else.

Julia instinctively felt afraid. She didn't want to look at it, or touch it. But she couldn't not. Her heart beat in her chest like a fist. Something about the antiseptic, cold colours of the stick - a body of baby blue with a cover of translucent white - told her this was from Barry.

Normally she'd have missed the postman, rushing off to work. Today she was a tad late but now, despite herself, she knew she'd be even later. She wasn't going to be able to do any work today until she knew what was on this thing. The problem was, she had no way of seeing what was on it without leaving a digital trace. She didn't know much about computers, but she knew that much. The battered laptop she shared with Paul sat on the kitchen worktop, from where she checked their email, facebook, the usual. No way was she inserting this stick into that.

She had cheated on Paul and felt sick. That was bad enough. She hadn't figured out what to do about that - yet - short of deciding to tell Barry that it had been a one-off. No-one must know. Especially Paul. And if he were to find out? And from his own laptop?

Was this Barry's response to her note? What did he have to say that he couldn't say to her face? How could she find out without looking at what was on it? She needed to find a way to check the contents without Paul finding out.

Julia waggled the stick in her hand and paced the length of the hallway. Up and down, up and down. Agitated and afraid, guilty and ashamed, her mind was abuzz. At the very moment she needed to most, she found herself completely unable to think straight.

The Chambers Cafe lies on the floor below the library in the Chambers Institute building on Peebles High Street. Library patrons are allowed to take books down the backstairs and read them at tables or in the sofas and armchairs that dot the large carpetted area in front of the coffee desk - as long as they return them back upstairs and don't waltz out of the front door with them and out onto the street.

Cullen sat nursing a pot of tea while waiting for the pelting rain to stop drumming against the windows to his right. On a small table for two in the farthest corner of the room, he had reassigned the other chair to a different table and sat hunched on one elbow, earphones jammed into his ears, stirring his tea listlessly with a plastic stirrer.

His mouth hurt still after his visit to the dentist, but in a more natural wounded way, rather than the raw unceasing pain which had gnawed its way through his lower face for the previous few days. His jaw itself felt bruised and battered, which it probably would be given the amount of force the dentist had applied in extracting the tooth - almost sitting astride him at one point in order to gain the necessary amount of purchase. Cullen couldn't avoid the feeling that, given the dentist's triumphant look as they parted, Sullivan had enjoyed himself a little more than was appropriate. An ember of anger flared briefly and then evaporated when he suddenly heard someone say "Hello, Julia."

He looked up and around only to see no-one. The voice continued briefly, clear and deep, then stopped in mid-sentence. It was a man's voice.

Sullivan's voice.

Coming through his earphones.

The second row of seats in the library, last cubicle on the left, was where Julia sat nervously tapping the USB stick against her glossy thumbnail and jiggling the shoe on her left foot on and off, her legs crossed under the desk. This was it.

No-one knew she was here, apart from Jennifer on the front desk. There were no internet cafes in Peebles but here in the public library you could buy an hour on a computer for £1, as long as you filled out a basic form with your name, address and scribbled a signature at the bottom.

She had slunk into the slot furthest away from anyone else and now sat staring at the grey monitor with the green light winking at her in the bottom bezel. She feared that the minute she touched the mouse the screen would spring into life, and a loud bing-bong Windows welcome tone would greet her. She reached for the volume control knob on the desktop speakers and turned it off.

Taking a deep breath, she grasped the mouse and entered the username and password Jennifer had given her. She inserted the USB stick into one of the front sockets and sat frozen, waiting for a window to open. When it did it showed one file only on the stick - a video. Julia felt a knife in her throat. Heart pounding, she clasped both hands in her lap and looked down at them, seeking some sign of comfort or peace. None came.

Head still down, she slowly scanned the room, lifting her eyes beneath her fringe to see if anyone was watching her; if anyone could see her screen. Like a child in a church pew, she slowly raised her eyes to the multi-coloured icon and double-clicked. Another window opened on a black screen with a play timeline at the bottom reading 14:45 and the cursor started to move. The black dissolved into a smiling head-and-shoulders shot of Barry Sullivan sitting in his blue scrubs, his head halo'ed by the bright surgery room lights behind him. He started talking but there was no sound.

Julia reached for the volume control and twiddled it. Barry continued on blithely, trundling along, smiling confidently in silence. Then she realised she had turned the speakers off so as not to be greeted by the login tune. Sweating now, she pressed the On button and, again, twisted the knob left and right trying to hear what he was saying. Still there was no sound!

Cullen put his head down and sat motionless as if any movement on his part would prevent him from hearing the voice again. Sullivan's speech was snatching on and off; there would be a gap, then his voice would return, louder for a few words then growing quieter before being cut off again. Cullen listened intently until the volume spiked suddenly and he yanked the buds from his ears and held them at arm's length until he could tell that the sound had faded. Tentatively he held one bud to his ear and heard Sullivan's greeting again: "Hello, Julia."

This time the volume stayed steady and he listened for another minute or so until Sullivan's voice stopped and was replaced by eager moaning and groaning. The audio quality was poor but this was undeniably the sound of two, or possibly more, people engaged in sexual activity of some kind. Cullen reddened, scraped his chair back to stand and shoved the offending earphones into his coat pocket.

Julia had wrenched the controls like a mad fool, dragging the cursor back to the beginning of the timeline and hitting play again. Still no sound. No static, nothing - even when she bent her head straining towards the speakers. She sat, appalled, as Barry mouthed silently to her and then the scene cut to a close-up of an untidy double bed and a naked couple writhing upon it. Recognising herself at once, she frantically closed the video window and jabbed the power button on the PC, shutting it off. Sick and slick with sweat, she pulled the

USB stick from the slot and sat shaking. Her jaw and hands were clenched tight and she jammed her eyes shut trying not to cry. Cry: with anger at her own stupidity; rage at her lack of self-discipline and the jeopardy she had now placed her marriage in; shame at herself for submitting and succumbing to the overtures of a man who now clearly showed himself to have the moral compass of a greasy, effervescent turd

And beneath the rage, just the slightest curiosity as to why Barry had not bothered with sound. If this was an attempt at blackmail he surely wasn't relying on sign language or his skills at mime, was he?

Jennifer watched as the tall man in the cowboy hat approached the enquiry desk from the backstairs. He was holding a pair of tangled earbuds in his hands and, as he placed them on the desk between them, his knuckles shone white.

"These are... yours." He seemed unsure quite what to say. "Your colleague lent me them to listen to an audiobook on one of the PCs? I've just been down to the cafe and forgot to return them. Sorry."

"Oh, right. Thanks." She swept them up from the counter and crouched down trying to find a home for the earbuds in a drawer. Cullen looked down at the register on the table, a list of names of those who had booked out the library computers. The name beneath his own was Julia McInnes.

"These are those new bluetooth ones aren't they?" Jennifer said as she stood to her feet. "Do they work ok?

"Work?" Her question had seemed to wake him.

"Yes. I mean, you know clarity? Range? These wireless

things, they're not supposed to be as good quality as wired headphones are they? And I have no idea how far you can be from the sound source before they cut out. Although, if you're just sitting at a PC that's not really an issue is it?" She smiled politely.

"Yes. Fine, yes." He looked at her squarely. "The range is excellent."

# PART THREE

## NOTHING BUT THE TRUTH

# EIGHT

Cullen pulled up the collar on his waterproof against the wind, crammed his hat more firmly down and headed over towards the bus stop. The only other occupant of the shelter when he got there was the receptionist who had waved him into his appointment two days before.

She was sitting hunched, head down, threading the fingers on one hand through the fingers of the other, over and over. Every now and then she gave a tiny sniff. Cullen stood away stiffly to one side. When she looked up and saw him, she'd been crying.

"Oh, hello again." The girl wiped a snotty nose on a wet woollen sleeve and attempted to dab her eyes dry with one cuff of a jumper under her coat. "Mr... Cullen, isn't it? Did Mr Sullivan fix your tooth?"

Cullen silently dug his hand into his pocket and retrieved a greying hankie, spattered with dried blood, and unveiled its cargo.

"Ugh!" The girl recoiled and searched his eyes keenly. "Are you ok? That looks like it... might have hurt a smidge?" She tried on a smile of encouragement.

"Better out than in." Cullen ran his tongue across the wounded gap in his teeth again, tasting imaginary blood.

"That's unusual." She looked puzzled. "They're supposed to avoid having to do an extraction, you know? Did he not offer you any alternative treatment?"

"No." Cullen considered this information for a

moment. "It was an emergency."

"What's that got to do with it?"

"Dunno. Cost me too. Emergency fee."

"What? There's no such thing!"

Cullen scrutinised her face. "No?"

"No." Janine protested. "He's just a bloody robber and sadist. As well as a sex pest!" This last phrase was spat out with real venom and she immediately burst into tears again, covering her face with her hands.

Cullen remained rigid for a few seconds, unsure how to respond. In the end, he moved closer and sat down next to her, wanting to - but afraid to - put his arm around her. She looked terribly young. He was wondering quite what to say when she spoke up, saving him the job.

"I'm sorry." She sniffed. "He's such a bastard."

"The dentist?"

"Yes, Barry bastard Sullivan. Barry bloody bastard Sullivan. Barry bloody bastard beaver Sullivan!"

"Beaver?"

"Yes." She stifled a laugh. "It's his nickname. Pathetic isn't it?"

"Beaver?" Cullen frowned. "Builds dams or something?"

"What?" It was her turn to screw her face up, her tears forgotten.

"Chews pencils?"

"Beaver! You know..." she waved her hand with a flourish over her lap. "Women."

"I don't..."

"Never mind." She wiped her nose on her sleeve again and looked at Cullen smartly. "He likes women. A lot."

"I see."

"Too much."

Cullen raised one eyebrow but remained silent.

"Except me." She crossed her arms. "He fired me."

"Because he doesn't like you?" Cullen was struggling to stay on the rails of this youngster's train of thought.

"He fired me because I don't like him!" She jutted her chin out. "Or, should I say, I don't fancy him as much as he fancies himself."

Cullen thought for a moment. "Is that a job requirement then?"

"Oh yes! And agreeing to blow him."

"Blow...?"

"You know!" She made a strange gesture, rocking a small fist in front of her mouth while simultaneously poking her tongue into her cheek.

"Ah."

"Yes, ah. I told him to fuck off."

"Right." Cullen nodded.

"So he fired me."

She burst into tears and Cullen looked uncomfortably up the road for any signs of an impending bus.

"I'm going to tell my Dad. He'll have his guts for garters."

"Is that wise?"

"Wise? Who the fuck cares? Wise! He's sacked me and I've not even been there a week. I have rights you know."

"Yes. But as an employee with such a short time in the role -"

"Fuck off!" Janine swung her small handbag at him. "I made your appointment - remember?" Cullen's tongue unconsciously reached for the hole in his gum again. "Next morning, he told me off. Said I shouldn't have done it. I told him it was actually my job to make appointments. He said this was... different. 5 o'clock appointments are different. Apparently. How the fuck am I supposed to know? Said he'd forget all about it if I... you know." She made the strange gesture again and wiped her nose with a tissue. "Ha, I bet he was surprised to see you in his 5pm slot! Serves the fucker right."

"What do you mean?"

"You're not his 5pm type." She looked him up and down, smiling. "Wrong sex for a start. That's his beaver slot."

Cullen eyed her, interested. "His beaver slot?"

"Aye. And you wouldn't have got it at all if Mrs McInnes hadn't cancelled at such short notice."

"McInnes? Would that be Julia McInnes?"

"Yeah. She was next up, I reckon. Can't keep his hands to himself or his dick in his pants. Fucker!"

"Ok." Cullen straightened in his seat, checked to see there was still no bus on the horizon, and then bent towards Janine, speaking quietly. "What can you tell me about Barry Sullivan?"

Janine jiggled the keys in the door to the dental surgery and tiptoed in, waiting until Cullen had fully entered behind her before locking the door again. Cullen turned all the lights in reception on.

"What are you doing?" She squawked. "Someone will see us!"

"And? You work here - as far as anyone else knows - and you've every right to come back to the office at..." he consulted the clock on the wall "5.40pm, to retrieve something or whatever. Perfectly legitimate and nothing to act surreptitiously about."

"Surrep-what?"

"-Titious. Furtive." Her face still drew a blank. "Sneaky?"

"Well, yes actually." Janine nodded. "I've been fired, remember? I'm not supposed to still have these keys."

"Well, can you show me a list of all the people who have had 5pm appointments with Sullivan in the past few months? Then we can leave."

"In for a penny." Janine sighed, turned the desktop PC on and waited for it to go through its startup motions. When she logged on and brought up the calendar list of appointments it showed six different names in the past three months. All women.

"Can I see the patient details for these women?"

"Erm... well, no. That's not allowed actually." Christ, hark at her! She sounded just like Alison. "Patient confidentiality, you see. What are you looking for?" She peered at him, beneath her damp fringe.

"Well. Answer me one thing. I don't want to see their details. Just tell me if they are married or not."

Janine eyed him suspiciously and then tapped away at the keyboard for a minute, scrolling and searching. "Done."

"And?"

"No, now you tell me why you're doing this. Then I'll tell you if they're married or not."

"Hmm." Cullen looked half-annoyed, half-admiringly at this slip of a girl, capably standing her ground. "Sullivan certainly met his match when he hired you didn't he?"

"Technically, he didn't hire me. Alison did." She smirked. "But, well, compliment accepted."

"Ok." Cullen started ticking off the fingers on his right hand. "Firstly, he harassed you and then fired you. That's not... nice. And it's not right. Second, I'm going to bet that all of these women are married?" He looked at Janine for any indication that he was right but she raised an eyebrow and folded her arms. He continued. "I bet they are and I further bet that he has been blackmailing some, perhaps all, of these women into having sex with him. And if they don't, he threatens to tell their husbands. Which is also not right."

"Or nice."

"Or nice." It was his turn to raise an eyebrow. "Does that mean they are married?"

"All of 'em."

"Ok. So, I think it is time our Mr Sullivan was taught how to tell right from wrong."

"Hmm. Any other reason you're doing this?"

Cullen pushed his tongue gingerly once more into his wounded gum, then looked her in the eye. "No."

Janine considered this for a moment. "Ok. So, what now?"

"Now? You show me how you make 5pm appointments."

"What time did you say?" Julia whipped her neck around to face Paul. She stopped chopping the onion and froze, waiting for his answer. Paul was casually unloading himself from his overalls and hanging them up by the door. He looked vainly for his slippers.

"Five."

"PM?" Julia felt her heart stop.

"What do you think?" Paul asked, searching under the sofa. "Have you seen my slippers?"

"5pm. Tomorrow?"

"Yes." Paul was becoming slightly irritated, distracted

from his slipper search. "Where're the dogs?"

"In the back garden." Julia replied on auto-pilot. She willed herself to calm down but felt the blood pounding in her throat. "Who with?"

"I don't know." Paul was not a regular dentist-goer and didn't actually care who he saw or didn't see, as long as he was able to experience a pain-free visit. He opened the back door and his two terriers rushed to meet him. "Somerville, is it? Summerfield? Summat anyway." He knelt down to be submerged under soggy dogs. "Hey fellas! How's it going, huh? Miss me?"

"Sullivan?"

"Prob'ly."

The gulf between how concerned Julia now was and how unconcerned Paul appeared could not have been wider. Her fate was sealed. Barry had obviously decided to not only go through with some kind of blackmail, but seemed intent on doing so straight away. She quickly reviewed the four options she could see:

1. Prevent Paul making the appointment. Perhaps this wasn't needed as his natural unreliability meant he'd probably miss it, or forget it, if simply left to his own devices.

2. Rearrange his appointment to buy her more time.

3. Try and contact Barry before Paul's appointment and see what she could do, if anything, to stay his hand.

4. Come clean and 'fess up to Paul and take the consequences. Perhaps all would be forgiven? She looked at him as he rough-housed with his dogs, his hands like meathooks. He had never hit her, but there was always a first time. Or maybe he'd hit Barry! That would be helpful. Or not. Ok option 4 was her last - *last* - resort.

"You ok?"

She glanced over to see Paul looking up at her, one eye squinting into the sunlight shining low in through the kitchen window. "Yes. Fine, fine. Just remembering I need to make myself an appointment."

"Didn't you just have one the other day?"

"I did." She snapped instantly back to indignation. "I cancelled it so that I'd be here for your bloody delivery, didn't I?"

"Oh." She swore sometimes Paul lived off-planet. "You didn't need to do that. I told you I'd be back in time."

She looked daggers at him. "But you weren't."

"Wasn't I?"

"No."

"Oh." He stood up, his dogs entertained enough for now. "Soz." He sauntered over to the fridge, took out a cold beer, twisted the top of the bottle and flipped it into the sink with practised ease.

"Can you put those in the bin please? Where they belong?" Julia snapped.

"Soz." Paul leant into the sink, snatched the bottle top up and dropped it into the swing bin. "Again." He muttered under his breath and shuffled off to the lounge.

Julia stood frozen at the worktop, gazing at nothing out of the kitchen window. After a while, she looked down at the knife in her hands, the onion skins on the chopping board, the sound of the fan in the warming oven, the familiar homeliness of this little scene.

And silently began to cry.

# NINE

Jake sat in reception. Today was his tenth wedding anniversary and he had bought his wife, Susan, a gift. These last twelve months had been something of a rollercoaster in their marriage. He had had an affair and Susan had been on the verge of finding out when he came clean and admitted it. She had thrown him out for a fortnight and then he had managed to crawl back into the house and start the slow, slow process of rebuilding trust and rekindling the love that had been there all along, lying forgotten and unnoticed. They had managed to keep it from their children, he believed, although Susan had told her best friends about it (she'd later informed him). A year of reconstructing their marriage and, whilst they weren't completely out of the woods, they had talked and talked, reignited their passions for each other and his past behaviour now only re-emerged in fleeting and rare occasions when a random word or scene on a TV show would remind her of it and there would be an immediate and noticeable temperature drop. A real tumbleweed moment where Jake would hold his breath and hide his eyes, waiting to deploy the right word or gesture to smooth them over this hump and put the needle back into the groove.

He watched the clock hands tick around towards 5pm and worried the eternity ring box in his jacket pocket.

Davy was genuinely pissed off. He threw his coat and scarf on and bustled out of the office, stalking head-down over the river Tweed to the surgery. He hated going to the dentists, retaining a deep fear of them which he had harboured since childhood. Combined with sensitive teeth and receding gums, he lived in particular fear of the water-pick they used to remove tartar and other buildup on his teeth. Every time he went he asked them to use the old steel scraper jobby, and every time he allowed the dentist to persuade him that it would be ok and there really wouldn't be any discomfort. And every time, the dentist would be right: there'd be no discomfort - just a shitload of pain. Searing bolts of nerve-cold would shred their way into him and he'd dig his rigid fingers into the arms of the chair and stiffen his legs, bracing himself for the next shot of agony. And if he ever needed a filling - oh man, the injection! Feeling the penetrating needle and the icy novocaine squirrelling into his gum. His jaw would ache for days afterwards, whether from real or imagined bruising he could never tell. Even when the dentist had extended the time between check-ups from twelve to eighteen months, these visits still came around too frequently.

Jean, his wife, would have told him not to be a big baby and to man up, but he had never let on that this was a big deal for him - he didn't need the ridicule or sympathy or comment. He might tell her one day but sharing wasn't really his thing. His view on life was very simple: you found a partner, moved in, got married and that was that. Life's mission was complete and you could then get on with your career and stuff. It was all straightforward and he couldn't understand why others made everything so complicated. When colleagues at work would bemoan their own relationship troubles, Davy would smile and trot out a little anecdote of his own. Some time ago, when they'd been married about three years, Jean had asked him where he thought their relationship was going. He'd just laughed at her and said "Going? It's not going anywhere. It's arrived!". She'd never mentioned it again. Other marriages might be pairings of incompatible souls but he and Jean were both on the same page.

He swept into the dental practice reception wearing a mask of grim determination.

Tony paced up and down outside the dentist's gulping down the last of his cigarette. He didn't have any more gum on him so if the dentist complained about his breath he could go fuck himself. Cheryl was always banging on about it to him as well - not his breath so much as the stench on his clothing and in his hair. Plus his stubble and dirty nails. God, she could go on. Usually took a good belt around the ears to shut her up. Or a smack on the back of the head. Nothing that would show. No need to make it anyone else's business, was there?

He stubbed his cigarette out in the metal ashtray attached to the wall below the window and lit another.

Julia stood in front of the wardrobe mirror shaking, both arms held tightly across her chest. She'd been so fucking stupid. The minute hand on the clock ticked round to 5pm and she realised she'd better get her skates on. She opened the suitcase on the bed and started to pack.

Barry pulled his last pair of latex gloves from the dispenser and snapped them on, checking his appointments screen as he did so. Wendy had been dismissed, it was 5pm and his final assignation for the day was... Cullen? That couldn't be right. He scrolled across to check the notes against the appointment, assuming another mistake by the newly-fired Janine.

On cue, the man himself walked into the surgery and Barry exploded at him. "Mr Cullen! I told you last time that simple etiquette requires you to wait until your name is called before entering my surge-. What are you doing?"

Cullen had closed the door behind him and snicked the lock into place. He turned menacingly back to Barry, his eyes hard and cold. "Time we had a wee chat." He said, stepping towards the dentist chair.

Barry pushed his own stool back towards the window, its castors spinning on the polished floor. He quickly scanned the room for a way out, or a means to defend himself - his visitor's intentions now alarming him. He saw Cullen, too, cast his eyes around the room as if looking for something and then move over to the computer on the counter top. While he fiddled with something, Barry seized his moment and grabbed for the catch on the window behind him. He struggled with it between the vertical blinds but managed to free it and push the lever up, swinging the window ajar. As he pushed his weight down on his stool ready to launch himself at this novel escape route he felt an arm around his throat and he shot back across the room, hurtling on screaming wheels, coming to rest only when his face crumpled into the all-too-solid hydraulic lift of the dentist chair. Barry put one hand to his mashed face and tasted blood.

Cullen picked him up like a cold bag of loose giblets and tossed him into the dentist chair, swinging the instrument tray across Barry's body in one smooth move, trapping him in place.

"Talk."

Barry probed his teeth with his tongue, delicately checking for damage. He grimaced as he did so, eyes warily looking up at Cullen beneath a bloodied brow. For a moment the pair locked eyes, silently weighing each other up. Barry broke his gaze away first and tried to push one index finger into his mouth. Cullen grabbed at it and pinned it to the arm of the chair.

"Talk."

"Mngh mmng mnwn." Blood dribbled from his lips and down his chin.

"Spit." Cullen nodded to the faucet and spittoon. Like an obedient patient, Barry tentatively leant over and spat into the shining drain.

"Rinse." Cullen nodded. "Good dental hygiene."

Barry swigged the pink mouthwash, swooshed then spat before Cullen thrust him back down into the chair

"Right. Now, talk."

"About what?" Barry wiped his mouth with the back of one hand, recovering a little composure. "This is assault, you know? I'm going to prosecute you for this."

"Really?" Cullen looked amused, his eyes glistening. He leant his face right into Barry's and growled: "Tell me about Julia McInnes."

Barry frowned. He'd thought this lunatic was exacting some kind of revenge for his rough-handling of his tooth pain the other day. "What?"

"Julia McInnes."

"What about her?"

"Tell me about her." Cullen swung the overhead armature above Barry's head and shone the lights right into his eyes. "And the others."

"What others? I don't know what you're talking about." He blinked rapidly, his breath ragged. He could smell the sweat of his attacker and see all the stubble and pores in his face.

"Yeah you do." Cullen reached behind Barry, out of sight, and when he brought his hand back into view it was holding the dental drill. The tiny motor whined into life.

Jake was the first to tune into the conversation being broadcast over the intercom. He cocked an ear and caught the eye of Davy in the process. The pair smiled, embarrassed, and then both listened to the two men's voices - one low and calm, the other higher and much more tense - until they heard the names of their respective wives mentioned and their smiles promptly dropped. When Tony sauntered in and saw two blokes gawping with their heads tilted, Jake put a finger up to his lips and looked at him.

"Fuck off!" Tony glared. "Don't shush me, you fucking-" He stopped short when he heard Cheryl's name being spoken by the higher pitched voice.

The more this man fed names to him, the more Barry warmed to his theme. He had no idea what Cullen's game was, and he was going to make sure the police threw the book at him when he managed to get free from his current predicament, but he found himself unable to resist this golden opportunity to brag about his conquests. He realised he'd never had anyone he could share this information with before and now he had a captive audience - even if it was himself who was currently playing the role of captive.

"Nice piece of skirt, that Cheryl. Everything in good working order, if you know what I mean. Don't look at me like that! Nothing wrong ... two consenting adults. No-one else's fucking business. Certainly not yours." Barry raised his eyebrows meaningfully. "Got a lovely little tattoo of a dolphin. Just above her pubic hair line. Well, I say pubic hair. She doesn't really go in for that much, if you catch my meaning. Suits me - I like a clean work surface."

There was a sudden series of banging noises that shook the floor, and a gathering rumpus that quickly culminated in the surgery door being violently hammered from the other side. Barry tore his face from Cullen's and looked anxiously towards the door. The lock held for mere seconds and when the door flew open there was a large furious man standing in the doorway, with two more red faces peering from behind his bulk. Realising that, perhaps, it was better the devil you knew than the devil you didn't, Barry turned back to seek reassurance from Cullen, but his former assailant was nowhere to be seen. The only other movement in the room came from the vertical blinds swaying erratically in the open window.

Big Paul pulled into the car park in his white van and exhaled with a groan. The clock on his dashboard said 17:32 and he figured he'd missed his appointment, but he clambered from his van and walked over towards reception. A tall figure in a cowboy hat appeared from between some bushes and came towards him, pocketing his phone. Paul looked askance and picked up his pace.

"Surgery's closed." Said the stranger.

"Huh." Paul shrugged. "Light's still on."

"Cleaner."

"Is that right?" Paul attempted to push past the man and got a distinctly off-colour whiff of something as he did so. "Guess I'll just double-check, as I'm here."

"I... wouldn't."

"I've got an appointment." Paul winced. "Had an appointment. 5pm. Bit late, I guess."

The man stood his ground as a number of sirens keened in the night, swiftly followed by a police car which fishtailed around the corner in the snow and skidded to a halt outside the dentists. Two patrolmen got out just as an ambulance hustled into view from the other end of the street, pulling to a stop alongside the police car.

The blue lights strobed the two men as they stood watching.

"What's happened?" Paul wondered, out loud.

"Whatever it was, you missed it."

After a while one of the policeman reappeared, scanning the car park and street as he returned to his car. The man in the cowboy hat turned to go and nudged Paul as he did so. "Come on. Don't want to be mistaken for witnesses, do we?"

Paul looked at the man with interest, seeing something in his face. What was it: honesty? Concern? "Not a fan of Old Bill then?" Paul asked.

"Not... as a rule." The man smiled thinly.

"Me neither."

They walked back to Paul's van in silence, the man still giving off a strong unpleasant odour. Paul wondered if it was the chemical element, Ew. There was the sound of frantic scuffling and barking emanating from the back of his van.

"Well." The man checked out the livery on the van and smiled to himself. Blowing on his hands, he rubbed them together. "Haven't you got a wife and a home to go to?"

"Yeah." Paul looked at the man, searching his eyes. "Yes, I do."

"I'd do that then."

Paul pulled the van doors open and Penn and Teller shot out and immediately laid siege to the man, jumping up at him, scratching his jacket arms and rucksack. The man leant forward to pet Teller and then looked up at Paul.

"Your dogs eat cheese?"

"Eat anything."

"It's just that I read somewhere that cheese makes some dogs sick."

Paul shrugged. "If it does, they'll eat that 'n'all."

The man slung off his pack and reached inside. He pulled out a somewhat-squashed, large grey cylinder which was leaking pale cheese from substantial wounds in its sides. Paul realised this was the source of the man's stench.

"Stinking Bishop." The man offered the wheel to Paul who just nodded to put it at his feet for his dogs.

"Whiffs a bit. Any good?"

"Weapons-grade, you might say." He lay the cheese on the floor and watched for a moment as the two dogs devoured it. "Name's Cullen."

Paul shook the offered hand. "Paul. Mate's call me Beep."

"Beep?"

"Short for BP. Short for Big Paul." He smiled, a touch

embarrassed. The man just gave a small nod.

"Nice to meet you, Beep. Mind how you go."

Paul watched as the man gave his hat a small adjustment, almost by way of a farewell, and then turned and strode off into the shadows. When he was out of sight, Paul turned back with his dogs and sauntered over to the policeman who was calmly talking into his radio.

# TEN

Julia was standing, frozen, at the end of the bed, the suitcase in front of her piled with random items she had thrown in. She couldn't decide who was to blame for the pickle in which she found herself - Barry or Paul - but it certainly wasn't her. Oh no.

And even if it was, there was no point dwelling on it. She could almost hear Paul now: "Don't keep blaming yourself." He'd joke. "Just blame yourself, then move on."

Paul.

The sound of the front door opening jerked her awake and she panicked, jamming the suitcase closed and shoving it under the bed. Heart thumping in her chest, she looked at herself in the mirror, dabbed at her eyes with a tissue from the bedside table and smoothed her dress down with both hands. Taking a long, slow breath she set her jaw, straightened her back and strode out onto the landing.

Paul was shambling up the stairs, shaking his head.

"Murder." He sighed heavily and raised his eyes, catching Julia's worried look.

"Murder?" Julia felt goosebumps rise and her legs start to buckle. She reached for the bannister to steady herself.

"Fuck, aye." Paul let out another heavy sigh and ran his thick fingers across his bald spot. "You ok, babe?"

"Oh my God!" Julia one hand to her mouth, her eyes filling up. She felt her whole weight sag into the newel post. "Paul, what have you done?"

"Me? Ain't done nothing." Paul reached out to catch her, startled, but Julia's eyes flared and she backed away. "Everybody ruining it for everybody else, is what it is."

Julia stared at him, horrified. "What? What everybody else? Who?"

Paul's brow furrowed. "S'not my fault." He cast his eyes down and shuffled past her into the bedroom.

"Paul!" Julia grabbed his shoulder and wheeled his bulk round to face her. "What have you done? Look at me!"

Paul couldn't meet her gaze and stood, cowed, a man-child in front of her. "I missed my appointment."

She lifted his chin and then took a step back, searching his eyes. She didn't know what to say.

"I was late, ok?" Paul sulked. "Murder on the bypass. Bloody rush hour traffic. Didn't get there 'til half-past." He pulled his mouth into a small grimace. "I'm sorry. Really."

"What?"

"I'm sorry, alright?"

"You were late?" Julia felt relief flooding into her but wouldn't allow it full rein until she had more information.

"Yes." Paul's shoulders slumped again. "Soz."

"You were late." A statement, no longer a question. Goosepimples rose on her arms and neck.

"Aye." Paul dropped his hands and headed back into the bedroom, already starting to put his ignominy behind him. "Might have to see another dentist next time, mind!" He added, somewhat brightly, as he rooted through the wardrobe.

"What? Why?" Julia found herself waggling her head from side to side, trying to shake her thoughts into some sensible structure.

"Sunderland's had some kind of accident. Attacked or something. 'S what the copper said."

"You mean Sullivan?" Julia played with the stray curls at the base of her bob. "Barry Sullivan, the dentist?"

"Aye." Paul came back out onto the landing, casually wiping his nose with the back of a sleeve. "With his own instruments too! Neat, huh? Someone decided he'd been getting too friendly with one of his patients. Went all Marathon Man on him."

"Marathon Man?" Julia screwed her face up.

"Yeah. Is it safe? All that." Paul smiled at her, broadly. "Seems they eschewed anaesthetic 'n all."

"I'm sorry?"

"Esch-ewed." Paul enunciated deliberately. "Good word, innit? Means didn't bother with, apparently." He beamed again. "Looked it up on my phone. Coppers these days, huh? Getting some kind of education any road."

"Is he, erm, ok?" Julia didn't know what answer she wanted to hear but felt this was the question she needed to ask. She stood, swaying slightly, as if on the deck of a ship, while the world around her shifted and heaved. "The dentist?"

"I don't think so." Paul grinned. "Mouth ripped to shreds, face mashed to a pulp. Wasn't pretty. At all. Used the drill imaginatively, according to the copper."

"Why is it amusing?"

"Well, not amusing as such. Just that I'd heard a few stories - down the pub - about him, you know?" Paul looked at her, innocently. "Heard he liked diddling married women on the side."

"Really? Well, then. He deserved it, didn't he?" She looked at her husband, as if for the first time, and drank him all in. She cast her eyes over his strong shoulders, arms and hands, his trunk and solid stance; scanned his face and his innocent, trusting smile. And when she had finished, Paul standing there silently and slightly clueless while she did all this, Julia moved into his arms and squeezed him tightly round his midriff.

"Me and you." She said, into his chest.

"You and me." Paul replied, ruffling her hair.

"Lots and lots."

"For us to see."

"You and me."

"Me and you."

"Lots and lots."

"For us to do."

"Hey." Paul pulled himself away slightly and tilted her face up so he could look into her eyes. "I promise I will never ever be late again." He cradled her face in his meaty hands, thumbs brushing the tears away. "Ever."

"Yeah." Julia sniffed and smiled. "You will."

"I am not a fun sponge!" Alison protested, simultaneously indignant and confused as she was having to guess at what this new term implied.

Janine smiled. "Ok. If you say so." They were sitting back in Alison's office, once more going through the sheaves of forms and questionnaires required to be completed for all new employees. "It was my Dad's words, not mine." She lied. "I didn't ask him to write that letter, you know? I was upset and really - really - angry about being fired. I wanted to do something to complain but also wanted to wait until I wasn't so upset. He sort of took it on himself, you know?" She gave another apologetic smile. "Guess I've always been his little princess."

"What is a fun sponge anyway?"

"It doesn't matter. Can we drop it and start again? Please?"

Alison's world was still rocking from the revelations that were coming out about Barry. They had started as murmurings, and then she had begun the process of piecing things together. But once she found his 'tax returns' and viewed one - she could not bring herself to do more - she had handed them over to the police. In the days since then she had been operating in a kind of zombie mode, keeping things in the surgery moving, ensuring appointments were rearranged and starting the process of recruiting an additional dentist for the practice. There was plenty to do and she was able to keep busy. Until it was time to go home.

She spent her evenings hugging herself and tearing into box after box of tissues, her dreams in pieces. She wasn't experienced in the ways of love, had had only a few relationships - but she knew what men were like. She'd thought Barry was different.

What a stupid fool she'd been.

And then, beyond how he had hurt her, she had looked, appalled, at the stuff he had done to others. And the letter from Janine's Dad had touched a raw nerve. The realisation that her inability, or unwillingness, to see what had been going on around her, brought her to tears. She had called Janine immediately and asked her to come back in for a chat and, if she wanted, to resume her position as Junior Receptionist.

"Yes, we can start again." Alison reassured her. "I just want to make sure that we are both clear on how things should proceed and that we are both happy that a line has been drawn under this whole affair. I mean, business. A solid red line."

"I understand. And I agree."

"You will need to agree that, in the world of work, you have a lot to learn Janine. And while you are clearly a bright and capable girl, there are rules and procedures that need to be followed."

"I get it."

"Procedures which are there for a reason. Which help things run smoothly and which predate your arrival. Procedures which all other members of staff understand and are happy to adhere to."

"Yes."

"Procedures such as not arranging appointments for other patients in calendars above and beyond your pay grade."

"I'm sorry."

"Such as not gaining access to the premises once all other staff have left for the day."

"Yes."

"Or allowing non-members of staff to access patients' confidential files."

"I didn't let him!" Janine bristled. "I specifically told him he could not see that sort of stuff."

"Good." Alison brightened. "And if you wish to query any procedures, or even suggest improvements. Why, we have a Staff Suggestion procedure for just that very thing!"

"Does it have a form that needs to be filled out?"

"Of course."

"Right." Janine swallowed. "Ok. I shall... keep that in mind."

"Excellent." Alison smiled. "We will see you first thing tomorrow then."

"Do I need to wear the crocs?" Janine tried on a smile

she thought might suggest hope more than desperation.

It didn't.

Alison pursed her lips and then gave a long, deep sigh. "Let's... think about that, shall we?"

# POSTSCRIPT

**Barry Sullivan** lost all his teeth and was unable to afford a whole mouth dental implant after his wife, Melinda, filed for divorce on the grounds of serial infidelity and her lawyers took him to the cleaners. He retired from dentistry and is currently trying to build a second career as a motivational speaker. He has a new book out called *Happiness is a Worn Gum.*

**Alison Fairbright** decided to forswear men and devote her life to the optimisation of procedures and processes within the field of dental clinic administration. At a conference on How To Get ISO Certification for Dental Clinics she met a fellow Office Manager called Malcolm who is a stickler for process and a devotee of all the acronyms which make the lives of business administrators so fascinating. They have a second date next Tuesday.

**Janine Crombie** still works at the Peebles Dental Practice and was recently promoted to Receptionist Assistant (Grade 3) after Alison introduced formalised job and salary grades in order to qualify for the Investors In People (IIP) commendation now adorning the wall in reception. Janine received a pay rise of £0.50 per hour and was, obviously, thrilled.

**Julia McInnes** devoted herself newly to the nurture and

regeneration of her marriage to Paul. Confident in their new-found togetherness, she persists in believing that - one day - Paul will turn up on time.

**Paul McInnes,** along with his dogs Penn and Teller, developed a liking for strong cheese. He did not renew his missed dental appointment and has not been to the dentist again. He bumps into Cullen more often than you might think, usually while out walking his dogs.

**Mungo James Cullen** lives alone. Somewhere. When the weather is cold, his jaw still bothers him.

## AUTHOR'S NOTE

This is my first attempt at a novella and I would like to thank Claire, for giving me the belief and push to get it started. I could have done it without her, but probably wouldn't have. Also for her many constructive comments and insightful feedback on reading my early drafts.

My thanks, once again, to Big Paul for allowing me to depict him unrealistically. He won't read this either (prob'ly) and wouldn't want my thanks anyway. He'd much rather have a good bottle of Scotch - but this is cheaper.

Peebles does not have a dental clinic like the one I depict, nor does the Chambers Institute have a cafe as I describe. Neither is there, at the time of writing, a cheese shop on the High Street. Don't really know why I set the story there, now I come to think of it. Lazy, I guess.

Any other inaccuracies or omissions are intentional and not meant to represent a lack of research or thoroughness on my part. Honest.

Finally, I'd like to extend no thanks at all to the concept that is NaNoWriMo (if you are not familiar with it, be grateful and endeavour to keep things that way). Whilst I was able to use the month of November to focus my efforts in writing this story, there the usefulness of the whole enterprise ends. My condolences to anyone who has ever tried to complete a novel in NaNoWriMo and I genuinely hope that you manage to succeed once you have recovered from the whole experience.

Bah humbug and Merry Christmas.

mjf
20.12.2017

## Join the Cullen & Big Paul Fan Club!

If you enjoyed the adventures of Cullen and Big Paul, why not join their fan club? You'll get early notice of new books, special offers, a monthly newsletter from the author, unique free content, invitations for discounts and more!

JOIN at **download.markfarrer.com/signup**

## Tell others what you thought...

If you enjoyed this book, please leave a review on Amazon

## About the Author

You can learn more about Mark Farrer at **www.markfarrer.com** or follow him on Twitter **@mark_farrer.**

# BRONCHIAL BILLY

mark farrer

funny business press

BRONCHIAL BILLY



Published by Funny Business Press

*To Gail*
*For being there.*

# CONTENTS

## BORN ON THE FOURTH OF JULY

"What time do you call this, Billy Gillespie?" Maud was peering through the crack in the door, keeping it on the security chain so that Billy couldn't get in.

"Let me the fuck in, woman. It's my birthday!"

"No it's not." She checked the clock on the wall by the door. "Your birthday was yesterday. Go away."

"Please, Mo?" Billy crunched his face up into what he thought might look like supplication and apology. In reality, he just looked like Emperor Palpatine trying to be sarcastic.

"No. Go away!"

"Where to? I live here!"

"Not tonight you don't." Maud started to shut the door but Billy wedged a hand in and got it jammed for his pains.

"Ow, ow, ow. Fucking ow, Mo! What do you do that for?" Maud relented and took the chain off the door to see the damage she had done to his hand. He was holding it like it was his favourite vase from the Ming dynasty. "That's my shooting hand. Fuck, Mo. My shooting hand!"

He slumped onto the doorstep and dropped a large box of fireworks by his feet, the contents spilling out onto the garden path. Maud looked up and down the deserted street and then hissed at him.

"Get your sorry arse in here, you stupid barmpot. You'll wake the street!" Maud watched as her husband drunkenly scooped up the loose fireworks with his good hand and staggered into the hallway in a half-crouch. He slumped against the wall and started to slide down onto the carpet. He raised his wounded hand to his lips, eyes half-closed.

"Shhh. I'm being quiet, see?"

"Being quiet, my arse. Look at the state of you."

"What do you mean?" he slurred. "The state of me. What's wrong with the state of me?"

"You are drunk."

"No, I'm not." Billy giggled conspiratorially and tried to tap a finger against the side of his nose. He missed. "Just had a little cebel... cebelatory drink."

"Little? Little?"

"Aye. Just a tiny, wee-" Billy swayed forward, off-balance, and managed to grab onto the bannister post to stop him falling.

"Look at you, you can barely stand. Gaynor told me you got thrown out!"

"Gaynor? How...? What...?"

"Pete told her and she texted me." Maud's face was a stern mask of righteousness

"Fucking..." Billy muttered under his breath, vowing to get back at Pete when he next saw him. He leant harder on the post and the bannister started to sway alarmingly.

"And look at that!" Maud interjected. "That's not safe. I've asked you to fix it. Time and time again."

"I'll fix it." Billy puffed, staring at some invisible detail in the bannister from a distance of mere centimetres.

"When?"

"Tomorrow."

"Tomorrow!" Maud scoffed. "You mean today?"

"Whatever. Look, if I say I'll fix it, I'll fix it. There's no need to remind me every six months." Billy tried to look into his wife's eyes but was incapable of focus. "Come here, Mo, eh? Gi' us a kiss."

"Don't be daft!"

"Come on, it's me birthday!"

"No, it's not. Where've you been, hmm? Gaynor said you were thrown out hours ago."

"Wasn't hours... and I didn't get thrown out!" Billy cast his eyes around the hall floor wondering if there was a reason that the pattern on the carpet was slowly crawling away from him.

"You don't even know what time it is, do you? Oh, you're so drunk. You've been out drinking for hours!"

"Was just a wee cebel, cebel... birthday drink. Wi' Pete." Billy hiccoughed and wagged a wayward finger. "I am not drunk."

Maud crossed her arms and nodded to the hallway clock. "Really? Can you tell the time?"

"Certainly." Billy slurred. He slowly released his grip on the bannister and turned to face the opposite wall. Bringing himself up to his full height, he prodded his chest with his finger and spoke sternly at the clock. "I am not drunk."

"Give me strength." Maud rolled her eyes and watched her husband slide towards the floor and then mysteriously arrest his descent and grab onto the half-empty box of fireworks. "And what do you think you're going to do with them?"

"They're birthday fireworks! It's the Fourth of July!"

"Fifth."

"Still the Fourth. In America." Billy sneered, smugly.

"You're not setting them off in here."

"Of course not, my sweet."

"Good."

"I'm setting them off in the street. Just came in to get a lighter." The act of saying it out loud reminded Billy why he had come home and he turned and made to head off towards the kitchen.

"Oh no you don't, Mister!" Maud barred his way. "Get out! Get out now! And take your bloody fireworks with you."

"But my sweet-" Billy blurted out over her and Maud recoiled at his sour breath.

"Oh! Don't you *my sweet* me. Get out and stay out." She bundled him out onto the step, turned him round and pushed him down the short garden path. "And don't come back until you're sober and ready to apologise."

She watched for a few seconds as Billy scrabbled unsteadily once more to accommodate the last of the spilled fireworks into the battered box but, seeing a light come on in one of the houses opposite, hurriedly closed the door and snicked the security chain back into position.

"Remind me again, why this is a good idea?"

The lumbering Moorfoot hills to their right were all dressed in greens and greys as the sun started to caress the peaks and pull down the day onto the upper slopes. But Stinky Pete was too busy wrestling to keep the Flying Anglia on the road to notice. And the green look on Billy's face was evidence of his torment of wanting to be sick but being unwilling to contemplate the horror of decorating the interior of his car with whatever he'd last eaten

And with good reason. Billy's treasured, restored 1965 Ford Anglia Super was a beauty. Strawberry red with a pearl white roof and red leather interior, reupholstered, buffed and treated like nothing else in his life had ever been. Its gleaming chrome bumpers, taillights, sidestrip and radiator grill shone in the early morning half-light as they kangarooed down the ribboning B-road.

"'Cos I'm not letting some puffed up Yank tell me how to use my gun!" Billy pouted, his car suspension complaining about the undulating surface as Pete struggled with the temperamental synchromesh, terrified of losing control and sending his pal's cherished possession into a ditch.

"It's his place. His rules." Pete said.

"Fuck it is!"

"It is!"

"Ok, yeah. It is. But. But." Billy paused trying to rein his own argument into a semblance of order so he could articulate it convincingly. "It's my gun. First he had no right to take it off me."

"He did. You crossed the line with it."

"He's the one who crossed the fucking line!"

"No, I mean you took your gunbelt beyond the limit. You know the rules. There's signs up everywhere and you know the rules. No firearms outside the main hall."

"Fucking stupid rule."

"He's only doing it for us."

"How the fuck is taking my gun away doing it for us?"

"You break the rules, he risks losing his license. He loses his license, we don't have a club. Or anywhere for the gunfights."

"Didn't need to confiscate it." Billy sulked.

"That's true. But you were drunk in possession a firearm. And you were waving it around. And you did take it beyond the allowed threshold." Pete looked across at his friend. "And you did argue the toss."

"I didn't argue the toss."

"You called him a big black twat."

"He is."

"And you grappled with him when he took your gun away."

"He's got no right to take it. It's my property."

"It's his club. His license."

"My gun."

"Well, it's his now." Pete said. Then, seeing Billy looking genuinely upset, he added. "For the time being. You just have to apologise and ask for it back. Nicely."

"Apologise? Fuck off!"

"You're going to need it for the shootout on Friday."

Billy glowered out at the road in front of them. He was thinking, Pete could see. This scheme to break into Cass's Clays to let off his birthday fireworks, was starting to morph into something bigger and all-encompassing. In Billy's mind, the plan was literally coming together. The pair had parted ways after their forcible ejection from the Country & Western night at the Grand Ole Opry, but hours later Pete had been woken by the incessant ringing of his phone and looked out of the window to see Billy slumped on the damp pavement stabbing stubbornly at the phone in his lap. Billy had waved him down and prevailed upon him to drive. Now look at them: two bickering pensioners still dressed in over-elaborate cowboy attire, one of them still drunk, tumbling along an abandoned road in a showstopper of a vintage car, intent on breaking into a shooting range in the early dawn.

Last Of The Summer Wine meets Easy Rider.

"Don't stand there! You're blocking the Fire Exit."

"I'm not."

"Yes you are. And the sign says - there, look - Do Not Block Fire Exit."

"How can I possibly block a Fire Exit?" Billy failed to keep the exasperation from his voice. "How is that possible? I've got legs. And I'm flammable. It is not physically possible for me to block a Fire Exit."

"Why are you always so angry?" Pete asked.

"I'm not."

"Yes you are. You're always angry."

"I'm not always angry. Just sometimes."

"You're always angry with me."

"Just seems like it, is all."

"Why? Why are you always angry when you're with me?"

"'Cos you say stupid things. Stupid things which piss me off."

"Like what?"

"Like *'don't block the Fire Exit.'*"

"But it's the rules!" Pete protested. "The sign says."

"You and your fucking signs and your fucking rules." Billy sneered. "Pathetic."

Stinky Pete's face dropped further, a feat barely believable given his usual hang-dog expression. When God had handed out appearances, physical characteristics and cheery demeanours, Pete had been picking his nose and looking out of the window. His veined cheeks, normally leathery and speckled with stubble, were currently puffed out and rosy red from all the effort that had been required of him. With his pale forehead glistening in the dim light, his gimlet eyes shining black and beadily, combined with his stuffed cheeks, he looked like two currants atop a freshly smacked arse straight from the oven.

Beneath the biggest Stetson you ever saw. A black felt ten-gallon hat, which drooped alarmingly at the front so that he had to crane his head up to look at you when he was wearing it. The relative size of the hat, along with the necessary head-tilt required whilst wearing it, did Pete no favours in the physical stature department. Which was unfortunate, because it was here that Peter Blaikie needed all the favours he could get.

Pete was not a large man; 5'6" was a slight exaggeration which he maintained with a pair of elevated cowboy boots, which never left his feet. He had a dainty, fragile frame with long arms and small hands, and an oversized head shorn of hair. His neck was thin and it was fair to say that the word which best described him overall was spindly - if spindles were short and had a large bulge in the middle of them. Pete's proudest possession, after his enormous hat, was his beer belly. Although these days it was more of a leaking water pouch. It hung down from his torso like a goitre on a camel's neck, swinging as he walked and looking as if it could detach any minute - like a drop of water about to take its leave from the end of a tap. Possession of such a belly left him in the quandary common to many elderly men: where to position his belt.

A straw poll of the Gorebridge elderly community, of which both Pete and Billy were members, would have revealed that elderly men had three choices in the belt-positioning arena:

Go High - you went several trouser sizes up, pushed your beer belly down into your gusset, and pulled your belt up to your nipples. Result: enormous clown trousers with a fly two yards longs, an inability to see one's shoes and a rear view of a bloke with no arse in his trousers.

Go Low - you stubbornly refuse to bow to gravity's

demands and sling your belt beneath the extruding stomach, tremulously cradling the wobbly blob with a meagre strip of leather built merely to contain a cow's innards and not withstand such strain as this. Result: your shirts bloomed at the buttonholes revealing patches of pale, baby Rhino skin, and when you turned to face someone it looked awfully like a fleshy swing bridge being manoeuvred into place.

Go Large - insist that the only place for a belt to go was where your waist should actually be and ignore the fact that your waist was no longer one of the shortest distances around your anatomy. Instead buy bigger trousers and much, much bigger shirts, so that the collars gaped and crumpled, revealing folds of turkey neck and hairy moles, and you had to fold your sleeves back up over your wrists to prevent them from being dragged through the gravy of whatever pie you were trying to neck at the time. Result: grimy, grey unwashed shirts which unearthed themselves from your belly and hung loose down the back making it look like you had been caught short and had to hurry to catch your next pie.

Pete was a bold follower of Go High. So the complete picture he currently presented was of a wizened Gollum peering out from beneath an over-sized cowboy hat with the confused air of a partially-blind mental patient. He wore a black T-shirt with an obscured message above a nipple-high belt keeping a tatty pair of black jeans from crumpling to the floor where his pointy-toed cowboy boots shone dully under the Fire Exit light. All this, while suffering the slurred and still-slightly-drunken invective of his so-called best mate with whom he was not mentally equipped to compete in the ultra-competitive Scottish sport of insulting-wielding. The means of defence Pete had evolved to contend with this, was flatulence.

In short, then, Stinky Pete was not a catch. He repeatedly told people that he had taken his cowboy name from the gold prospector character in Toy Story 2 but this was, as everyone knew, complete hoo-ey. Some kind of lower intestinal issue, and a lifetime of tissue damage and muscle loss, seemed to physically prevent him from emitting gaseous reminders of his last meal. The farts would come - it was *when*, not *if* - and the only question would be whether they were audible or not. They would certainly smell.

Pete's intestines took this lull in the angry monologue which passed for Billy's conversation as an opportunity to fart wetly and loudly. Billy turned back to him with a fiery glare.

"Fucking hell!"

"Can't 'elp it." Pete muttered, then sniffed enquiringly. "Jalfrezi."

"What?"

"Jalfrezi." He repeated, as much to himself as anyone else. "Kinda fruity."

"You are a marvel, do you know that?" Billy didn't wait for an answer. "Who else would hang around with a human water treatment centre? It's fucking disgusting is what it is."

"Can't help it." Pete grizzled. "It's age."

"Is it bollocks, age. I'm older than you and I don't fart like a field full of fucking Highland cattle."

"Better out than in."

"No, it's not. Can't you just... I don't know, put a stopper in it? Just for now, so's we don't set any alarms off or anything?"

"Doctor says there's actually nothing I can do."

"Nothing? Like, say, *actually* trying to exercise some *actual* physical control over your *actual* sphincter?"

"At my age?"

"Will you stop banging on about your age? None of us are getting any younger, you don't hear us yakking on about it. What about charcoal tablets? If you can't stop the farts, can't you do something about the smell?"

"Tried them. They made everything smell... kinda smoky. Like all I ate was barbecued."

"Fucking marvellous." Billy put a fist theatrically up against one ear. "Excuse me, I'm looking for someone to help me with an illegal, covert operation. Wondering if perhaps you could recommend, you know, maybe a cat burglar extraordinaire or something? Oh, you're right out of cat burglars? Ok, how about Mister fucking Methane?"

Pete looked around, confusedly. "Who are you talking to?"

"Myself." Billy growled. "Only way I can be sure of intelligent conversation. Come on, let's get a fucking move on. Just... try and fart quietly."

"Okey-dokey." Pete said cheerily, letting another Jalfrezi reminder float quietly along the dark corridor as he followed Billy out into the early morning light clutching a semi-automatic pistol, a box of live ammunition and Billy's battered box of fireworks.

Cullen stared at the broken trinket box and felt his throat tighten. This was all he had left of her. Everything else he had burnt or walked away from. This he carried with him, always. Buried deep at the bottom of his backpack, he would dig it out whenever he couldn't sleep. Which was more and more these days.

Sometimes it was the recurring dream: the van, the photo, the injustice and rage which boiled up from within him and jolted him awake. Sometimes it was his mind racing, bouncing around when he wanted it to be quiet; at peace, when it wanted to keep searching. And sometimes, sometimes, it was the sound of the gunshot. He couldn't sleep through that.

And now he was awake. Those first few sounds perhaps weren't even gunshots, maybe fireworks, but they had woken him just the same. He had bolted upright, smacking his head on a low shelf and the box had fallen to the floor. He picked it up and saw that a small semi-precious stone had fallen from the inlay. He brushed the space were it had been with hands which were pale and scarred and scoured by age and weather. Outdoorsman hands. Whereas the box looked almost new, so small and polished, exquisite in its detail and its marquetry, the different woods expertly inlaid and beautifully crafted. It was a delicate, precious memory, untouched by time.

As she was.

His eyes pricked with tears as he knelt down on the floor in the half-light and started feeling for the tiny missing stone. The firing sounded again. Definite gunfire this time, echoing off the wet stone in the chill dawn. Now wholly awake, he grabbed for his hat by the side of his sleeping bag, clamped it on his head and pushed himself to his feet, hairs standing on the back of his neck, the precious box still in his left hand.

With a flame in his eyes, Cullen went to find the man with the gun.

"Loud, isn't it?" Stinky Pete ruminated as he watched

the grey smoke and splintered rock rise from the quarry wall. Billy was not a good shot.

"Loud, shmoud. No-one for fucking miles around. This is perfect!" Billy was marvelling not just at the setting, secluded and safe, but at the miracle of being able to fire this wondrous handgun loaded with live ammunition. "Wish I'd thought of this years ago!"

"Crime, you mean?"

"Crime, my arse!" Billy sneered, loosing off another round, this time into the log on which was perched the tin cans he was actually aiming for. "Is this, or is this not, a fucking firing range?"

"A closed firing range."

"Detail."

"And a stolen gun."

"I'm not stealing it!" Billy protested, waggling the pistol dangerously in Pete's direction. Pete leant back awkwardly, as if the unusual angle alone would prevent him from being shot if Billy's trigger finger slipped. "Borrowing it, is all. Using it for its intended purpose. Viz: shooting at stuff."

"Without a license."

"Fuck off! How many times have you seen me handle a gun?"

"A replica gun."

"That fires! How many times?"

"A lot."

"Thank you. And do I not know how to handle a firearm?"

"A replica firearm."

"Will you fuck off with the replica shit? What difference does it make?"

"This one fires real bullets. Bullets can kill people."

Pete was still warily watching Billy's less-than-tight grip on the pistol. "Would you mind not waving it in my direction?"

Billy ignored him, relishing the feel of the loaded metal as he brandished it generously in defence of his argument. "The point is-"

"Pointing at me." Interrupted Pete. "You well know, as someone who has handled a gun lots of times, that you should never - NEVER - point a gun at someone, loaded or not."

"It is not pointing at you." Billy retorted, waving the pistol sarcastically in an extravagant flourish.

"It's pointing in my general direction."

"I." Said Billy, articulating each word so as to avoid slurring them. "Am a CRACK shot."

"You mean crap shot." Pete smirked, nodding at the three tin cans, all still standing intact atop the pitted log.

It was five in the morning and the alcohol had only partially worn off. In the dawn light, Billy's bloodshot eyes clearly spoke of someone both familiar with excessive drink and recently acquainted with it. Since early yesterday evening until the time they had been ejected from the Grand Ole Opry, Billy had been continually drinking, swearing, complaining, arguing and ultimately resisting. Now he was doing all the shooting.

Cass's Clays was tucked away off a B-road near Heriot, a no-man's land where Midlothian met the Scottish Borders. In amongst a ridged landscape scarred by burns which had gouged deep troughs into the soft rock, there were many scattered abandoned quarries. Small reservoirs of stone which had been mined to build farms and outbuildings, walls and stells - and then abandoned to the sheep and cattle. Cass's Clays was one exception to this. A clay pigeon venue and outdoor shooting range, it boasted a single-storey wooden building which housed a reception, an office, a cafe, a gun showroom, a small shop, and a sprawling potholed car park. An intermittently planked wooden walkway threaded a route from it to three separate quarry sites, each containing two automatic traps from which clays could be shot into the air and fired on from four separate stands.

Billy fired two more rounds into the quarry wall and lowered the gun, seemingly out of breath.

"Fuck me, it's heavy."

"Heavier than Geronimo?"

"Fuck aye. Same calibre, mind. Must be these bullets." Billy marvelled at the gun in his hand, hefting it to more accurately assess the weight. He flipped the catch and pulled out the magazine from the grip and cast around for the box of bullets he had brought with him from the gunshop cabinet. "Why did this never occur to me before? It's genius."

"How?" puzzled Pete.

"Well, first off, we get to practice somewhere out of sight, not disturbing anyone. Second, it's free. Doesn't cost us anything and we get free ammunition."

"You mean 'cos you're nicking it."

"Detail. Third, it's real ammunition. Live bullets! Makes it all more real, more genuine experience."

"You don't have a license."

"Which is why we're doing it this way, lame brain. And why it is just so perfect!"

"And it makes the gun heavier."

"Yeah, and that is the genius part!" Billy gloated. "See, if I can practice quick-drawing with a heavier gun, when I get Geronimo back it'll feel lighter in my hand. I'll be more nimble. Faster. Muscle memory will expect the heavy gun and I'll be able to draw in the fight faster. That ten grand has got my name on it, baby! Guaranteed win!"

Geronimo was Billy's beloved pistol. A replica 1873 Samuel Colt Army Peacemaker single-action revolver, holding six blank .45inch rounds. One of the most popular handguns ever made in the nineteenth century, it had been manufactured in a variety of calibres and barrel lengths. Geronimo was a .45 with a 4.75" long barrel, shorter than those issued to the US Army, making it easier to carry and faster to draw. This was its strength and Billy knew it. Had researched it, in fact, at length. Then, having chosen his model, went in search of an elaborately decorated example. This was his Apache - delicate black leaf engravings on the gunmetal barrel and cylinder, an ornately decorated frame and hammer with antique gold finish and a polished walnut grip. Slung snugly into his buttery leather holster laden with deactivated brass bullets (for show) and loaded with blank cartridges (for shootouts).

Months spent practising in front of a mirror, watching endless Westerns, slo-mo'ing through the gunfights and later studying the quick draw tutorials scattered over YouTube. Billy might look down at his wrinkled hands, with their loose, mottled skin and gnarly old nails, but when he wrapped his fingers around the handle of his gun the decades fell instantly away and he stood young and proud, crouched ready to whip his pistol to his waist and fill an enemy belly full of imaginary lead, staring impassively on as his opponent writhed bleeding in the dirt.

"And if we get caught?" Pete whined and lifted his head so he could look Billy in the face beneath his towering hat.

He looked like a small boy with wrinkles dressed up in his father's work clothes. If his father had been Johnny Cash, dressed from a charity shop.

"Caught! Who's going to catch us?"

"Big V."

"First, can we not call him Big V? That is a self-appointed name made to make him sound cool and impressive - neither of which he is."

"What? He's a black guy. That's cool. And he's huge! He's what, six-five, six? He's like they crossed a fridge-freezer with the Lion King. That's impressive. He's one of those, whatdoyoucallems, giraffrican-Americans."

"He's a nignog and he's called Vince." Sniffed Billy, who refused to acknowledge the suavity and success of Vincent Cass, aka Big V, the owner of the Grand Ole Opry and Cass's Clays.. "Says it all, far as I'm concerned. No-one called Vince has ever been cool or impressive."

"Vince Hill." Offered Pete.

"Who?" Billy scoffed.

"Vincent Price?"

"Shut up."

"Van Gogh?"

"Look, I said Vince, alright? They're fucking Vincents. Not the same thing."

"Vince is short for Vincent."

"I swear to God, if you don't shut your cakehole I'll-"

Pete farted again, loudly. "Sorry."

"Give me strength." Billy shook his head and winced at the smell. "And they can't swim!"

"What?" Pete wondered if, in relaxing his bowels, he had missed some new signpost in the conversation.

"Coons. They can't swim, you know."

"Look you can't call 'em that, these days." Pete

protested. "And you certainly can't call him a black twat."

"But he is."

"You have to call 'em ethnics. Or people of colour."

"Jungle bunnies?"

"No!" Pete shook his head, exasperated. "And what do you mean, they can't swim? Course they can swim."

"Can't." Now it was Billy's turn to shake his head. "Ever watch the Olympics? Ever see an ethnic-" He loaded the word with dripping emphasis. "Ever? In a swimming race?"

Pete screwed his face up in thought. "No, you haven't." Billy continued. "'Cos they're runners. Look at the running races, all the fastest ones are darkies. They win everything. They run, we swim."

Pete relented. "Ok. So... what?"

"So shut up about him and us being caught. Do you really think that big Yankee Jungle Bunny has got CCTV or something?"

"Ethnic." Sighed Pete. "No I don't. But he might have an alarm for his gun cabinet and ammunition drawer."

"Ah." Said Billy, reloading.

If no-one could ever have imagined the sight of two badly dressed cowboys in a quarry at dawn, they would certainly never have offered odds on the chances of a third one turning up. But, when Pete looked up to where the quarry ridge-line met the dawn, that is what he saw. Silhouetted against the pale sky was a tall figure in a wide-brimmed cowboy hat, standing menacingly and certainly not intending to be hidden.

Pete froze, tried to swallow, realised his mouth had gone dry and managed only to emit a strangled moan. Billy looked across at him, distracted from his reloading, and when he saw the look on Pete's face he turned to look in the direction of his friend's gaze.

"Is it Big V?"

Pete remained dumbstruck. Billy unthinkingly shoved the clip into his gun and raised his arm to point at the stranger. Pete's eyes bulged.

"Don't point your gun at him!"

"Why not?" Billy jutted his chin out and thrust out his chest, the weapon boosting his adrenalin and machismo in one smooth slug of stupidity. Pete recoiled in surprise when the gun went off.

"Oops." Billy waggled his eyebrows and gave a lop-sided grin. Pete looked up at the empty skyline, a smeared after-image of the man's silhouette still on his retina. From somewhere he managed to rediscover his vocal cords.

"Did you hit him?"

"Dunno. Might have." Billy waggled his gun as if to say *With all this natural talent, why the hell not?*

"Fuck sake! Come on." Pete urged, tugging at Billy's sleeve. "Let's go! Before he comes back."

Billy, all bravery now fully inflated due to the absence of any visible threat, resumed his default state of unjustified belligerence.

"Let's be havin' yer, then!" He bellowed, his rasping cry ricocheting off the quarry walls, echoing through the cold dawn. There was an empty silence when the reverberations died away. Billy scanned left and right, looking for any signs of movement

"Fuck, Billy." Pete tugged again in a loud stage whisper. "Let's get the fuck away. Could be Big V. Could be the police."

Pete led a reluctant Billy away down the gravel path,

turning a corner down into a little winding valley of scree and heather slopes. Billy spun his head this way and that, eyeing the ridge carefully for any signs of the stranger reappearing. But they made it back to the main office without seeing anyone else. All was quiet and undisturbed - no car park full of police cars silently flashing their blues and twos, as Pete had feared.

"Let's put all this stuff back and get the hell out of here." Pete's hands and voice were shaking. "I don't need this. Not at my age."

"You're younger than me, you barmpot."

"Well we're both too old for this. Bloomin' stupid idea."

"It wasn't a stupid idea." Billy retorted. "Was going great until mystery man showed up."

"Well, you've had your fun. Had your practice. Let's put the stuff back and get out of here."

Billy baulked and hung back as they reached the office door.

"Come on!" prodded Pete.

"Kinda like having this." Billy hefted the pistol again, admiring its weight and presence in his grip.

"Put it back. Let's go." Pete hissed, looking anxiously around.

They passed through into the gun display area and Billy sulkily placed the pistol back in its place.

"Take the bullets out." Protested Pete.

"What for?"

"So they won't know it's been used. And so they won't get it out later and accidentally shoot someone with it."

"They'll know it's been used by the smell. And the residue. Need to clean it, really."

"We don't have time." Pete hissed again. "Take the

bullets out, put the unused ones back in the box and let's go. That'll have to do. Wipe your prints off."

"Hmmm." Billy said, thoughtfully, patting his pockets without success. "Box."

Cullen looked at the blood on the back of his left hand and realised he was trembling. Maybe it was the morning chill, because this was little more than a scratch, really. But the shot to his hand had made him drop the trinket box and it lay now in pieces on the stony ground. He absently raised the wound to his mouth, sucking it gently as he contemplated the shattered box and then bent slowly, gently, to his knees and started carefully retrieving the pieces he could see amongst the stones.

From away beyond the quarry edge he heard an engine start up, the punky, throaty roar of something unnecessarily souped-up. He hurriedly gathered what he could into his pockets and headed for the ridge. By the time he could look down to the winding track which led away from Cass's Clays, the car was spitting dirt up into a ragged cloud as it skittered towards the B-road. An old car. An old shiny red car with a shimmering white roof, its bumper and wing mirrors gleaming in the rising dawn.

He descended a scree-laden slope to the quarry floor and found a half-empty box of fireworks. Some roman candles, and Catherine wheels lay discarded on the ground and, a few yards away, a couple of rockets were planted unsteadily in the dirt. Over by a large rock lay the remnants of a box of bullets, and a pile of newly discarded shell cases amidst old clay pigeon fragments. He picked up an unspent bullet and weighed it thoughtfully in his right hand.

Back at the hut, Cullen gathered up the things he'd collected and stuffed them into his pack. He took out the box fragments from his pocket once more and fed them into a ziplock bag and then spent a fruitless hour searching on the floor for the tiny missing stone. As the warmth of the rising sun started to filter through the window and the noise of vehicles and staff arriving for the start of their day drifted through the still air, Cullen stood and wiped his brow sadly.

He slung his pack, wedged his hat firmly back onto his head and strode off towards the South, away from Gorebridge.

# THE MAN WITH THE OLDEN GUN

They called him *Billy The Kid* even though he was pushing eighty.

And they didn't call him that either, Billy called himself that. He figured (Americanism inserted deliberately - as was his wont), he figured that if he referred to himself in the third person using that name then, as sure as varmints were varmints, the rest would follow and soon he would be known as *Billy The Kid.*

It was a vain hope but one he clung to since, as far as Billy was concerned, there wasn't much in his life left to cling to. All hope may not have been lost for Billy Gillespie, but he sure felt his life had put hope down somewhere and now couldn't quite remember where he'd left it.

When Billy was a middle-aged man, his GP - tired by the many years of complaint, malingering and griping from this long-time patient - had recommended him for a psychiatrist evaluation. The psychiatrist's notes came back simply bearing the initials *PM* which, Billy's GP knew, stood for *perpetual malcontent.* In layman's terms, a miserable bugger. His GP had sighed in agreement and restricted himself thereafter to limiting his ministrations to trying to lure Billy off the fags so that he might extend the length of his declining years, and not bother himself with Billy's toxic mental hinterland. It was, after all, his GP thought, a Hippocratic oath, not a hypocritic one.

In the years since then, Billy's tendency towards miserabilism had deepened and widened, like the fat Mississippi as it churned and toiled sluggishly down towards the delta. In his twilight years, Billy was an intolerable, miserable old bastard with only bad words to say about anyone, and a resting face which made him look like someone was pressing down hard on his toes in steel-capped boots. A wheezing, whining, whingeing weasel of a man with the grace of Trump, the warmth of Scrooge, and a cough like a distempered hyena. If you were in range, it was often a choice between choosing to be sprayed with bronchitic sputum or listening to the diseased outpourings of a vile, ranting ignorant bigot. For many it was not an easy decision.

When he coughed, his body spasmed like a shitting dog; when he talked, his pallid jowls wobbled and shook, his rheumy eyes scowling at you beneath fevered lids. His face, partially hidden by stringy dirty-white hair which hung down over his brow in an unruly gobbet, was blotchy and pale. And, like the betting shops and pubs he patronised in his day-to-day existence, he was both gloomy and bitter. With a hangdog demeanour and globular facial shape, he had the look of a badly bandaged and permanently depressed poached pear.

Plus he was lazy. Words took time to think of, articulate and phrase. Who could be bothered? A scowl, frown or a simple hatched-faced look worked wonders on most people who had kindly (or unknowingly) initiated a conversation with him. They didn't do it a second time, and Billy was glad. The world was full of fucking idiots and morons, unthinking and uncaring sheep who did what they were told, believed what they heard, and followed the fucking rules. Billy knew better. The rules and procedures were there precisely for those cretins. If you had your head screwed on right, you didn't need procedures and rules - you could exercise your initiative, override the settings which authority imposed - because, 99% of the people in authority were those same unthinking, uncritical, uncaring cretins. Rank, privilege, wealth, seniority - the 99% were distributed evenly across society. No strata was exempt or more favoured than the next. A complete normal distribution across society, from top to bottom. And whenever someone asked him what "normal distribution" meant, he just gave them one of his looks and felt smug inside as the question proved his very point about the ignorance of the masses.

Billy knew better and that was that.

Billy woke and reached for the phone and then immediately wondered why he had done that. His head hurt like buggery and without his contacts in he couldn't make out the time. He hoped it was at least the afternoon given the night he'd had. This better be fucking good.

"Yes." If he could have fired the word more pitilessly down the phone to wound the caller he would have.

"Hi. Mr Gillespie? It's me! Sophie? How are you this morning?" The voice was as bright and shiny as a freshly vajazzled TV weathergirl.

"What?" It was still morning. Billy didn't like mornings. Or morning people. Or people.

"It's Sophie? From the house?" Another one of these fucking students, Billy thought. Workshy snowflakes, wasting their time doing media studies, political environmentalism or tattooing & relationship management. Making every utterance into a question when they should be out making a living, contributing to the economy instead of draining it. Generating wealth. That's what he did. Why couldn't they?

"What do you want?"

"It's about the washing machine? I was just calling to see if there was any repair on the, erm, horizon. It's been two weeks now and I've got a pile of dirty clothes here which-"

"Haven't you got a launderette?"

"Not nearby, no."

"How about a sink?"

"Erm, well, yes. We have a kitchen sink but-"

"Then use it."

"But we're paying rent for a house with a washing machine and it's not working and-"

"And, and, and. And what?"

"And I was hoping that you would be able to send a man out to fix it?"

There she was, turning sentences into questions when she had no business to.

"Plumbers busy right now. Have to wait until next week." Billy lied. Although it probably wasn't a lie, he had just omitted to contact a plumber since they cost money - and they were probably busy anyway.

"Next week? Can't you find someone-"

"No."

"But-"

"Next week." Billy growled and hung up. Fucking students. Being a landlord was a right royal pain in the arse. Surely there were easier ways for him to make his money work so that he didn't have to.

Billy was not a well-educated man. His gas fire had more certificates than he did. But he was vastly experienced in the ways of the world, hadn't been born yesterday and - where money was concerned (especially his own) - was as tight as a Scottish sprinter's hamstring.

Leaving school at fifteen, as you were allowed to then, he had become a plumber's mate but had quickly grown to hate the early morning starts and the days spent being cold and wet. A fortuitous accident, when he was eighteen and had fallen through a bedroom ceiling whilst attempting to remove a dead pigeon from a cold water tank, had given him a bad back and a year signed off sick. When his back recovered he found the will to work, never strong, had weakened through neglect and he was now a bona-fide skiver. He fell in with mates who spent their mornings lying in, lunchtimes down the pub, afternoons in the bookies, and evenings playing darts and pool down the Social. That was the Sixties. Easy dole money and a climate of strikes, walkouts, and civil unrest took care of the Seventies and Eighties where he was just one of the mass unemployed. By the time the Nineties rolled around and society was clamping down on the likes of him, he had gained such a mastery of the chronic but difficult to pin-down conditions which prevented him from working - stress, back, feet, RSI - he was a fully-paid up member of the long-term unemployed. With the rise of the knowledge economy, Billy headed into his fifties an unemployable dinosaur that society would rather shuffle off into a corner whilst it wrestled with the challenge of getting useful people gainfully employed.

It was just before the millennium that Billy finally struck gold. His mother died and he inherited her draughty terraced house in Dalkeith. In a fit of unexpected and atypical financial acumen, he had decided to rent it out as student accommodation. Blair's goal of getting 50% of young people into further education meant it was boom-time for anyone with rooms to rent to tenants who weren't too fussy about standards. The term slum-landlord was dusted off after a long absence and it fitted Billy like a well-tailored shroud. Within a year, he was no longer shuffling and skulking about the place, but standing looser and more erect - until the Benefit Office started to eye him suspiciously and he had to make a serious effort to maintain the gait and demeanour of a broken man, something which he had once done without thinking.

Ah well, no such thing as a free lunch, thought Billy.

Roll forward into 2010's and Billy's income through rent had increased dramatically as he had been able to keep squeezing it up in line with commercial rent rises, increases in student loan limits and rises in tuition fees. None of which had required him to lift so much as a finger to improve or modernise his property in any way. Yes, the interfering Health & Safety busybodies were continually popping up with new legislation regarding carbon monoxide detectors, smoke alarms, fire extinguishers, Legionella and God-alone-knew what else. Billy certainly didn't, as he had managed to finagle a way past all these by the sophisticated ploy of simply ignoring them and telling any students who came to apply for a lease that they could take it or fucking leave it. Most of them were unaware of their rights, as it was their first time living away from home as adults. They knew nothing about boilers, heating, consumer rights, or legalities. The *#metoo* snowflakes were far too busy poncing around on social media complaining about safe spaces and Brexit to spare any thought for practicalities like their own safety or consumer rights. Say what you like about this generation, Billy mused, but they were as gullible and exploitable as they were impassioned. Bless 'em.

And the University Housing Association was a running joke. Staffed by student representatives, each limited to a tenure of one academic year, it meant there was no continuity, no follow-through. And when said student representatives would much rather play politics, shoot for President of the Union, or spend their time making Points Of Order and reading Trotsky, it meant that, for students, the UHA was a pointless, toothless irrelevance; for Billy, it was a ticket for the gravy train.

So, each year, a fresh batch of students showed up, applied, requested improvements, were told to lump it or leave it, ended up lumping it and paying Billy handsomely for the privilege. This year's crop were no different - Sophie and whoever-the-hell-else was sharing the house with her. Billy felt he might need to put some effort into clarifying the division of responsibilities of landlord and tenant a tad more clearly. Viz: he, the landlord, got to do what he damn-well pleased and could leave his property to rack and ruin if he so chose - and, in fact, he did so choose; she, the tenant, could go swivel and should forthwith restrict herself to ensuring he was paid each semester in advance and then shutting the fuck up.

"How'd you find me, then?"

Cullen shrugged and pushed another pint towards Paul. "It's your local."

"Aye. But I'm not here 24x7 you know."

"No?"

"No!" Paul was indignant. "Out looking for Miss Right

the rest of the time."

Cullen sipped at his own iced water and stayed silent. Ant and Dec, Paul's two Jack Russell terriers, lay contented in front of the fire raging in the grate, even though it was summer outside.

"Got a date on Friday, actually. Blind one."

"Huh."

"Been shopping for a new outfit." Paul patted the ballooning shopping bag on the floor beside him.

"Why do you need a new outfit if she can't see?"

"She can see. We just haven't seen each other yet."

"So why are you meeting her then?"

"Because it's a date. Duh!" Paul scrunched up his face, wondering if his friend's ignorance was genuine or put on. Sometimes with Cullen it was like talking to an unmade bed with a head injury.

"Why haven't you seen each other yet?"

"My niece, Sofe, set it up. Says we're perfect for each other, apparently."

"Well, if she's never seen you before, why do you need a new outfit? Any outfit would be new to her."

"Because it's a date. Want to look my best. Jeez!" Paul was beginning to regret starting the conversation now. It had gone from complete silence to the Spanish Inquisition in a heartbeat.

"Hmm." Cullen nodded, not bothering to bring himself to understand.

Paul looked his friend over, weighing him up. His usual hat clamped down over protruding ears, a few stray greying curls escaping beneath the brim. His face lined and worn, wrinkles and ridges etched deep in his forehead and around his eyes. He wore a few days stubble and it looked like he had the startings of a cold sore on his bottom lip.

Cullen had a general stillness about him which put a lot of people off-balance. There was something in his silence and demeanour which made people think they were being assessed, unfavourably, failing to come up to some unspoken standard or other. Probably correctly, but it was unnerving and most folk took it as a sensible cue to keep their distance, leave him be. As a result, Paul knew, Cullen had few friends. Possibly none. And he was happy with this outcome. But today, rather than looking at ease with himself, he looked adrift, forlorn. Amidst the chatter and hubbub of the Lamb & Flag, he looked like an isolated castaway in an ocean of sociability.

"You're not chatty much today are ya?" Paul attempted. "Not that you're chatty any time, mind, just saying you seem particularly... reticent at the moment."

"Reticent?" Cullen frowned, whether at Paul's choice of words or the thought of him ever being un-reticent, Paul couldn't tell.

"Aye. I do know what it means."

There was a long pause while Paul continued to observe Cullen closely. His steel-grey eyes looked cold and he seemed older, more gaunt, more fragile. He waited but Cullen stayed silent.

"What happened to your hand?" Paul nodded to a dirty dressing plastered to the back of Cullen's hand. His friend glanced down at it and shook his head slowly.

"Nothing."

Paul sighed, took another drink and then tried another deduction punt. "You ill?"

Cullen shook his head again and dropped his eyes to the tabletop between them. "I need a favour."

"So you said."

Cullen looked up into Paul's eyes, serious and cold. "I

need your help."

"Yeah. Got that." Paul tried to make it light but Cullen's face wasn't interested.

"Can you fix this?" Cullen produced a ziplock bag from a pocket and pushed it across the table. In the bag was what looked like a dirty handkerchief wrapped around something small. Paul looked askew at Cullen and then gently opened the bag, unwrapping the hankie to reveal the remnants of a wooden box, polished and inlaid. It's lid was severed at one hinge, one side was split, one was hanging by a thread and there were several splinters of wood lying inside the empty box.

Paul brushed the lid with one enormous finger and prodded the splinters around the table. "I was going to ask what is it, but perhaps I should ask what *was* it?"

"A box."

"No shit, Sherlock." Paul sneered. "You do know I am a woodworker, yeah?"

"That's why I came to you. Can you fix it?"

Paul looked at the shattered box, no bigger than a tobacco tin. "What happened to it?"

"It broke." Cullen looked into Paul's eyes, intently. "Can you fix it?"

"Well." Paul bit the inside of his cheek and turned the shattered box over in his hands. "Bit smaller than stuff I usually work on. Craftmanship this. Quality work, is what it is."

"You're a craftsman."

"Aye." Paul puffed his chest out and nodded. "Need special tools for this kind of thing, though, you know? Can't go putting a twenty-five-mil chisel through something like this."

"No, you can't." Cullen made a sudden grab for the box

but Paul's huge fist closed over it.

"I'm joking."

"Don't." Cullen's face was ashen and Paul squinted at his friend.

"What's the story with this, then?"

"There's no story."

Paul brushed an enormous thumb over the inlay pattern in the lid. A cursive string of tiny semi-precious stones set into the wood spelt out the name *Eilidh*. There was a stone missing where the dot of the second "i" should have been.

"You want me to fix it? Tell me the story."

Cullen seemed horrified. "I can pay you."

"I don't want money."

Cullen raised his eyebrows.

"Yeah, I know right." Paul smiled and his eyes lit up. "I mean, I do want money. I'm not stupid and I am skint. But not for this." He leant in, conspiratorially. "I want you to tell me about this box. Payment in kind, as it were."

"Why?" Cullen had pulled back as Paul had leant in, as if they were connected by a fixed-length steel rod.

"'Cos I'm interested." Paul grinned a winner's grin, folded his arms and waited.

Tom Corcoran sat in his new office and gazed out over the campus feeling pleased and proud of himself. The official Senior Housing Officer in the University, like all the other officers, was appointed right after the madness of the exams when the previous reps disappeared never to be seen again,. He and his cohorts were left to handle the trickiest task of the year - with no prior experience - addressing the needs of the new intake of freshers requiring accommodation come September and the start of the next academic year. There was a lull, obviously, until then. But someone needed to mind the shop and handle the trickle of emails and letters which the dog days of summer yielded up.

And in the afternoons, there was always the window to stare out of.

So, yes, right now it was boring and, yes, it was glacially slow, but you did get to finish at four and spend the long sunny evenings with your pals in a beer garden or watching the golf on TV. And at some point soon, something interesting would fall into his lap.

"Hello?"

Hello yourself, thought Tom as he looked up at the face peering around his office door, now if she would like to fall into his lap...

"Is this Student Housing?" Her hair was a muss of thick, blonde bedhead tangles and her eyes were innocent and cute. Yeah, cute, thought Tom. He nodded dumbly and she stepped into the room.

She was a little shorter than Tom, dainty, delicate and diminutive, like a large doll. Dressed in a tight-fitting mustard T-shirt and pale blue calf-length jeans she had smooth, slender arms and great legs. And a tremendous chest. Tom watched in awe as the cotton fabric of her shirt strained as she walked across the room towards him, every movement yielding a new sensual curve and contour.

He motioned for her to sit in the chair on the other side of his desk and tried desperately to maintain his composure as he watched her slip into the seat. She had slim fingers with one hand full of chipped and individually painted glitter nails and a tiny tattoo on the heel of her palm that Tom couldn't quite make out. There was something about the secretive nature of it that made him want to reach over the desk and kiss it. He stopped himself.

"How can I be of assistance, erm...?"

"Sophie." Said the angel in front of him. "Sophie McKay."

"Sophie. Ok. How can I help?"

Tom listened, gazing gormlessly, while she explained the reason for her visit. Not all her words registered, but he got the gist. When she had finished, he looked down and saw that he had made a series of almost legible notes on the pad in front of him.

"Well, if Mr.... Gillespie, wants to remain on our approved housing and landlords register then he will have to comply." Tom said. "Any complaints are dealt with very seriously. You get a verbal warning, then a written one and if you don't respond to a third and final request then we take them off our list. Three strikes and you're out. Simple as that."

"Is that really such a big deal?"

"Depends. Getting on the housing ladder is tough - so I'm told." He smiled, meaning it to reassure but unsure that it did. "So rental demand is always high. There are always more prospective tenants than properties. If a property is in good repair, attractive and can demand market rent then there is no particular reason for a landlord to focus on student tenants. He can take his pick. But if a property isn't-"

"Oh, it isn't." Interrupted Sophie. "It's a shit-hole."

"Really?" He could barely contain himself at the way she had uttered the swearword. It was perhaps the sexiest thing he'd ever heard.

"Really." Sophie insisted. "We're all sorry we live there

now. If we knew then what we know now, we would have looked elsewhere. Absolutely."

Tom sucked his teeth in thought, gazing at her, imagining her lying, vulnerable and warm - and naked - in a filthy, insanitary hovel. He heard her clear her throat and snapped back to attentiveness.

"Yes. Well, leave it with me. I will give him a call. I expect you'll see an instant response." He smiled helplessly at her.

"Thank you."

She stood to leave and he lurched forwards in his chair. "Can I have your number?"

She blushed, and he joined her, adding quickly. "So that I can... let you know... the outcome of the call?"

She smiled shyly and scribbled a number down on his deskpad.

He watched her as she swayed towards the door and out of the room and it took him several minutes to realise he was standing, leaning on his desk with his fingertips, in an empty office gazing at the open doorway. Gathering himself he strode over and closed his door and then stepped over to the filing cabinets lining the wall opposite the window. In the top drawer labelled A-G, right at the back of the hanging files, he found the Gillespie file.

It was three inches thick.

"Tell me about the car again." Paul narrowed his eyes and looked tenderly at his friend. Cullen had spoken for several minutes, haltingly, threading his fingers together on the table in front of him, eyes downcast. Paul had never heard Cullen talk - really talk - about his past and, while he couldn't help feeling that he had been given only the most meagre details, it had been enough to melt his heart and soften his view of this solitary man with steel-grey eyes.

Now that he had finished, Paul was trying to keep his own composure by changing the subject away from the trinket box.

"Old car."

"How old?"

"Old." Cullen shrugged, cars clearly not his thing. But what was?

"Old as in Chitty Chitty Bang Bang, old as in Herbie, old as in Inspector Morse, or old as in Starsky and Hutch?"

"Watch much TV do you?"

"No." Paul sighed. "Come on, gimme some idea. How old?"

"Can you give me some frame of reference that makes any sense to me?"

"Apparently not."

Cullen chewed his lip for a moment. "Sixties or Seventies I'd say. Small car, two-door. Before they made hatchbacks."

Paul pulled a face but couldn't rustle anything up. "Colour?"

"Red with a white roof. Lots of chrome. Very good condition. Very good. Obviously well-loved. Someone cares for it."

Paul's face lit up. "Well, why didn't you say?"

"I just did."

"I meant earlier. I know whose car it is."

"Whose?" Cullen leant forward, his eyes flickering with a once-familiar fire.

Paul smiled and nodded at his empty pint glass.

"Mr Gillespie?" Tom's appetite for this conversation was bellying out rapidly. So far, it had involved him trying to finish sentences and Gillespie interjecting, either an endless stream of *what's* or brandishing a large array of novel declensions of the word *fuck*.

"What?" There was another one.

"I'm just trying to explain to you that-" Tom gritted his teeth.

"Fuck off!" And again. "I don't want your fucking explanations!"

"It's just that, well, these complaints are long-standing and-"

"So am I. And so's my house."

"But these complaints... It's my job, you see, to-"

"You don't have a fucking job! Call this a job? Get a proper fucking job instead of badgering honest landlords like me."

"Mr Gillespie-"

"Never mind the Mister Gillespie's son. Get off my fucking case. My tenants have signed a fucking lease. With me. Got that? With me, not you. You are fucking irrelevant."

"Mr Gillespie, I can assure you-"

"A lease. A legally binding document. Do those words mean anything to you?"

"Well, of course-"

"Good."

"But you see-"

"Never mind the fucking *but*'s either, son. *But*'s don't mean jack."

"Mr Gillespie, if I could-"

"I swear to God, if you *Mister Gillespie* me one more

time, I will come round that University and insert a large implement into a small orifice!"

"Sir, please." Tom was endeavouring to keep calm and finding that this constant interruption was burrowing into his thin crust, marrowing perilously down through his calm mantle which he was nurturing, patiently, to prevent his molten core from exploding upwards and spurting volatile magma into the conversation. He paused, involuntarily, as he realised that this analogy made him think not of this conversation, but of his client - Sophie - and himself. She was why he was making this call, and it was her he was seeing in his mind's eye while this ranting arsehole spewed venom down the line at him.

"I think we're done, here, son."

"Yes." Tom swallowed. "Thank you, Mr Gillespie."

"Don't you fucking-"

Tom dropped the handset into the cradle and breathed out slowly. He hoped he had made himself clear. The file in front of him made dismal reading: damp and mould, draughts and a leaky roof, lack of hot water, broken showers, unrepaired appliances, neighbour complaints about the garden and exterior. Tom wondered whether any of the previous inhabitants of this office had ever done any work, given they had allowed the complaints, warnings and failures-to-comply for this property to recur, year after year.

He scribbled on the last page of the file and placed it back in the tall cabinet. That was warning Number One. He made a note in his diary to follow-up in a week's time to check if the landlord had actually paid a visit and attended to matters.

Better still, he thought, crossing out the note - why not make a note to call Sophie instead?

Billy stood at the front gate and contemplated the dilapidated hulk before him. It was all his and it made him a nice income but even he couldn't bring himself to say it was a good-looking property. A three-storey, end terrace in a row of similarly down-at-heel dwellings. The front garden was a few square yards of weedy crazy-paving containing a crumbling stone bird-table. The only greenery on display was the mould on the wheelie bins.

Fucking students should be grateful for a roof over their head, never mind complaining about this, that and the other. Bad enough that he had to fork out for things when these careless, stupid tenants broke them. Getting a verbal warning from the University Housing bloke or whatever he was because he wasn't... whatever he'd said - well, that was a fucking liberty.

The paintwork on the door and windows was peeling and the letter box cover was hanging off. He walked up the short path and looked at the brickwork, in sore need of re-pointing. Certain that the doorbell wouldn't be working, he knocked loudly and peered through the two stripes of frosted glass either side of the scabby plastic number 9 nailed to the centre of the door.

The girl who answered the door was wearing a brushed cotton nightshirt, faded and shrunk, revealing pale skinny legs like wishbones and arms with the translucency of blown eggshells. The garment hung open at the neck and a single glance told Billy that there was nothing to see beneath it of any interest to him. This girl had the contours of a coathanger and a face like a slipped disc.

"Sophie?"

"Jenny. Sophie's out." Her voice, matching her build,

was reedy and thin - like an old gramophone playing in a cold back room. She seemed in a bad mood. That makes two of us, thought Billy.

"I'm your landlord. She said something about a washing machine not working."

The girl turned silently and padded barefoot down the lino'd hallway, leaving Billy on the doorstep. Shaking his head slightly he stepped inside, closed the door and followed her. Jenny stood waiting for him in the kitchen, one hand resting on the lid of the washing machine. Someone had pulled the machine out from underneath the worktop revealing stains, mould and fluff all over the unpainted plasterwork behind it. There was at least a week's worth of dirty dishes in the sink.

"It's about time." She grumbled. "We've been waiting weeks."

"It's the parts." Billy countered, retreating into his usual scowl.

"What parts? You don't know what's wrong with it yet."

"Ach, it's always the same thing with this - er, these machines." He corrected himself quickly. There was no need for her to know that this machine was a decade old and that former tenants had required regular repairs. Billy was no stranger to this particular scenario: disgruntled tenant complains about broken appliance unfixed for weeks. "As a reliable landlord I feel it is my duty to have a supply of relevant spares on hand for when things, inevitably, break down." He gave her what he considered a thoughtful and compassionate look and placed his toolbag gently on the floor. "What *is* the problem with it?"

Jenny ignored the obvious bollocks he was feeding her and raised her eyebrows. "Knackered isn't it? I mean, look at it. It's older than me!"

"Yeah, well I've got underpants older than you."

"Wondered what the smell was." Jenny sniffed, unimpressed.

Billy bristled. "Perfectly good machine this. They don't make 'em like this any more you know. Know why?"

"Because it's the 21st century now? The iron curtain's down. We have electricity, the internet. Soap." She sniped, sarcastically.

"Not at all. Models like this will last a lifetime, is why. Simpler in them days. None of this internet connectivity, sticking a computer into anything with a plug. Simple. Nothing to go wrong. Nowadays, any breakdown, you got to throw the whole machine away. Disposable society. This-" he patted the washer affectionately. "This predates that. Comes from a simpler time when manufacturers had the decency to make machines that worked and lasted and you could fix yourself."

He patted the washer again to emphasise his point. There was a loud clink and something dropped to the floor. Jenny looked at him archly. "You were saying?"

"Something and nothing." Billy waved his hand dismissively. "Have it fixed in a jiffy."

"I'll leave you to it, then." She said, and tripped out of the kitchen.

When she returned fifteen minutes later, Billy was furtively looking through the kitchen drawers and cupboards. He jumped guiltily at the sound of her voice.

"Find anything?" She spat.

Billy scrunched up his bulldog face and scratched his stubble. "Don't have the parts."

"Yeah, you said." She put her hands on her hips. Billy wondered how she found them. "*Before* you even looked at it."

Billy held up his hands. "I do have the parts, just not this one."

"Simple, you said. Fewer things to go wrong, you said." A gathering storm of indignation clouded her features.

"It's the drum."

"I don't care if it's the string section!" Jenny raised her voice and started to shake her head as she spoke. "We've been without a washing machine for fucking weeks. I want you to fix it. Now!"

"Can't. Not right now."

"But I need it!" Her voice fast turning into a whine. "It costs a fortune down the laundrette. You're my landlord, you have a duty to provide me with a working washing machine. We're paying you rent!"

"You've been using it."

"Of course I've been using it!" She spat, incredulous. "I wear clothes, they get dirty. It's a washing machine, I use it to clean them!"

"Can't fix it today." Billy restated. "Need a part." And the stomach to spend money on it, he thought.

"Well get it!" Jenny persisted, her voice raised and her face flushing. Billy thought perhaps she wasn't such a sexless thing as he had thought. Being angry suited her, brought her eyes alive. He realised she was glaring at him, waiting for some response.

"Hmm?" Billy managed.

"Today!" Jenny demanded. "You're the fucking landlord of this piece-of-shit house. Look at it! We've had nothing but problems since we moved in here. It's cold and it stinks and nothing fucking works." She was really worked up now and Billy found himself getting aroused. "So, of course this doesn't fucking work either. Just like its fucking landlord! We call and we ask and we wait and we fucking wait and you eventually turn up and then go away without doing anything. It's a fucking disgrace."

Billy felt sure he should be defending himself or otherwise retaliating to this onslaught but the passion and fire in the girl's face had turned her, in his suddenly swimming vision, from a pikestaff into a passable beauty. He imagined her young lithe form sliding over him, worming her way down his torso until she buried her head in his groin. He felt himself harden and then, before he could think, the words were out of his mouth. "What's it worth?"

"Excuse me?"

"I can order the part but it'll take a few days. You want it fixing sooner..." Billy swallowed and then straightened himself up. He was committed now. He raised his eyebrows, he hoped meaningfully. "What's it worth?"

Jenny looked into Billy's face, disbelief making her eyes widen and her face contort. "Are you for real?"

Billy ran his tongue over his teeth, the anticipation of a positive outcome growing inside him. He waggled his head from side to side, playfully he hoped, considered his response and then thought his best prospect was to remain silent and appear teasingly enigmatic. Her face fell swiftly into a stone-cold slab of disgust.

"Get lost, Granddad." She spat. "You're a fucking pervert. A sick, twisted, disgusting old man who should be locked up."

Billy was still lost in his imagination, her furious words echoing emptily somewhere beyond his reach, not registering. It was the cold, unexpected slap in the face which snapped him back.

"Go fuck your shitty old machine." Jenny ranted,

storming from the kitchen.

That wasn't the outcome Billy had had in mind.

# THE GRAND OLE OPRY

Maud could only presume that the reason she had stayed married to Billy all these years was because she was a Virgo. Virgo's understood patience, servitude, forbearance, devotion. Duty. And she remembered her mother's words. "Mo." she had said. "Always keep your man happy. They're simple folk, just keep 'em fed and watered and - you know. And if he still isn't happy, it's him not you. It'll pass. Head down and do your job. Keep on keeping on. Do your duty."

And that was what Maud had done. She'd kept keeping on. For fifty-seven years.

Maud looked at herself in the mirror now and wondered where all those years had gone. She herself had not long turned seventy-nine, but didn't look it. She still had her figure left. Just. Always an hourglass, now there was inevitably too much sand in the glass. It had entered her system somehow over the years - osmosis perhaps - the incessant grit and grind of rubbing up against Billy's moods had eroded this irritant down into fine sand which had somehow wormed its way into her metabolism, and much of it had somehow got wet and now clumped at the bottleneck in the middle of the timer.

The girdles helped. Not called girdles these days, of course. Shapewear. Same difference. It was a bugger to get them on and when you got them on, they smoothed out the humps and lumps by spreading the excess around to make it look less noticeable. But there was only so much dirt you could brush under the carpet before you started to stumble and roll as you walked across it. "Keeping your man happy" involved looking good for him, too. Even if the bugger never noticed. He'd clean and fondle his precious gun, spend hours lavishing attention on that bloody car, but look at her? Fat chance.

So, yes, she looked good for her age. Look at her pals down the club - they had a hard time making themselves look human, never mind attractive. Here she was, after years of frequent perming, drying, colouring and back-combing, still with a full head of bouffant hair. Autumn Fire (it said on the bottle), her normal tint, covered up the grey nicely. But even if she was fooling nobody - and no-one was ever going to be checking to see if her collar matched her cuffs any more - there was no doubt she cut a smart and snappy dash amongst what passed for the Gorebridge pensioners posse down at the Grand Ole Opry.

And, tonight - Grand Ole Opry night - her outfit in the mirror was her most glamorous one. Black satin slacks, a snug and streamlined trim around her backside and thighs, tummy tucked in and no VPL thanks to the Shapewear. Boot-cut legs flared nicely down to her shiny cowboy boots which had silver toecaps and block heels, and after-market fake spurs added as a nice feminine touch, which tinkled and jangled when she walked. *After-market* meaning that she'd bought them *after* the shoes, down the *market.* Money didn't grow on trees, she could hear her mother intone.

Around her strapped-in midriff she wore a thin silver belt into which was tucked a black polyester long-sleeved top, garnished with silver sequins across the chest, front and back, providing the illusion of a silver-tassled cowboy jacket, with breast pockets and buttons, the whole affair sensitively done, she felt. She was modelling her look on Olivia Newton-John, not Elton John.

Topping off the whole ensemble was a black felt Stetson with a sparkling silver hatband and a glittering thread of chin strap. She didn't like the hat - it had been a present from Billy and, unusual for no other reason than that, she kept it and wore it to and from the Opry. It protected her hairdo from the elements well enough, but if she wore it for too long it would press down on her perfect coiffure and make her look like an underdone orange - ahem, Autumn Fire - souffle when she took it off. So, she essentially perched it lightly atop her head and kept it in place with one hand if the wind suddenly picked up.

Thusly dressed she was ready to lead the dance floor. And this was Maud's moment of the week. These hours between eight and eleven pm on a Friday she lived for, and looked forwards to from 11:01pm that night until 7:59pm the following week. The lights, the live music. And the floor.

Oh, the floor. A floating square of twelve metres by twelve, edged with a chrome strip which transitioned to the sticky patterned carpet of the rest of the club. That dance floor was the thing. Her thing, her domain, her floor. Smooth, sleek, smart. You crossed that silver threshold, beneath the rolling spotlights which glimmered and shone, changing colours as they roamed across the space - like American suns seeking out their kith and kin to bestow their heat and light and glory - the reflections shimmering and moving on the sequinned tops of the arrayed dancers.

Dancers in a line. Line dancers.

Although *trancers* might have been a better word. The dancers may be lost in the glamorous dream and delusion of some US altered mind state, but outwardly they moved robotically, stiffly - emotionless. A joyless rote each followed as Maud led. A middle-distance stare from those who knew the steps; a nervily attentive head-swivel from those still unsure, watching dancers to their left and right, ahead and behind, as they moved in sync with their compatriots, turned and spun and side-stepped, heels and toes tapping. A stifled parade of procedure in a way that, perhaps, Brits alone could muster. One could only imagine the vibrancy, life and exuberance of their American counterparts - whooping and hollering, gleaming smiles and brilliant teeth, luscious hair and healthy skin sending waves of vitality and joy from the dance floor into the cheering and appreciative crowd.

Cut to Gorebridge: a robotic parade of the mentally absent or furiously concentrating, intent on getting it right. Not having fun, getting it right. Following the steps. If you got it right, *then* you had had fun. Like completing a Sudoku - it was a foreign, alien, compelling puzzle to complete. You worked it out, filled in the grid and had the quiet satisfaction of seeing everything fit neatly into its allotted place... before quietly moving onto the next one. A puzzle, a dance, a conundrum, a song.

You'd never know from watching them that they were having fun. And perhaps they weren't? Maud was, but she wasn't going to let on. She had responsibilities. She had taken on the self-appointed role of leading the floor. This enthusiasm to know all the steps, be confident with all the right moves, had started like a new hobby: a hunger to discover the information, learn it and demonstrate it to others. Soon it had been distilled down into a lean, efficient process of cataloguing and cross-referencing songs to dance moves, recording and remembering them so that, when each new tune was announced Maud was ready. And what tyranny was this? She led so others could follow - but she had to lead every dance. The duty, the responsibility! She hadn't asked for it, hadn't meant for it to happen this way, but here she was duty-bound to spend the night - like Marley's ghost - haunting the arena, doomed to repeat it each and every Friday so that others could benefit and learn from her. Joy? Yes, there was joy. Beneath the duty.

And it was through duty that she clung to Billy, and clung to weekly line-dancing. Once upon a time, there had been happiness in their marriage. She presumed. She couldn't remember any. Like a dredger ploughing the Mississippi delta, when the bucket came to the surface, any fine sediment laid down during the initial marital years was now lost amongst the rank, foul muck which polluted the later ones. This harmless pastime, which allowed her to shine once a week, had become a lifebelt to keep her afloat on this deep, rolling river of mediocrity and disappointment. A lifetime of treading water with Billy Gillespie.

Maud sat at her usual table and sipped her rum and coke. She had spent the time gluing on fake rhinestoned fingernails and rubbing handcream into the backs of her hands while she waited for her small entourage to assemble: Gaynor, Pete's wife, who worked part-time in the Town Hall and had a birthmark on her neck which looked like Alabama (the birthmark, not her neck); Elsie, on a widows pension, who volunteered three days a week in the Macmillan Cancer charity shop on the High Street and walked with a stick; June, a no-nonsense octogenarian with a fierce head full of white hair and opinions equally as strong, whose constant complaint in life was that she had the misfortune to marry a man with better longevity and health than she was encountering.

This was Maud's posse.

Gaynor appeared first, hustling in with her coat on. A second or two behind her appeared June, carrying a plate steaming with something hot.

"How are you, both?" Maud asked, knowing full well that, in Gaynor's case, this was completely unnecessary since she knew what Gaynor's reply would be. Was always. Any time anyone ever asked how she was, Gaynor would always reply: "Och, no' three bad. No' three bad. Yersel?" What perhaps had once been a cute little joke she had first heard at her mother's knee and chuckled at, had now become a verbal tic, an irritant that no-one listened to, cared about or found amusing. Much like Gaynor herself.

"Och, no' three bad, hen. No' three bad. Yersel?"

Maud gave a small, almost imperceptible nod of her head and then indicated to the plate June was placing down on the table in front of her chair.

"What have you got there?"

"It's new!" June smiled appreciatively. "Big V's got a new menu."

"Hmmm." Gaynor pulled a face. "I think I'll give it a week or so masel'. Wait until the kitchen's got the hang o' it, an' that."

"Oooh!" Maud was immediately interested, enticed as much by the notion that this was Big V's doing as of the fact that it might actually be a first tasty output from the club's Cantina. "Smells good. What is it?"

"Gumbo."

"Gumbo? Eeurk." Gaynor pulled the face of someone who had been told her medication required her to stir a tablespoon of desiccated dog-dirt into a glass of her husband's phlegm. Every four hours and again at meal times.

Maud grabbed a spoon and helped herself to some of June's gumbo while she cast her eyes around the gradually-filling club, looking for either Big V or Billy. Her husband was sitting with his gunfighter pals, lounging on seats against the far walls, as removed from the dancing as it was possible to get. Partially, she felt, this was to avoid the prospect (however remote) of being dragged up onto the dance floor by their wives. And partially so that, when the time came, they could saunter through the crowd to the shootout, weaving their way through the tables giving everyone sufficient opportunity to admire their outfits, their insouciance and their guns. It wouldn't have surprised her if she had known that another partial explanation was that they did it in tribute to old Westerns where the gunslingers sneak into the bar unnoticed, and lean against the saloon walls in the shadows until emerging to call out the one person at the bar who they really should know better not to rile.

Men.

So Maud and Billy, like all the other long-suffering couples, went together to the club. Billy would split off as soon as they crossed the threshold and plonk himself down with his pals, leaving Maud to anxiously scan the scattered tables or find a loud Elsie yoo-hoo'ing her from the far side of the dance floor and pointing to an empty seat beside her with a big, stupid smile on her face.

But Maud was old school. Not old school as in Harrow

or Eton; old school as in born before the Second World War, familiar with going without, outside toilets, loveless marriages and having to enjoy tripe and spinach. All hangovers from soldiering on, making do, stiff upper lip. Doing one's duty.

And another thing Maud was familiar with was the image and reputation of wartime Yanks - overpaid, oversexed and over here. That was the mantra during the war and one her mother had referred her to later during her teenage years. She may have been too young in the '40's, but not now. Now she was very much thinking of making up for lost time. At her ripe old age, she was flushing and fumbling like a schoolgirl at the thought of her very own big, brash American idol.

Big V.

The V was for Vince; the Big because he was a tall, black American who looked about at home in Gorebridge as a dill pickle in a Scotch pie sandwich. And he wasn't just tall, he was 6'7" and rangy - a former basketball player in college who had done his knees in and now buckled slightly when he walked, a bit like his accent: loose and twangy. But his voice was deep and sonorous and sensual - like James Earl Jones getting a rubdown with a chamois leather - and with a mouth that was nearly always open, either displaying a dam-full of gleaming teeth beneath chortling eyes or emitting that beautifully rich sound, it soared and ricocheted off every surface creating a kind of sonic boom. You always knew when Vince was in your postcode.

And he wasn't just black - he was almost blue he was so black. As if deploying some kind of alien light-absorption technology which hoovered up the photons and only spat back one in ten. From a distance he looked like an enormous obsidian obelisk: smooth, solid, impenetrable. Recent discoveries in Egypt tell of rock formed from beyond the solar system and carried here as meteorites. Rock which was perhaps formed in a star before our own sun even existed. And, in a similar way, Vince himself was other-worldly, not quite belonging. Because Vince had a secret.

He wasn't really an American at all.

Vince was one of the Windrush generation. His parents had come over from Antigua to Scotland after the Second World War - and absolutely hated it. He had been a babe-in-arms at the time, knowing nothing of the experience, but his mother and father had been enticed by the prospect of coming to the home of the British Empire and building a new life for themselves, only to find that mangoes were unknown, chilblains were the norm and everyone looked at the colour of their skin and either avoided them, insulted them or assumed they lived in trees.

They stayed less than a year before fleeing for the warmth and promise of America and its Deep South. Paperwork and administration had been something of a joke in those days, so Vince's understanding of his date and place of birth, exactly where he had lived and when, were all passed down verbally from his mother. As he grew, his parents had slowly completed the transition to US citizenship and at some point in the proceedings a birth certificate was conjured forth and became the official record for Vincent Bradley Cass.

Ironically, over the years, the family's brief Scottish fling grew grander and more romantic in the telling - by his mother in particular. In the cultural melting pot that was Baton Rouge, having an exotic backstory was a thing and his mother built and polished this transitory Scottishness until it glittered and shone. It wasn't until he was much older that he began to understand the true nature of his heritage but, by then, it was too late. He had not just come to believe his mother's fancy, he had adopted and devoured it until it became a burning definition of who he wanted himself to be. He didn't deny his origins, just saw them as irrelevant - his Caribbean roots may have been transplanted into Cajun soil but the seed of his soul was wrapped in tartan, and he was determined that one day the flower of Scotland within him would rise and blossom.

His life in America had been successful, if unspectacular. After failing college due to his basketball injury, he had started as a sales rep for a vacuum cleaner company, selling door-to-door, and then worked his way up the chain until he was sitting, dumb, fat and happy, in an office in New Jersey, pushing paper around his desk and counting the money from the pyramid-scheme frenzy below him. When his wife died of cancer in her mid-fifties, Vince cashed in on her life insurance, withdrew all his savings and decided he too may not have many years left on the planet. It was finally harvest time, so he sold up, bought a one-way ticket and found himself in the arrivals hall at Edinburgh airport with little clue where to go, or what to do.

And what he'd found had shocked him. Vince hadn't expected Scotland to be the same as Louisiana but he had been unprepared for the little things which seemed to make such a difference. At the national level, there were some obvious similarities. Tribalism in national politics for example: In America, presidential campaigns continually pitted feral bible-belt Republicans (who wanted Jesus-shaped fighter jets to drop gay people on Isis) against east-coast intelligentsia Democrats (who pulped books on trickle-down economics to make same-sex marriage placards they could wave at climate change rallies). In Scotland, everyone hated the English and thought that Westminster politicians of all stripes were venal, lying bastards whose unspoken and eternal goal was to screw Scotland out of everything in every single way they could.

And there were some national differences: Scotland's main exports were whisky and drunken aggression; America's were generously-proportioned tourists who blocked the view to anything while loudly asking if it was edible.

But here in Midlothian, these generalities were eclipsed by the mundane and the everyday. Gorebridge, for example, was very much a neighbourhood where dentistry still had a lot of heaving lifting to do. Where possessing a full set of teeth was frowned upon in polite company - unless you were going to vote, or to a funeral. The latter being a more frequent and well-attended occasion than the former.

His initial question of "How do these people eat?" had been answered when he saw the food. There was not a lot of call for biting as far as the local cuisine was concerned. Haggis, neeps, tatties, fish, chips, burgers, pizzas, mince. Almost all food produce was mashed, scrambled or somehow squashed into a protein carrier to provide rapid access to its contents and fast transit to the stomach, without the awkward encumbrance of hanging around in the oral cavity for any longer than was absolutely necessary. And, Vince considered, if you looked at it from the poor food's point of view, how could you blame it?

Nevertheless, Vince had come to these shores with a mission: to bring quality and American values to his ancestors' homeland. It had been a labour of love and sweat, tenacity and persistence - but his efforts had paid off. Fifteen years later he owned a clay pigeon-shooting business and an outdoors experience company which hired out quadbikes, canoes and mountain bikes for tourists wishing to feel the clean Scottish wind through their hair.

And he was also the proud owner of the Grand Ole Opry, Gorebridge.

When Vince had acquired the club it had been the Gorebridge Miners Welfare and Social Club, a faded working men's club that, when empty, projected a dismal abandoned air of stale beer, cleaning fluid and day-old urine faintly wafting through from the lavatories. Low Formica tables, dark red, hosted pale beermats surrounded by upturned wagons of padded benchseats, the occasional rip in the faux-leather exposing old foam which had been stabbed and scooped out with the tips of black biros.

It had been a place of smoke-stained wallpaper, naked striplights and dusty photographs on the walls of the old collieries and mining communities which had once dotted the hills of Midlothian. Every former mining town had "a Social" and they all looked the same. Vince had seen it, yet not seen it - in his mind's eye it was a blank canvas on which to paint his dreams and he had set to work.

From the outside it still looked like Fort Apache: The Bronx - a single-storey pebble-dashed toilet block with chicken wire over the frosted windows, a flat bitumen roof surrounded by razor wire, with a minefield car park reached through a pair of cement gateposts, on one of which was attached a peeling wooden sign bearing the legend WE COME. But inside it had been transformed, through the devoted application of love and money. The smooth, rich patina on the mahogany woodwork everywhere, polished until it shone, was a true reflection of the attention, time and care Vince had lavished on the place.

Double swing, slatted saloon-style doors led from the reception area into the club proper, a large rectangular space with an elevated stage at one end. Vast floor-length professionally-painted murals ran down both sides of the hall. On the left, the mesas and buttes of Monument Valley in the background loomed majestically over a foreground scrabble of US cavalrymen charging after a scattering band of Apaches, dust kicking up from the horses' hooves as they swerved in and out of sagebrush and the geographic anomaly of saguaro cacti. Down the right, a desert sunset, where an impossible night of stars twinkled down on a campfire of cowboys drinking coffee and cooking beans under the eerie branches of a Joshua tree.

At the near end, opposite the stage, was the bar area which Vince had turned into an old-time gin palace model of a Texan saloon from the Old West - a shining silver dollar nestling in a dark cave of a place, all mirrors, glass and polished chrome. Shot glasses, optics and bottles gleaming from recessed spotlights and the bar, backlined with etched mirrors, was bedecked with scattered Country & Western memorabilia, horseshoes, gunbelts and miniature Confederate flags.

A slowly-rotating disco ball lorded it over the large wooden dance floor in front of the stage. Either side of it were a pair of fire doors, usually propped open with extinguishers, which led to the toilets and then out to the Fire Exits proper. The lavatories themselves had also undergone a dazzling makeover of glistening porcelain and dark wood wall panels. Hand-carved silhouettes on the doors showed pistols for the Gents, holsters for the Ladies.

Such was this place re-branded as the Grand Ole Opry. A place where the tired and weary elderly Gorebridge residents came to escape their tawdry lives and be transported back to the time of Wild Bill Hickok, Jesse James and Buffalo Bill. Twice a week it hosted Country Music nights, twice a week Bingo, and once a week a combined Country & Western Music & Gun Club night, where a variety of over-enthusiastic, over-age, over-anxious pensioners came to test themselves against each other to see who was the fastest gun in a vest.

So here he was, lording it over the South Scotland C&W fraternity. The irony was not lost on Big V. Firstly, he had come to Scotland seeking a fictitious heritage only to find himself foisting a pastiche of his own fictitious past on them; secondly, he absolutely hated Country & Western music.

Vince looked out over the blue-rinsed heads of the murmuring crowd, their fat fluorescent dabbers hovering expectantly over their cards. Here was another British ritual he didn't understand - this fixation with Bingo. Back home they played Bingo, but it was either part of some weekly Church gathering or part of the overall experience when you visited a Casino. Here it was a standalone fixture in many people's social calendar and, more importantly as far as Vince was concerned, a perfect party piece to fill 20-30 minutes of dead air while the musicians took a break between sets and a nice little money-earner which threw the slant off a little from the gunslinging, macho overtones that gun club nights could so easily possess. The permed and sequinned old dears would shuffle in on their husband's arms, only to separate at the threshold and split into their gender-specific parts - like some miniature Hadron Collider experiment where tiny particles, themselves already insignificant, were suddenly accelerated and split into their underlying male and female quarks: The men, *machons*, slung outwards by some invisible centrifugal force, congregated around the walls of the hall, comparing their pistols and their gunbelts; the women, *silvikrins*, flung inwards, clumping into clusters of female particles, complimenting each other on the latest sparkling addition to an outfit and readying dabbers from their handbags.

Whilst Vince could maintain a proprietorial air when surveying proceedings, it was difficult not to be judgemental about his regular clientele. The hard and vacant looks on the faces of many told their own story. It was as if these people had never made the, oh so British, mistake of developing self-esteem. What they had was embarrassment so that they could dress up and pretend to be someone else, thus saving themselves from being regarded as show-offs or better-than-us. These poor people, for many of whom their one night of the week here was an undoubted high-point, looked like they had long ago squandered whatever potential they might once have had, and were now just eking out an existence on the little of what was left. Like last year's Christmas tree lights - half of them didn't work, and the other half weren't all that bright.

Vince fired up the machine and picked up the microphone with a weary sigh. Another soul-crushing step downmarket was underway.

"Eyes down, look in. Your first number: On its own, number two. A meal for two with a hairy view, six and nine. Sixty-nine."

Vince wanted his place to be a palace, a shrine to the Old West and his adopted home country. But these Brits turned everything to dust, sucked the joy right out of it and made it tawdry and lowest-common-denominator. He had tried to educate and resist the pull, but the punters voted with their wallets and he hadn't been able to find a way to balance a unique high-end experience with their low-brow tastes and budgets. Neither had his accountant.

"Ray Charles, Eight-oh, blind eighty."

He wanted china and fine Dixie dining, they wanted plastic cutlery and deep-fried crap; he wanted glamour and glitz with a honky-tonk pianist and a chorus line of Parisian showgirls, they wanted line-dancing and a chintzy Country Duo called Red River Gulch; he wanted an array of Tennessee whiskey and chrome-plated beer pumps serving foaming tankards, they wanted cheap, watered-down blends and Tennants Extra at £1.80 a pint.

"Five-oh, Five-oh, it's off to work we go. Snow White, blind fifty. Unlucky for some, one and three, thirteen."

If the drink was too expensive, they wouldn't come. If the food was too fancy, they wouldn't eat and his margins would be shot. He needn't worry about the ambience - this clientele reduced everything to a cross between after-funeral drinks and carpet bowls in a retirement home for the incontinent.

Something had to give. He was at the end of his tether.

His final throw of the dice was this scheme to expand and upscale the gunslinging element of the Country & Western experience, maybe even get it to the point where he could brand it, license or franchise it. He had travelled the length of Scotland meeting and cajoling other C&W clubs and owners and roping them into his new Fastest Gun in Scotland extravaganza. A £10,000 cash prize, a blaze of publicity and a breath of energy and vibrancy injected into the moribund venture it was becoming, this was it for Vince. Either he'd be able to attract a new, more upmarket clientele, or the whole thing would go down the pan and he'd sell up and move back to the States. He'd already had some unsolicited interest in the place from Midlothian Council who wanted to turn it into a pre-school nursery or after-school club. That was his backstop but it was very much unwanted - Vince was going "all in". If he went down, he wanted to go like Butch & Sundance, with all guns blazing.

"All the beans, five and seven, fifty-seven."

"House!"

"Hold it there, please, ladies and gentlemen. We have a claimer. Don't go anywhere while we check the numbers."

Vince scanned the pale faces around the room as they alternately craned their necks to see who had called out, whilst simultaneously cursing under their breath and commiserating with each other that they only needed one or two more numbers for a line themselves. He sighed again and checked the clock above the bar.

"It's a win, folks." He declared when the card was checked. Vince looked up to see the winner coming towards him to collect the prize of a crisp £20 note and a bottle of cheap Scotch, and was momentarily captivated by the vision that was Maud.

Maud tottered towards the stage, holding her stomach in, watching Vince with hungry eyes. Her shapewear was at full stretch, literally, beneath her black sequinned top and she had been practising each day, in front of the mirror, trying to give it all the help she could whilst maintaining an expression of serenity with just a dash of a twinkling come-hither. She gazed at him, entranced, as he smiled at her like a beacon.

He was wearing a snappy tan dress coat with black velvet lapels, bootlace tie, flat-topped, broad-brimmed Texan hat and a pair of gleaming leather cowboy boots which, unlike every other pair on display here or any other day, were the real deal and had been hand-crafted from the hide of a US-reared, fed and slaughtered prime Texas Longhorn. His broad shoulders and chest all snugly contained within this Colonel Sanders-style getup, managed to turn his standard wattage into a dazzling brilliance. When the disco ball spun bursts of light his way he was spotlit like some alien god beamed down onto planet Gorebridge, a superior, perfect, genetically-engineered vision that didn't belong here and yet somehow did. He was here to show us all what we could become if we lived healthily, believed in ourselves and loved everyone. Or, at least, paying customers.

Maud had married at twenty-two, primarily because she had to. All girls had been fools in the years after the end of the Second World War, their heads easily turned. The taps of restraint and constraint which had been turned on by the American freedom surge and their invasion into the

UK had transformed the country overnight from a black-and-white smog-filled station where Brief Encounter was set, to a colourful kaleidoscope wonderland of music, dance and smooth-skinned movie stars who were wealthy, generous and charming. It was like the scene from the Wizard of Oz where the dreary farmstead reality turns into a Technicolor fantasy. And for Maud, unfortunately, the fantasy was real. Billy was a jerk; always had been. She had just been too anxious, and too blind to see it. She had wanted to grow up so badly she had flung caution to the wind and ended up growing up far more badly than she had ever expected.

Here she was now, realising belatedly that her life was behind her, she had little to look forward to and somehow, without thinking about it, planning to or meaning to, she had somehow missed her turn. She had been standing in the queue waiting for her life to start, waiting so long, watching the queue stretch out ahead of her. And when she got to the front, she found it was the wrong queue and she had to join another, longer line way over there and the Bouncer on the door was telling her she was now too old to get in. Somehow life had passed her by and she was sitting in Death's waiting room.

But here was Vince and she dreamt that this was a possible final chance to really live. The first time she had set eyes on him, he had had his expanse of back to her, peeling tenners from the till and stuffing them into a wallet in his jacket pocket. He had been wearing his hat so she had been startled when he had turned, as if feeling her eyes on him, and revealed himself to be a black Adonis, eyes sparkling beneath a mile-wide brim. She felt sure her eyes had bulged as she ran them over his frame. There was something quite unbelievable about him - his size, his manner, the way he dressed, his bearing. He had huge, manicured hands and a smooth dexterity with his fingers that made her feel like a twenty-year old again. When Maud had first mentioned her crush to Gaynor, her friend had smirked and elbowed her in the ribs.

"Once you go black, you never go back!" She had twinkled, and Maud had snorted, blushed and then spent the rest of the evening fantasising just what she would find if she ever got her hands inside his Corby-pressed trousers with a side-stripe.

The contrast between her husband and Vince could not have been more pronounced. Billy was coarse, ignorant, loud, odious, rude, unhygienic and belligerent; Vince was refined, intelligent, discrete, charming, courteous, smooth and clean-as-a-whistle.

She was prepared to bet.

And she really quite keen to blow his whistle.

Maud was a stalwart at the Grand Ole Opry and, for that reason alone, Vince would have liked the cut of her jib. Lord knows she stood out from the crowd in her dogged determination to make the best of things - whether that referred to her marriage to a man with a history of miserablism longer than the Bayeux tapestry (and probably older), or her desire to define a high line-dancing standard and help others keep to it. Vince was all about high standards and so, from the get-go, he held Maud in high esteem.

But Maud also took care of herself and her appearance. Present-day Gorebridge represented something of a throwback to Britain in the 1970's - a time of callipers, cleft palates, lazy eyes and very bad haircuts. And that was just the women.

So to see a well-turned out, conscientious, intent woman who was smartly dressed, as trim as could be expected of an octogenarian on a Scottish diet, and who would throw themselves heart-and-soul into a course of action she believed in - well, she was a rare treasure indeed. And Vince had decided that Maud was to be treasured.

Not for him an obsession with the shallow, the surface appeal that young people these days thought passed for substance. Like a wine connoisseur, Vince appreciated age, maturity and a full body. Throw in the wee twinkle in her eye when he caught her looking at him out of the corner of his eye and, yes, there was definitely something about Maud - something he couldn't quite put his finger on, although he very much wanted to.

He watched her as she shimmied towards him. And it was a shimmy. In her smooth-soled boots and tight black slacks she needed to adjust her gait across the slick dance floor in order to maintain a straight course. This was something she did automatically while dancing, sort of sliding then wiggling to prevent herself colliding with the dancer next to her. But when this was translated into a simple walk it somehow transformed itself into sexy swaying, a smooth manoeuvre which indicated there was no arthritis in her vicinity. And, as much as her sprightliness of spirit, Vince was interested in her physicality. If you don't use it, you lose it, and since the passing of his wife Vince had had little time for dalliances or romance - business had been all. But that had been a long time ago now, and he had no desire to join the queue for blue pills at the pharmacy, thank you very much. He may have just turned seventy, but he was still packing a pistol that was very much in full working order.

And they didn't call him Big V for nothing.

He beamed at Maud as she claimed her prize and, as she took the bottle from his grasp, their hands touched and lingered just long enough, and longingly enough, for Vince to confirm that there was indeed some mutual attraction here and that, if he wanted to capitalise on it, all he had to do was ask.

"Maud, isn't it? Would you mind if I asked you something?"

# GUNFIGHT AT THE UK CORRAL

"What happened to your hand?" Sonya asked, concerned,

"Work injury." Paul grinned sheepishly and tried to hide his bandaged arm behind his back.

"What work you do?"

"Woodwork." God, what was wrong with him? "Carpentry." He clarified.

"Ah, yes." Sonya nodded. "Like Jesus."

"Ahm. Yeah." Paul was nervous, feeling exposed and uncomfortable. And when he felt uncomfortable he drank too much. And when he was comfortable. And sometimes he would take a drink to work out whether he was comfortable or not, before deciding he was, and therefore deserved another drink.

Usually this wouldn't have mattered, because Paul was a big man who could take his drink. In fact Paul, at 6'5" and closing on the thick end of seventeen stone, was widely known as Big Paul, and - amongst close friends - as Beep (short for B.P, which was short for Big Paul). And Big Paul could absorb all manner of liquid punishment with ease, on a normal night. But tonight he was drinking too quickly and, because he had rushed due to being late - because Paul was always late - he was drinking on an empty stomach. An empty, nervous stomach.

And he was nervous because his date was sitting next to him, dressed to the nines and looking even less comfortable than he was. Like an elegant long-necked swan, she had swooped down to an inviting lake only to find it frozen over and she now wore the look on her face of someone uncertain as to her fate but sure that skidding out of control as the icy surface ahead of her grew smaller, she was about to collide with something uncomfortable. She didn't know exactly what it would be or how it would feel, but she wouldn't be recommending it to her friends.

She was, Paul assumed, regretting this whole thing - and she didn't have the comfort of being able to self-medicate on cheap booze to get through the evening. He reached down for his pint automatically and then had to readjust and use his left hand instead. He looked unhappily at the bandaged monstrosity that was his right hand. The doctor in A&E had presumably done the best he could - Paul had all but passed out at the sight of the stitches going in so was unable to comment any further - but the dressing was ridiculously huge. Anyone would think he had a total hand transplant whereas they'd told him that the gash in his hand would heal in a few weeks, the stitches would naturally dissolve and he would have full movement in a couple of months. Meanwhile, he had to go around looking like some kind of superhero who had grown a giant cottonbud for an arm.

Paul sipped his drink glumly, unable to conjure up conversation for fear that anything he could say would be too uncouth, unbecoming or mark him out as ignorant, politically-incorrect and a short-lived prospect as far as this woman was concerned. And, unusually, in this regard Paul was completely right. In the first fifteen minutes of meeting Sonya he had discovered that she enjoyed playing the saxophone, kept herself in shape by jogging daily and regular gym membership, and was contemplating going vegetarian. Paul was aghast - the only instruments he'd ever handled had been sharp (he had waved his hand as Exhibit A) or blunt, his idea of exercise was improving his pie-arm and playing darts, and the mere thought of going a day without bacon in some form or other was simply unfathomable. He was convinced she was out of his league - her favourite dessert was probably mint Vienetta.

But.

But.

Paul was lonely. Had been for a while now. His marriage had ended, abruptly and unexpectedly and even his natural happy-go-lucky nature had had a tough time seeing the blue amongst the grey which had been clouding his sky for over a year. Now, there had been plenty of opportunities for a good night out and a chance to clear the custard, as his mates so charmingly put it. But he was coming to the surprising conclusion that perhaps he might have become institutionalised by marriage and, frankly, missed the regularity and rhythm of being with someone, sharing and being relaxed in the sheer comfortableness of another familiar person.

So tonight he was presented with a quandary. A woman who was here, so he was told by Sofe, because she too was looking for a new partner. Whereas he could clearly see they looked as incompatible as it was for any two people to be - at least on paper. He kept looking hopefully over at Sofe to see if he could make eye contact, signal for help, but she was away on the dance floor learning the moves to whatever song was blasting out from the two-piece up on stage. Why had he listened to her and agreed to this? This wasn't his scene - although it seemed more his style than Sonya's. Sitting next to him, she was gazing forlornly around the Grand Ole Opry like a regretful sheep found buried in snow on the Pentland hills, unhappily stuck and doing her best to be stoic. She was a handsome woman, early forties, elegantly dressed with chiselled Slavic cheekbones, a lovely smile and trim figure - maybe they'd be incompatible on paper but very compatible on sheets, Paul considered.

He took another swig from his pint glass and tried to strike a conversation, but the music was loud and he had to almost shout to make himself heard. He leant into Sonya so that he could talk into her ear.

"What do you do, Sonya?"

"For work?" She had a strong accent - Eastern European, maybe even Russian. Paul nodded, finding it quite sexy.

"I am shepherdess."

Paul was gobsmacked. She certainly didn't look like a shepherdess in her smart outfit and perfectly-applied makeup.

"Really? Wow, I've never met one of those before."

Sonya seemed surprised. Maybe a Russian thing, thought Paul. Perhaps all these rich Russian oligarchs kept someone on the payroll to look after their own sheep on their private estates.

"Do you get a lot of work?" He called into her ear.

"Hm-mm." She nodded. Paul was unsure how to follow up. Sonya wasn't showing a great urge to chat here.

"Do you have a dog?"

"No." She looked at him, furrowing her brow.

"Oh." Bummer. What else would shepherds use, Paul wondered. "Well, are you a good whistler?"

"No." Now she was definitely looking at him strangely.

"Ah, right. Ok, well do you have a -" What did they call those things? "A crook?"

"No. Sorry, what do you think I said I do for a living?"

"You're a shepherdess."

"No!" Her eyes widened. "I said I am chiropodist!"

Sonya burst out laughing and Paul, feeling that this had almost certainly put the tin lid on any chance he had of making a success of his evening, gave her to understand (through the use of universal sign language) that he was going to the bar to get a refill and did she want one. Sonya shook her head, still smiling, and Paul shrunk away to the bar and ignominy.

"Bloke and his missus, sitting in their living room one night, right?" Billy was shouting to Pete over the racket coming from the duo on stage. As far as Billy was concerned, these musicians were putting the sick into music. He wasn't prepared to verbalise what they had put into country.

"He's on his armchair, she's knitting on the sofa. Bloke looks at his watch, gets up and says 'I'm off down the pub. Get your coat on.' His missus looks up at him, astonished and the beginnings of a wondrous smile appear on her face. 'Am I coming with you, then?' she asks. 'No' says the bloke. 'I'm turning the fire off!'

Pete looked blankly at Billy. "I don't get it."

"God, you're a stupid bastard." Billy sneered, picking up his pint, shaking his head in despair as he looked around the hall. "Probably missed a key word 'cos of these fuckers on stage. I wish they'd shut the-" He stopped mid-sentence and let out a sharp whistle. "Fucking hell. You don't get many of them to the pound, do you?"

Pete turned to follow his pal's gaze and his eyes alighted on a young woman with an enormous chest.

"Kilo, I think you mean." He leered.

"Christ, do you think they influence the tides?" Billy couldn't peel his eyes off her. She was dressed, quite inappropriately for a Country & Western night, in a pink wig, a sequinned boob tube, spray-on black latex trousers and silver stilettos. The only thing thematically consistent was her white-tassled cowgirl hat and a glittery sticker in the shape of a Sheriff's badge stuck to her beautiful collar bone.

The contrast between his wife and this girl could not have been greater. Maud was sitting off to his left, stiff and upright, strapped in by her undergarments with her posse of old crones; this creature was loose and lithe and free, her young flesh on show and bouncing with vitality.

If it was a choice between his wife's posse and this girl's Sheriff badge, it was no contest.

But it was her bosom which drew him in like some kind of dazzling tractor beam. Two disco balls bouncing dangerously and enticingly around, seeming only loosely secured to her upper torso which was quite inadequate moorage for such fleshy cargo.

He watched as she tottered to the edge of the dance floor, her arm around the shoulder of a similarly skinny, but flat-chested, pal. The pair of them stood giggling unselfconsciously trying to learn the movements off the grid of women going through the line dancing routine to Achy-Breaky Heart. Oh, the innocence and beauty of youth, he thought. How pleased he was to be no longer subject to its trials and tribulations; but oh how he would love to get his hands on it.

Stinky Pete nudged him from his trance and when Billy turned, annoyed, to his friend, Pete had a grin plastered all over his face. Like a game-show smile transplanted onto a greying bandage. Sans white teeth.

"She must be all of twenty."

"Yeah." Said Billy, wonderingly. "On a scale of one to ten."

The girls were obviously part of some Hen Night or Girls Night Out group who had all clustered around two tables they had shoved together, laden with pint glasses and three pitchers of something pink, on the far side of the dance floor to Pete and Billy's normal station. Eight or so young women, and one slightly older one, were all done up to the nines in garish and skimpy outfits, taking photos of each other on their phones and taking it in turns to get up and dance or visit the lavatories. Both in twos and threes.

After a while, Sheriff's Badge picked up a silver clutch bag and began winding her route towards the Ladies, arm-in-arm with her pal, looking suspiciously like this was primarily for support. The route to the toilets passed right by Billy's table and he pulled himself upright in his chair and sucked in his belly as she came near.

He kept his eyes on her face, determined to meet her gaze if she looked at him - which she didn't. The pair swayed right past him and all Billy got was a nostril-full of scent and a bewitching, tantalising swish of young firm flesh as her arm came within a whisker of brushing his sleeve. As she did so, her friend staggered slightly which pushed Sheriff's Badge off-balance and she bumped into Billy's chair.

"Soz." She slurred as she glanced briefly over his face and then disappeared behind him.

Billy turned, and watched them delightfully disappear into the toilets. His eyes widened in wonder. The skinny pal who'd bumped into him had been that miserable, argumentative, shin-splint tenant, Jenny. Did that mean that Sheriff's Badge, with her magnificent headlights on full beam, was his other nagging tenant, Sophie?

"Sofe." Paul confessed. "I'm done here. Me and Sonya, we're just not right for each other."

"Oh, Unka Po!" Sophie draped her arms around Paul's neck and breathed alcoholic fumes into his face. Her eyes were unsteady as she spoke. "Don't be so.... hasty." Her vocabulary was shrinking alarmingly as the evening wore on. "You look lovely together."

Paul shook his head, sadly. "I'm sorry, sweetheart. She's too, um, refined for me. Trust me. I can tell."

"Really?"

"Really." He smiled kindly at her and tried to pull away. "Look, I'm going to take her home."

"But they haven't done the... gun thing yet!" Sophie protested. "C'mon, Unka Po. You got to give these things a chance."

"I'm sorry, Sofe. It was a nice thought. But my head hurts, this music's too loud, and I don't think this is her cup of tea."

"Unka Po." Was about all Sophie could manage now.

Paul had to admit that, much as it made him sound like one of the Tellytubbies, he loved being Sophie's Unka Po. She had called him that when she was little and first learning to talk, and it was so charming it had stuck. He had used it to refer to himself, she had used it, so had her mum, and her sister (Paul's ex-wife, Julia, was Sophie's aunt). It had stuck and here he was, some eighteen years and one divorce later, with an ex-niece who called him on the phone once a fortnight, regular as clockwork, and who was one of the very few people Paul knew whose birthday he always remembered.

It was this easy intimacy and frequent contact, for Paul, which had caused him to open up to her about his loneliness and his sadness about his failed marriage in the first place. Sophie was a natural listener and a very determined young lady with strong views and she had shushed any qualms he had expressed when she proposed fixing him up with a blind date. Women knew these things, she had said. Just wait, she had said. I knew someone who is just right for you, she had said.

Sonya, the shepherdess.

"It's ok. You enjoy the rest of your night, ok? I'll see you soon." He unbundled her arms from around his neck and stood to go.

"Oh! Oh! Unka Po! Unka Po!" Sophie was suddenly agitated. "Don't forget my washing... thing. Machine."

"Ah." Paul grimaced. "Problem." He held up his large cottonbud and waggled it.

"Ohhhhhh." Sophie's eyes rolled back in her head. "Bollocks."

"It's gonna be a few weeks before I can take this dressing off. Can it wait 'til then?"

"No!" She cried. "Oh, bollocks bollocks bollocks. It's costing me a fortune down the laundrette."

"I'm sorry."

"Might have to suck off the old pervy landlord after all."

"What?" Paul peered anxiously into her face, looking from one unsteady eye to the other.

"Oopsie. Did I say that out loud?"

Paul was suddenly on alert. "You said something. Do you want to repeat it?"

"No." She shrugged. "Doesn't matter. No biggie."

"Sofe." He held her by both shoulders and gently shook her. "Tell your Unka Po."

Sophie let out a loud, wet sigh. "Our shrunken old bastard of a landlord seems to have swapped strategies. He used to stay out of the way to avoid fixing anything, now he just pops round asking for payment in kind."

"Billy Gillespie?"

"Yeah." She said, dejectedly.

"Old Bronchial Billy? That old miserable fucker?" Paul felt his chest start to burn and his teeth set. "Are you telling me..." He whirled his head around and scanned the room. "The fucker'll be here somewhere. He's always here, isn't he, with his stupid fucking-"

Paul locked eyes with a leering, salivating old man sitting in the corner, like some grey wolf. "There he is."

And Paul barged between the tables, one chair toppling, and headed like a missile for Billy Gillespie.

Stinky Pete, swept through the swingdoor from the Cantina. He plonked a grey plate of something in front of Billy, settled down on the velour stool next to him and started tucking into a bowl of chips.

"What's this?" Billy sneered.

"Grits." Said Pete, through a mouthful of chips.

"What the fuck's *grits*?"

"Dunno. Nobby said it was tonight's Special so I thought I'd get you that."

"Did I ask for something Special?"

"No." Admitted Pete. "Thought it was, you know, fitting."

"You know what thought did? It followed a shit wagon

and thought it was a wedding." Billy snorted and steered the grey stuff around on his plate. "This looks like it should be used in Chinese medicine."

"Well, try it!" said Pete. "What's it taste like?"

"You fucking try it." Billy pushed the plate towards Pete and glared. Pete intrepidly dunked a chip and popped it into his mouth.

"Tastes like Pot Noodle."

"Great."

"But I like Pot Noodle!" Pete said, dipping another chip.

"Hey!" Billy dragged the plate back towards him.

"I thought you said you didn't want it?"

"I never said that. I said I didn't ask for it." Billy grabbed one of Pete's chips and dipped it into his grits.

"Hey!" Pete complained, but Billy ignored him, pondering the taste sensation in his mouth. He pulled a face and took a swig from his pint.

"This." Billy considered. "This doesn't taste fresh."

"The pint?"

"The grits."

"Aw, it's alright." Rejoined Pete. "You just need to... squint your tongue a bit." He reached over with another chip but Billy pushed his hand away.

"Off."

"But it doesn't taste fresh, you said."

"I'm hungry and I paid for it. I'm having it. Eat your chips."

Pete shrank back on his stool and sulked. "I paid for it."

Maud had been waiting for the barman to change a

barrel, watching her husband's pathetic leering and listening to him and Pete exchanging their appalling banter.

"Blimey. Look at the clunge on that!"

"Cameltoe, eight o'clock."

"Christ. She's got pissflaps like Audie Murphy's saddlebags!"

When she was finally served, she tottered over to her husband and stood over him.

"You're disgusting. The pair of you!"

"Bugger off, woman!" Billy batted at her protests away like midges in July. "Leave us in peace."

"You're both as bad as each other. You, I almost expect it from." She slapped the brim of Billy's hat. "But you, Pete Blaikie. You should know better. You're just two dirty old men spouting filthy abuse."

Pete shrunk back in his seat and cast an anxious look over at his wife sitting at Maud's table.

"Yes, you do well to look sheepish." Maud nodded, ceremoniously. "Just wait 'til I tell Gaynor what you're up to."

"Bugger off, you interfering cow. Harmless fun is all it is." Billy made a face to his friend as if to say *Don't listen to her, she's always like this.*

"All you're missing is dirty raincoats." Maud sneered and Billy, not wanting to appear hen-pecked in front of his pal, stuck his neck out and together he and his wife began trading verbal blows. It was a smooth, professional performance. Like two heavyweights coming out of retirement for one final payday in the ring, they metaphorically circled each other, footwork immaculate. The old jabs and lunges familiar - still able to score points, but no longer capable of wounding.

Somewhere inside the routine, Maud found the ability to step outside herself and examine this situation. It was all too predictable and she had simply been following a script written over the course of a married life. Like some compilation album, the old arguments came rolling out like Greatest Hits. Resentments and rows from years ago where you thought: *oh, I'd forgotten this one... but, hey, I still know all the words.*

The pair of them were lost in the middle of their set-list, Pete observing silently from his stool, nobody else paying the slightest attention, when they were interrupted by a looming figure carrying one hand which looked like it had been wrapped in a hot towel.

"You." The giant with the goatee prodded Billy with his good hand and Billy reeled back, initially shocked, and then visibly scared as he weighed up the man's bulk. But like the veteran he was, he wasn't going to take any shit from some stranger in front of his wife and best friend. He held both hands in the air, palms out, and adopted an affronted air.

"Hey! What's your game? I'm having a row with the wife here, butt out Goliath!"

"You touch my niece and you're a dead man, pal."

"Don't you threaten me!" Billy tried to square up to the man but came barely to his chin. But, like a terrier snarling at a Great Dane, there was something unexpected about it which unsettled the giant and Billy seemed to scent it. "I'm not your pal. And you're not mine. You don't frighten me, you gormless twat."

The big man hesitated and Billy pushed on, while the momentum was with him.

"I fought in the war to defend the likes of you." He lied briskly. "Look at you." He indicated the man's bandaged hand. "You can't even give yourself a wank."

The man recovered himself and pushed himself forwards, towering over Billy. "If you so much as talk to her again I'll break every bone in your body."

"I don't know what are you on about, you pillock. What's your game, eh? Threaten an old man would you? A war veteran?" Billy was bobbing and shaking in a pretence of machismo but Maud could see quite clearly that he was alarmed at his inability to select his preferred option of flight over fight. If he wasn't careful, he would provoke this bodybuilder into inflicting some serious, potentially fatal, damage. Despite the appeal of the latter, she felt her marital instinct kick in.

"Now, now." She forced herself like a wedge between the two men, her husband obligingly sliding back to allow her to do so. "Show some respect, young man. He may not look much to you, but he's my husband and he's all I've bloody well got."

"Unka Po!" From nowhere a very busty young girl in a pink wig appeared and grabbed the man by his good hand. "Leave it, he's not worth it. C'mon. Sonya's waiting."

The man's eyes narrowed as he glared at Billy, but he heard the girl's voice and Maud could see him soften. She turned her glare on Billy who quickly slid his own eyes away from the girl's chest and onto the floor, affecting innocence.

Maud bristled but kept her tone calm. "Go on. No harm done. Let's all enjoy the rest of the evening, shall we? Shooting'll be on in a minute." She looked over hopefully at Vince, setting up on the stage now that the music duo had departed. "That should all... calm us down." She finished lamely.

The big bear poked a finger one final time in Billy's

direction. "You've been told. One finger." And, with that, he turned and, led by the hand by this little slip of a girl, he threaded his bulk back between the tables. Maud watched him go and then turned to Billy, her face resuming its former sharpness.

"You and me..." She steamed. "You and me will get to the bottom of this when we get home."

Up on the stage, Big V materialised out of nowhere and grabbed a microphone.

"Fucker doesn't need a mike." Growled Bill, grateful for the distraction. "Needs a silencer."

"Lay-dees ah'and gennelmen. The gunfights will be starting in ten minutes. Tonight is the first round in our new national Fastest Gun in Scotland competition. First prize, ten thousand pounds." An enormous *ooh* rang out and then turned into a cheer. "Please fill your glasses and then take your seats. Gunfighters, can you please come down to the side entry here and register for the competition so we can make the draw. Thank you."

Billy curled his lip and shot a sideways glance at Pete. "Fucker's still got Geronimo. How'm I suppose to enter if I don't have a gun?"

He adjusted the empty gunbelt at his hip and stomped off down the edge of the dance floor. On his way, Billy swung past a fussy, stout lady all dressed up in a ruched burgundy taffeta gown. She looked like a superannuated whorehouse madam and her cleavage wobbled precariously on the edge of her Victorian ruffle like a Stilton souffle as Billy barged past.

"Ooh, how rude!" The woman protested to her friend, sitting next to her in a bright yellow satin number, her hair back-combed and bouff'ed up into a nest of ringlets and tumbling curls. "Guns kill people you know." She said, in a raised voice to no-one in particular, but clearly meant for Billy's benefit.

Billy swung his head menacingly towards her, without missing his stride. He dropped his hand to his empty holster, spite in his eyes. "Yeah. And spoons make you fat."

"Ooh. How rude!" The woman repeated and pulled a schooner of dry sherry to her thin beestung-painted lips.

Vince laid down the microphone and walked down the steps to the left of the stage, clipboard in hand. An orderly queue of fancy-dress gunslingers was already forming, some he recognised, some he didn't.

"Gunfighter name?" He asked each one, wrote it down, then directed them over to the Fire Exit at the right of the stage. "Wait in that corridor until your name is called. Check your pistols and be ready. No practising allowed past that point."

He looked up at the next entrant to see Billy snarling into his face. "Where's my gun?"

"Billy The Kid." Vince said, calmly, as he wrote the name down.

"Where's Geronimo? I can't enter without a fucking gun!"

"Go and wait over there with the others. I'll bring it over when I'm done here." Vince looked past Billy over his shoulder. "Next?"

As the line dwindled down, a couple of assistants were hustling around the floor in front of the stage. They were arranging two large folding cubicles, three panels of Perspex standing shoulder-high, hinged together, with the fourth side absent. Each of these booths was positioned at opposite ends of the dance floor, their open sides facing each other. The people sitting at tables behind each of the booths looked nervously at each other, some making efforts to edge their chairs back or to one side.

Vince noticed the unease and grabbed the mike again. "Ladies and gentlemen, while we're setting up, let me explain what is going to happen, for any first-timers here tonight." He bestowed his widest smile and warmest looks on the audience near the booths. "Your safety is paramount to us all and these booths are here to protect you from any stray sparks from the gunfire. Let me reassure you that these weapons are replica guns and only fire blanks. There is no way in which you can be harmed, and these booths are purely a belt-and-braces approach to satisfy the pesky health-and-safety folks." He smiled as if to say "*you know the way it is, it's a load of nonsense but these people need to earn a living too and if we don't go along with their unnecessary precautions they'll close us down.*" A murmur of understanding rippled through the crowd and some of the people sitting nearest the action even started to poke their noses and chair forwards to get a better view.

When the queue had gone, Vince handed the clipboard to Irene who had shuffled up from the sound booth. "Can you see if you can find some intro music for each of these, please?" Irene took the clipboard and shuffled back. Vince looked over to Maud and gave her a nod. She shot up from her seat and almost sprinted over to his side.

"I'm just going to get your husband's gun." He rolled his eyes at her. "If you could just stand over there, opposite me now and wait 'til I get back. Then we can start." He held her briefly by the shoulder a moment longer than necessary before he turned away, and he saw Maud's eyes light up.

Billy sat down in the toilet cubicle and rolled himself a scabby cigarette. He coughed as he lit up and scratched his stubble. The cigarettes sort of helped and sort of hindered: calming his nerves would make for a smoother, faster draw; increasing the likelihood of him coughing at an inconvenient moment risked screwing with his chances altogether.

*Fuck it,* he thought, taking another sweet drag. He sat back on the lavatory, closed his eyes to try and focus, and blew the smoke slowly up into the air.

His brief meditation was shattered by the shrieking of a smoke alarm.

Forgetting his advancing years, Billy bolted for the door like a Thomson's gazelle in a trolley dash.

"What the hell is it now?" Vince muttered under his breath as the piercing alarm echoed down the corridor into his office. He grabbed Billy's gun from his safe and strode back out to the main hall, looking left and right for any member of staff who could point him in the right direction.

"Men's toilets!" Shouted Irene helpfully from behind the bar. Vince dashed across the dance floor between the Perspex booths and out into the corridor where the gunfighters were queueing patiently. He scanned the line of faces and, dissatisfied, looked into the eyes of the nearest cowboy to him. "Where's Billy?"

The tall cowboy looked blankly and shrugged.

"Give him this." Vince thrust the pistol into the cowboy's hand. "And tell him if I have to confiscate it again, it'll be the last time he sees it."

Vince turned on his heel and sped down towards the Gents at the end of the corridor and pushed the door open. The alarm waxed louder and then waned again as the door closed behind him.

Billy ground out his cigarette butt on the step and slipped back into the corridor through the fire door he had left ajar. The alarm was still ringing out behind the lavatory door and Billy sheepishly crept up towards the line of cowboys waiting at the entrance to the main hall. As he joined the queue, the man at the back of the line turned round to face him. He was holding Geronimo in his hand.

"Hey! That's my-"

"He told me to give it to you." The man's voice was like a stone dropped into a cold pool.

"Oh. Ok. Thanks." Billy hefted Geronimo in his hand and brushed his thumb across the barrel engraving. Quickly he flipped it in and out of his holster, and twice more, recalling the muscle memory to create a smooth movement. He looked back up at the cowboy he had taken it from, the tall figure's eyes hidden beneath the brim of his leather hat.

"Do I know you?" Billy asked, feeling hairs starting to prick on the back of his neck.

"No."

Billy rattled through his fading memory of faces and names trying to identify the nagging sensation he felt, but at that moment the whirlwind that was Vince sped by, his frock coat flapping as he headed for the stage, muttering. Billy reflexively turned his face to the wall and waited in the silent corridor hoping to be unnoticed.

"The only warning I will give." announced Vince. "Is that some of the guns are quite loud, so please be ready for the sound of gunfire when the contest starts. Each contest is between two gunslingers. I will call their names and they will step forward and position themselves in each of these booths facing each other. I will then count One-Two-Draw! And they will both draw their weapons and fire. Maud and I will decide who drew fastest." He nodded over at her and Maud almost purred with delight. "Each contest is best of three. It is a knockout competition and the winning gunslinger from this group will go through to the next round."

Maud was still standing at the opposite edge of the dance floor, positioned out of the line of fire midway between the booths, a serious look on her face. "Are we ready?" he asked her.

Maud nodded. Vince looked down at his clipboard and called the first duel.

"The Hangman!"

A pale, lanky middle-aged man dressed all in black, strode through the Fire Exit to the rhythmic strumming of *The Man Comes Around* and took up his place in the left-hand booth. He flicked open the cylinder of his revolver and checked the chambers while his theme tune faded down.

"Wild Bill Hitchcock!"

The gritty vocals of *Three Wheels On My Wagon* blared out and an ironic cheer piped up from somewhere near the bar. A man in matching buckskin leather jacket and trousers appeared and swaggered, his jacket fringes swinging, into the other booth. He theatrically unsnapped the closure from his holster and articulated the fingers of his right hand in preparation and then lifted his face towards The Hangman.

"Gunslingers are you ready?" called Vince. Both men gave a curt nod.

"One. Two. Draw!"

There was a sharp, empty bang and a small cloud of smoke from Wild Bill's booth, but The Hangman - who looked like he had actually drawn first - was pulling the trigger on his pistol disconsolately, his gun having failed to fire.

"Round One to Wild Bill." Vince proclaimed. "Gentlemen, please check your weapons."

The Hangman fiddled with his revolver and checked the hammer action. Satisfied, he looked back up at Vince expectantly.

"Gunslingers, are you ready?"

Again, both men nodded and waited, primed, for the countdown.

"One. Two. Draw!"

This time there was no doubt. Both men's guns fired, The Hangman's larger .44 making a boomier sound and doing so a fraction earlier.

"Round Two to The Hangman." Vince announced waiting for the gunsmoke to leave the stage front, the smell of fireworks drifting out across the tables.

"Billy The Kid." Called Vince, announcing the next contest.

Billy emerged and shuffled unsteadily across the floor. He tried to narrow his eyes but scrunching up his face made him cough and he brought up some sputum. He cast around vainly for a spitoon, then glanced over at Maud who glared at him and he unhappily swallowed it back down and turned into the right-hand booth.

"The Man With No Name." Announced Vince.

Paul was sitting right behind Billy's booth when his mouth fell open. He looked around the room, checking to see if everyone else was seeing what he was seeing. No-one else looked amazed, just him. Paul looked back at the target of his disbelief and tried to take it all in.

Was that Cullen? It looked like his hat but the rest of his outfit was a calf-length Driza-bone range coat, just showing the tattered edge of black jeans over unpolished boots. He wore scuffed tan leather gloves and a dirty-white neckerchief pulled up over his lower face as if he was about to rob a bank. The haunting whistle of an Ennio Morricone score howled out from the speakers as the figure strode calmly across the floor. All that was missing was the sound of spurs jangling and some dry ice.

Once in his booth, he pulled back one half of his coat like a stage magician to reveal a dark grey revolver tucked into the belt of his jeans. He held his right hand outstretched, far away from his gun.

Paul glared at the figure, directly opposite him now, daring him to make eye contact or give away some unambiguous sign that it was Cullen. Nothing doing.

"Gunslingers, are you ready?"

Billy tensed and brought his hand into position, inches over the grip of Geronimo. The Man-Who-Might-Be-Cullen didn't move, his hand still with plenty of distance to travel before it reached his own gun. Paul shifted in his seat, adjusting his position so that he was looking right through Billy's booth, across the floor into the masked face of the far gunman. Paul was somewhat shit with names, but faces? And Cullen's face? It had to be him, didn't it? But he would never dress up like that. Never attend something like this. Never handle a gun - even as a bit of fun, like this. And he would never, ever, do something for a bit of fun.

Nah, couldn't be. Paul watched mesmerised as this bizarre, unreal scene unfolded in front of him. He couldn't tear his eyes away and he realised he was holding his breath.

The crowd hushed.

"One... Two... Draw."

Paul's crystal-clear view of events shattered into a red mist and there was yawning gap, which was probably only a split-second but felt like minutes, to a huge ragged BANG and clatter as Billy's gun dropped to the floor, Billy collapsing immediately behind it. The Perspex walls of his booth were splattered with blood and the firework smoke hung stale and poignant in the air around it. There were screams from the women behind him and Paul felt Sonya's hand grip his arm and time sped up as the ringing in his ears faded.

"Ladies and Gentlemen, please!" Vince was shouting, the distortion fragging over the sound system. "Please stay calm. There has been an accident but there is no cause for alarm." People were rapidly splitting into two groups, unheeding his words: most of the women and the more infirm were collecting up their belongings and hustling towards the exit at the far end of the room; the younger, drunker and braver folk were scrambling over upturned chairs and the styrofoam-littered floor, making a beeline for the bloody booth and a closer look at Billy lying on the floor. Vince stood magnificently on stage braying deeply through the mike, being completely ignored.

Paul got to his feet and leant on the Perspex like some kind of gore-seeking Kilroy, taking in the scene. Billy was curled up foetally on the floor nursing his right hand with his left. He was crying out, ranting and shouting abuse, all interspersed with expletives indicating that it hurt like fuck. The floor was slick with blood and Billy's boots slipped and slid in it, leaving whorls and smears as he cycled his legs in pain. He writhed and turned and, as he did so, Paul saw the right side of his face was a bloody pulp.

Stinky Pete had scurried over, concern all over his sunken face, and was holding Billy by the shoulder, digging into a pocket to bring out a hankie which he offered his friend.

"Fuck off!" Billy waved it away.

"Are you ok?"

"Course I'm not fucking ok! Fucking... fucking... ow!"

"Are you hurt?"

"Hurt? Fucking look at me! It's blood isn't it? Of course I'm fucking hurt! Fucking gun's gone off in my fucking hand."

"And your face." Pete added, not altogether helpfully.

"What?"

"Your face. It's.... " Pete scrutinised his friend like a vet who wasn't sure whether he was going to get paid for this.

"I can't see!" Billy shrieked, as if only just realising it. "It's all red in one eye!"

Pete was still staring at Billy's face now, horrified. "You must be in shock. Are you in shock?"

"How the fuck should I know?" Billy raged, twisting himself in an attempt to rise but the floor was too slippery. "Get me a mirror! No, wait. Get me an ambulance, dickhead!"

"There is an ambulance on its way." This was Vince, in reassuring tones as he appeared over Billy, towering over the scene like a butte in Monument valley. "Don't move. Don't try and get up. Wait for the paramedics." He glanced up from Billy to the receding crowd, as the curious finally dispersed, being shepherded away by Maud and Irene.

Vince turned to Paul. "Did you see what happened?"

"Er..."

"You were right behind him weren't you?"

"Er... Aye, yeah. Yeah."

"I can't be the only one who witnessed it." Vince said, concerned. "They'll need witnesses."

"Er... Well, I was looking at the other guy. Mainly." Paul finished, weakly.

"The other guy. Yeah." Vince said, as if awoken from a dream. He twisted his head this way and that to see if he could see the masked man. "Where did he go?"

Paul shrugged and ran the shootout through his memory to see what he could recall.

"I was just watching and then... all this blood hit the screen. Like a tin of red paint exploded."

"Yeah." Vince turned away from Paul, perhaps realising that his search for a corroborating witness needed to be widened. "Wasn't a tin of paint, though. It was his gun that exploded."

"Can they do that?"

Vince looked down at Billy, still keening on the ground. "Seen it once before. When some idiot tried to fire a live round from a replica gun."

"Right." Paul said, absently, casting around for any sign of The-Man-Who-Might-Be-Cullen.

"This is your fucking fault!" Shrieked Billy. "You fucking did this!"

"I fail to see how I can be held responsible for you firing your own gun." Vince said, not irrationally.

"You fucking big, black American... twat!" Billy blurted. "You put a live bullet in my gun! You knew this would happen!"

"No." Vince said, doing his utmost to remain calm. He glanced up as two paramedics entered the hall on the far side and acknowledged them with a tilt of his head.

"You fucking did. Fucking barred me. Threw me out. Took my gun. You've had it all this time. You put a fucking bullet in it!" Billy spat, blood and sputum flecking his pale stubbled chin as he ranted, his right eye socket like a strawberry smoothie.

"No. I did not." Vince could feel his heart starting to thud in his chest.

"Yes, you fucking did! Who else had my gun, huh? No-one!"

"Well, actually, I gave it to-"

"You put a live bullet in my gun so I would shoot myself!"

Vince forced out a grim smile. "Why would I do that?."

"Fuck you!" Billy wiped his mouth and nose, his sleeve coming away crimson. "Fuck you and your club." He struggled to his feet just as the lead paramedic reached him, then slipped to unconsciousness as he slid in his own blood and smacked his head on the dance floor.

"Whoops." Said the paramedic, who had held out his arms to catch the crumpling man but had been a foot too distant to reach.

Maud came rushing over, having finished sweeping the last of the attendees out into the night.

"Is he ok?"

"Um." Said Vince.

As the paramedics stretchered Billy out of the club, Paul belatedly looked around for Sonya. His date was nowhere to be seen. He followed everyone outside to the waiting ambulance, its lights flashing blue and red. There was a small crowd of spectators hanging around, waiting to see what bounty was being delivered from the maw of the club.

Beyond the watching gaggle, flirting with the shadows from the strobing emergency vehicle lights, a tall figure in a long coat and a cowboy hat slid away into the summer night.

# KISS KISS BANG BANG

"So, what do you reckon?" Paul winced as Geoff turned the trinket box in his hands and tapped it with a little hammer.

"Yeah, I can do it." Geoff looked up quizzically, and removed the jeweller's eyepiece. "But so could you."

"Tried that, mate." Paul waggled his bandaged souvenir. "Didn't go too well. Those little tools, too tiny for me. Slipped and went clean through... well, everything. Thumb, palm tendon. I'm never touching something that small again."

"Keep away from the urinal then!" Geoff grinned.

"Good one." Paul gave a tight smile. "Sarcasm won't get you anywhere, you know."

"Well it got me to the Sarcasm World Cup in Ottawa in 2008."

"Really?"

"No."

Paul set his jaw. "Look, will you do it or not?"

"Aye. For a hundred."

"A hundred!"

"Minus this tiny stone that's missing. Probably some semi-precious bit. Not my area." Geoff sniffed.

"A hundred!" Paul's repeated, distraught.

"Cash. Take it or leave it."

"When can you do it by?"

Geoff thought for a moment. "Maybe Tuesday?"

"Tuesday?" Paul's eyes bulged. "Can't you do it any sooner?"

"Like when?"

"Like tomorrow?"

"Aye. I can do it for tomorrow. For two hundred."

Paul considered his situation. "I'll see you Tuesday."

Vince was sweeping the floor behind the bar when Maud crept into the club and stood watching him until he noticed her.

"Maud." He acknowledged, glumly, continuing to sweep.

She smiled at him, standing awkwardly in her coat and looked around the chilly hall. The patter of light summer rain on the roof above was the only sound. She walked towards the bar, footsteps echoing on the wooden floor, and glanced nervously at the spot where her husband had fallen. The space was surrounded by metal barriers sheathed in thick polythene and DO NOT CROSS police tape. Through the translucent material she thought she could still see dark stains on the golden wood.

"How are you?" She looked into his face and tried to see the booming self-confident giant that usually strode the stage. Instead, all she saw was an emptiness behind his eyes and an unwillingness to hold her gaze. She had a weird sense that, somehow, he looked paler.

Vince sighed and leant on his broom. "I'm done here."

"Are they...?" She nodded towards the dance floor and raised her eyebrows in a unfinished question.

"Crime scene." He shook his head, looked over at the cordoned-off area and then up at the ceiling and around the hall. "Closed me down. Forensics first. Then some

Health & Safety guy came round and, charmingly, told me my license was being suspended pending an investigation. Said it could be weeks... and chances of getting it reinstated were quote *slender* unquote. Headlines in the press and word of mouth did the rest. I don't think there's any coming back from this."

"I'm sorry, V." She had never used this abbreviation for him before and, as the words left her mouth, she wondered if she had breached some etiquette guideline. Vince didn't seem to notice.

"Yeah. Well..." He scrunched up his face and then blew air out of from his cheeks. "These things happen. You know, I imagined sometimes all this coming to an end - failing to take off and having to rein it back somehow or morph the club into something else. I never saw it ending like this."

"It doesn't have to be the end." Her eyes widened in alarm, too many unwanted prospects for her to contemplate: losing her line-dancing role, the lights and music, the regular camaraderie of her friends, the absence of Vince's presence. All of a sudden, she felt overwhelming emotion and her eyes began welling up.

"Hey, hey, hey." Vince put his broom to one side and strode over, huge arms engulfing her shoulders. "It's only a club. Nobody died."

"No." She sniffed, unsure whether this was a good thing or a bad one, and allowed herself to nestle into his chest. "What are you going to do then?"

"Me? I'm going home." Vince declared to the empty hall.

"Home?"

"Louisiana."

Maud pulled away and looked earnestly into his face.

He held her gaze this time - honest and open, even allowing himself a smile. Her lip started to tremble. The absence of Vince's presence in the club was not the same as the absence of Vince period.

"Really?"

"Yep. Nothing for me here, now."

Maud brushed a tear from her cheek and asked: "Nothing?"

The figure shambled out of the derelict caravan and started to piss against one of the flat tyres. His chest and feet were bare and he wore only striped pyjama bottoms with a cord at the waist. One hand leant on the side of the caravan, green with mould and mildew. Steam rose like mist from the warm stream as it gushed audibly in the silence of the forest. Out of nowhere, a Jack Russell terrier trotted up amicably to take a sniff and the man looked down, startled.

"Sorry, mate!" Paul called as he reached the edge of the clearing. His dogs, Ant and Dec, were both well ahead of him. "Didn't mean to disturb your morning wossname. Ablutions!"

Dec scampered up next to Ant and the pair both cocked their own legs to urinate onto the wheel where the man had been.

"Marking their territory." Paul laughed. "This caravan's theirs now!"

"No." The man said with finality. "It is not."

Paul was slightly put out by the coldness of the remark. "Only joking." He regarded the dilapidated wreck in front of him and screwed up his face. "Looks like it's only the mould and stains that's holding it together!"

The man turned to glare at Paul, his rugged face a 'Fuck Off' in flesh.

"Mungo!" Cried Paul. "Didn't recognise you there for a moment. You know, without your hat."

Cullen maintained his glare, unhappy with this use of his first name, and finished watering his caravan wheel. Paul strode cheerily across the clearing towards him.

"This yours then?" He scanned the exterior and the small clearing it was in. "Nice. Very... bijou."

Cullen disappeared back into the caravan without responding. Paul screwed his face up and sighed. This was not that an unusual start to encounters with his odd friend. He followed Cullen inside, ducking his head as he entered the cramped vehicle, the small caravan wavered unsteadily under the combined weight of the two men.

"Here, I've been looking for you all over!" Paul said, scanning the interior crammed with piles of boxes, crates and assorted junk up to the ceiling. Cullen was sitting on a half-cleared bunkseat, a navy sleeping bag pushed back against the backrest to reveal a stained orange-patterned seat cover riddled with tears and holes. Next to him was a stuffed black bin bag that he was lazily rooting through. Ant & Dec scampered up the step into the caravan and started sniffing energetically about. Cullen scowled at them and they froze, looked at Paul for a cue and then retreated back outside.

"Why?" Cullen resumed scooping through the bin bag, for all the world as if Paul wasn't there.

"Why what?"

"Why are you looking for me?"

"Ah, well. Two reasons. First - and I know this is a silly question - were you at the Grand Ole Opry on Friday night?"

"The where?"

"The Grand Ole Opry." Paul watched Cullen closely, tuning in to the slightest indication that might signal a lie. "I mentioned the place when I told you about Billy Gillespie?"

"Oh right." Cullen gave an almost imperceptible nod. "Why would I have been there?"

"Just, you know, wondering. There was a bloke looked just like you. In a gunfight with Billy."

"I don't like guns."

"All the same-"

"I really don't like guns."

"Aye, well, they're not real guns are they? Only fire blanks 'n that. Mind you, Billy-"

"What?"

"Well he didn't come out of it too well. Real guns or not." Paul sniffed. "Seems them replica guns aren't made to fire real bullets. Almost lost an eye."

"Huh."

"Shame about that *almost*."

Cullen looked up from his bin bag, suddenly interested. "Why?"

"Dirty old bastard had it coming."

"Really?"

"Oh aye. Sofe, my niece, she's a tenant of his. Place is a total dump, natch. Apparently he's been trying it on, suggesting that he can fix the place up if she, you know..."

Cullen's eyebrows rose, questioningly.

"Payment in kind, so to speak." Nodded Paul.

"Oh."

"Yeah. I tried warning him off at the Opry, not sure it sank in, mind. I'll make sure it sinks in once this comes off." Paul waggled the large cottonbud at the end of his arm, and Cullen noticed it, as if for the first time.

"What happened?"

"Erm. Nothing." Paul stiffened and quickly put his bandaged hand behind his back.. "Not related to your box. At all."

"My box?" Cullen eyed Paul suspiciously.

"Oh yeah. That's reason number two." Paul scooped a paper bag from his pocket with his good hand and offered it to Cullen, beaming. "Ta-da!"

Cullen wiped both hands on his pyjama trousers before gently opening the bag to reveal the patinaed trinket box, its marquetry gleaming in the pale light filtering through the grimy window. He pushed it open, tenderly, with his index finger and then turned it in his palm, stroking the hinges and the smooth polished lid.

"Thank you." Cullen kept his head down and still and the words were little more than a whisper.

"Did it all on my own!" Paul cried. "Not a bad job, if I do say so meself. Needed to dust off some old tools, mind. Keep a steady hand an' all."

"It's lovely." Another whisper.

"Couldn't get a stone to fit that *i* hole, though. You'll need a jeweller for that."

"It doesn't matter." Cullen brushed the tiny indentation with a grimy finger and said to himself. "An eye for an i."

"Right. Well. Don't suppose..."

"What?"

"Just... you know... a bit short right now, is all." Paul nodded meaningfully in the direction of the repaired box.

"What do you mean?"

"Nothing. I was just hoping. You know..." Paul waggled his head from side to side but Cullen was still busy caressing the inlaid box lid. He looked up suddenly, eyes gleaming into Paul's.

"You know, you don't need to wait to mark Billy's card." Cullen said softly.

"Don't I?" Paul screwed up his face, confused.

"No." Cullen dipped into his bin bag with a sly smile and offered Paul a large battered box of fireworks. "Ta-da!"

Billy felt his good eye pop out when the gorgeous girl opened the door. She was wearing a thin silk blouse which was bursting open, several buttons undone, under the strain from its cargo. Her nipples thudded against the material like rivets from the Ark Royal and she had a sheen of sweat on her vast cleavage which made her chest look like it had just been removed, dripping, from a can of peeled peaches.

She was wearing a pair of tight denim cut-off shorts, so short that the pocket linings were hanging down below the hem of each leg. He stared at her legs and the perfect pink toes which wiggled delightfully on the cold linoleum floor. Her hair was tousled and provocative and she had sleepy eyes, her lips slightly parted to reveal a hint of dainty white teeth.

He was staring at a centrefold.

"Sophie?" He managed, hopefully.

She didn't speak but just nodded her head and opened the door further to invite him in. Billy looked up and down the empty street, trying not to seem furtive, but feeling very much like he was in a second-rate porn film. Sophie turned and padded barefoot down the hallway, leaving Billy gazing at her legs as they swished delightfully ahead of him. Heart thudding in his chest, he stepped across the threshold into the cool hallway and closed the door softly behind him.

At the entrance to the kitchen she stopped, leaning on the doorjamb. She ran a hand through her heavy head of hair, tossing a huge flap of it back over her head. Billy thought it was one of the sexiest things he had ever seen, but she was oblivious.

"I'll be upstairs when you're done." She said, and tripped out of the kitchen.

Billy stood in the kitchen, the washing machine still alone in the centre of the room, like an unwanted ex-boyfriend in a family photo. He knelt down, opened the mouth of his toolbag and peered inside - tilting his head at a funny angle to allow his good eye to survey the contents. He had an erection the likes of which he couldn't recall and, when he reached inside the bag to pull out an adjustable wrench, he realised he was shaking and sweating.

Billy closed his eye, forcing himself to breathe slowly and then swallow hard. In his head, he saw the two of them entwined naked on silk sheets, her young lithe form sliding over him, perfect skin smothering him with kisses, her mane of golden hair worming its way down his torso until she buried her head in his groin. This was the stuff that dreams were made of. But *she* had called *him* - in a way he had only been able to imagine: all breathy and reluctant and too, too sexy for him to bear. *Yes*, she understood what he was proposing. *Yes*, she was prepared to pay the price - she just wanted the machine repaired. *Yes* she would stay right there until he arrived.

Now here he was, and she had gone upstairs to wait for him. He opened his eyes, took a deep breath and set to work on the washing machine.

When he was done, he stood and rubbed both hands down his overalls. This was it.

He strode excitedly down the cold hall and, just as he turned to climb the stairs, he saw a strange flickering through one of the frosted glass panels in the front door. Something about the image scratched at his brain and he hesitated for a moment. Then there was a sudden bang, followed by several more. The hairs on the back of Billy's neck stood straight up and he flung open the front door in alarm.

The cabin of his beloved Flying Anglia was in full flame. Billy stared, horrified, as two rockets exploded out from the shattered windscreen and screamed up into the warm summer sky.

# POSTSCRIPT

**Billy "The Kid" Gillespie** never fully recovered the sight in his right eye. His precious Flying Anglia was declared a write-off by the insurance company and Billy elected not to replace it, as it would just be one more thing **Maud** would get half of in their divorce. As it was, she got their marital home and he got the student house in Dalkeith in which he now lives - in squalor, as he slowly saves money from his state pension to cover the cost of gradually making it fit for human habitation.

**Vincent "Big V" Bradley Cass** eventually found a buyer for Cass's Clays and sold the Gorebridge Grand Ole Opry to Midlothian Council who re-purposed it as a pre-school nursery. He flew back to the USA and is now happily retired, living in Riverbend Lakes, Baton Rouge.

**Maud Gillespie** packed her bags, left home, and applied for a divorce. She met **Big V** at the departure gate for United flight 39 out of Edinburgh. The £200,000 she received from selling her home was pooled with Vince's money to buy a bungalow, where they now live, overlooking the mighty Mississippi.

**Sophie Jane McKay** was re-housed in Halls of Residence after St Margaret's University removed **Billy Gillespie's** property from their approved list. She has a date with

**Tom Corcoran** on Friday.

**"Stinky" Pete Blaikie** hung up his gunbelt with the closure of the Grand Ole Opry and now stays in on Friday nights, with his wife, **Gaynor**, who is not three bad.

**"Big" Paul McInnes** had two more blind dates, courtesy of his niece, before going online and failing to find love there as well. Then, one day, he walked into Greggs Bakery in Peebles and found himself asking for Shirley Stevenson's phone number. His injured hand is now fine.

**Mungo James Cullen** still carries the trinket box in his pack. Somewhere in Cardrona Forest is buried a black bin bag containing an oilskin trail coat and a Smith & Wesson Model 10 handgun. The revolver has only ever been fired once, many years ago.

## AUTHOR'S NOTE

As ever, this book involved some research, and (given the way I do it) the receipt of some suspicious and/or funny looks in the process. I guess it's bound to happen if you visit a nuclear power plant and ask "How could someone could break in here?", or ask a policeman "Is anyone on night duty at the station over the Xmas period?", or ask a rugby club chairman "Is there an alarm on your trophy cabinet?". Very often the answer is the same: "Get off the premises."

For this book, I visited the Grand Ole Opry in Glasgow. It is nothing like the one I describe (although the drink is very *very* cheap) and there is no equivalent in Gorebridge, or anywhere else in Southern Scotland that I am aware of - otherwise I would have gone there instead. I asked one of the gunfighters "Could I put a real bullet in your gun and shoot someone with it?" The answer to that question is one reason why you have this story.

I did no research whatsoever regarding the way Universities staff or operate any kinds of Housing departments for their students, apart from being a student myself far too long ago to have any relevance. Nor did I visit any clay pigeon shooting establishments, other than walk past a quarry used for these purposes at the foot of the Pentlands, near my home. I figured the exercise I gained from the walk was enough.

Also, as ever, I need to thank some people:

First and foremost, Claire, for giving me her invaluable feedback and being willing to engage in prolonged conversations about plot, tone and character so constructively and patiently. And for living with someone with a head full of bits and pieces of Paul, Cullen, Barry, Billy, Conrad, Tony, Duffy, and the all the rest of the weirdos and oddballs in my books. It can't be easy.

Thanks also to my fantastic Beta readers Deidre, Jane, John, Mike and Pete. They're ever so good and I can highly recommend them... and no, you can't use them. They're mine!

I am also hugely grateful to my cover designer, Jonathan, for coming up with a cracking illustration at really short notice and doing a belting job. As always.

Finally, a shout-out to all the members of the Peebles Writing Group. Whilst they didn't directly help me with this book, they were my first step on the road to writing several years ago and I am, and always will be, grateful to them for that. I still attend every month when I can and, if you're ever in Peebles on the first Monday of every month, pop in and say "Hi."

Aside from all the above assistance, this is entirely a book wot I wrote. Any creations, flights of fancy, omissions, stupidities, inflammatory comments, insults or unfunny jokes are all mine and I take full responsibility for them.

But you bought this book, so you need to take responsibility too.

*Caveat emptor* and Merry Christmas.

mjf
18.12.2018

## Join the Cullen & Big Paul Fan Club!

If you enjoyed the adventures of Cullen and Big Paul, why not join their fan club? You'll get early notice of new books, special offers, a monthly newsletter from the author, unique free content, invitations for discounts and more!

JOIN at **download.markfarrer.com/signup**

## Tell others what you thought...

If you enjoyed this book, please leave a review on Amazon

## About the Author

You can learn more about Mark Farrer at **www.markfarrer.com** or follow him on Twitter **@mark_farrer.**

# PALE ALE RIDER

mark farrer

funny business press

PALE ALE RIDER


Published by Funny Business Press

*To the soup*
*For being so trustworthy.*

# CONTENTS

# ONE

Tyler McKenna was a complete bastard. Complete in the sense that he didn't want for anything. Because if he wanted something, he took it.

And he was a bastard in the literal sense of the word: born out of wedlock; illegitimate. His mother, Angela, had fallen pregnant while still at school and his father, Iain, had legged it before the birth and never been seen again. Well, almost never seen again - he was later spotted on Crimewatch.

The way Tyler saw it, his future had been predetermined. Raised on a sprawling estate, guns everywhere, one parent mostly absent, his father from a dysfunctional family with a long history of joblessness. An insightful observer could have pointed out that the same could be said for Prince Harry and he'd turned out alright - but there weren't many insightful observers in Tyler's orbit.

But despite this - or more correctly, perhaps, because of it - Tyler never had a problem coming into money. Usually because the money he came into was other peoples'. At school he had effortlessly acquired the dinner and pocket money of other children through ransacking of coats in cloakrooms, lockers in corridors, bags in changing rooms. Outside school, the money he acquired was his mother's. Dipping into her purse, nicking the odd quid here, a spare fiver there. She never noticed, or if she did she never said anything. Angela had an air of permanent exhaustion about her, a constant harried look - no doubt due to the fact that she held down two jobs to make ends meet. Not that this was in any way acknowledged or appreciated by her son - her absence at work, and the resulting lack of time spent with him, was just seen as further illustration of the parental neglect which had made him the way he was.

Even his mother's loving attempts to spend time with him went largely unappreciated. One of her jobs was at the Brewery and, from an early age, she had taken Tyler to work there - first as a kind of free creche and childcare facility where the other women on reception could coo and cuddle while she expressed milk; later, when she had taken on the job of delivery driver, she would let Tyler ride along in the cab with her during school holidays. What she might have considered entertainment, even education into the world of work, was certainly not what Tyler would call quality time. It was a chore, a drag and time spent away from his primary occupation: theft. An occupation which Tyler pursued smoothly and efficiently.

Because Tyler was smart and sly, and had no lack of planning or attention to detail. He would never take money where it would be unambiguously noticed - one pound coin from a purse containing several; just enough from a kid's coat to make them think they might have dropped some; graduating onto a few tenners from the Brewery Shop till loaded with them (never a twenty, or the highest denomination in the till). There was a permanent air of plausible deniability about any disappearance when Tyler was around - maybe it was him, maybe it wasn't. Or maybe there hadn't been any loss in the first place? Were you sure?

And it wasn't just cash. Tyler, like the taxman, was never happy. If someone had what he considered to be "too much" (and the strict definition of this term amounted, really, to "more than him") he had a roving eye and creative imagination.

When Tyler was six, his friend Joe (who had parents wealthy enough to afford two cars and a double garage to put them in) had put his hand in a garage door and then the door had slammed shut - in the wind, it seemed. Joe lost two fingers.

When he was eight, his next-door neighbour had three beautiful pedigree dachshunds which she was devoted to. Tyler had released four bars of Green's Organic Dark Chocolate from her kitchen cupboard onto the floor, testing out whether dogs could survive eating chocolate. They did - just. But shat all over an expensive Turkish rug and vomitted across a brand new sofa which never olfactorily recovered.

And later, at the Brewery, one full crate of beer amongst fifteen or so might cause Freddie doing the stock take to scratch his head and correct last week's figures. Tyler would never take one if there was a round number or an even, regular stack - but if there was a pile, he was in gravy.

No-one had a good word to say for Tyler, not that Tyler gave a toss. No-one, except for his mother. Angela wouldn't hear a bad word said about her beautiful baby boy - a child she doted on and had dedicated her life to raising and loving. Any criticism, accusation or negative feedback she heard about her son simply could not penetrate this confident forcefield of devotion. Were they sure? Everyone makes mistakes. Surely they were mistaken? Not her Tyler.

Like a weary pensioner with cataracts, Angela didn't so much navigate by what she saw as by the memory of what it had been last time she'd seen clearly. However long ago that was, probably the last time she'd had any energy to spare.

So Tyler slid through childhood and puberty like a shark, threatening but largely unobserved, and never in the vicinity when the damage was discovered. He wasn't some muscled or unintelligent thug - he was slight, not even that tall, and didn't look particularly prepossessing and certainly not intimidating. As an infant, he'd had the resting face of an angel - a cherub with apple cheeks, large liquid eyes, and a dimple in his chin which grew when he started to blubber. The slightest little thing could reduce him to tears, as if Bambi's mother had just died.

As he grew, his youthful chubbiness transformed into wiry, gawky pubescence, but he kept the almost baby-faced innocence, the demeanour of a pleasant if underachieving youngster. He had a shock of short, dark hair atop a narrow face of soft pale cheeks and a once-freckled stub of a nose.

But catch his face, one time, out of the corner of your eye. Or keep an unwavering gaze on him when he was unaware you were looking, and his face would somehow slacken. His facial muscles would loosen, skin tone switch and his eyes darken and you were looking at a different face - that of an unfeeling, dead-eyed man-child who could snap and spit, wound or injure without the slightest remorse. Insolent, hooded eyes which looked through you and dared you to react. Waited. Incited. Hoped.

And if you did, you never did it again.

But look again, and it was just Tyler, gazing at you enquiringly: *What?*

Tyler had the eyes of a serial killer. Could, perhaps one day, even become one - if only he had the ambition.

Tracey Mulhearn had ambition. She was the youngest of four girls, the other three all much older than her. Four daughters to four different fathers: Tyra, Tiffany, Teri and Tracey. Her elder sisters had all but left home by the time she was ten and her mother figured that, having taught her first three kids how to grow up, the last one would somehow pick it up through a kind of sororial osmosis. Plus her mother had quickly tired of the whole parenting lark: birthing four kids was quite bad enough without having to care for them alone when their co-creators had all fucked off at the first whiff of a full nappy.

Tracey's mother had had a hard time holding onto anything: boyfriends, money, reality. So Tracey had lacked a lot growing up, but she did have mental and physical energy to spare - and had needed to find outlets for it before she literally exploded. School certainly didn't do it for her. Not that she wasn't bright - she was; but the whole dull and grinding system and structure of study, revision, testing, attainment - endlessly repeating. She wanted more. She wanted X-Factor and recording contracts and blogging millions and... everything. Or, at least, anything but this boring nothingness which her painful teenage existence in some rural backwater involved. Biggar wasn't all that bad, she rationalised, but it wasn't New York, or London. Not even Manchester or Leeds. It was a sleepy, provincial town huddling nervously between Scotland's industrious central belt and England's domineering call and, like the red ribbon on a tug-of-war rope between two teams both tired of the game but too stubborn to quit, it was pulled this way and that but over the years the overall effect was that it essentially didn't go anywhere at all.

And if she stayed there, neither would she.

Tracey wanted more. She wanted excitement and danger, thrill and exhilaration. She wanted the needle to move and to hell with it.

And that was how it started.

"Hey." Tyler had pulled his mouth to one side, partly to exhale the smoke away from the girl, partly because he thought it might look cool.

The girl in black looked sullen and quiet, but very pretty nonetheless. Her hair was bright orange and chopped cruelly short and uneven, as if she'd been attacked by an aggressive strimmer, and she had artfully daubed on makeup - the way young girls do - attempting to achieve a unique look whilst ending up as a clone of all the other punk rebels in Biggar (there being nothing so unifying as a rebellion against one thing to make you resemble each other).

She was thin, almost gaunt, with hollow cheeks and narrow lips but bright round eyes which sparkled and flashed emerald. When she laughed - a dirty cynical laugh which sounded cruel and harsh - she rocked her head back to reveal a translucent, delicate neck with a perfect pale clavicle, partly-concealed by a washed-out grey T-shirt. Over this she wore a short black puffer jacket, shiny with wear. A badge on one lapel said "Nuclear Power: Yes Please"; the other lapel badge said "Nuclear Power: No Thanks". Her drainpipe black jeans, stick-thin, came to an end above a pair of Doc Martens trimmed with neon green socks peeping out the top. From one ear dangled a crucifix on a long chain, a blood-red metallic Christ painted on its silver cross; the other ear was penetrated by a gleaming sword, its hilt sitting outside her eardrum, and from its tip beneath her lobe dripped a small solitary ruby.

She looked up from her phone at Tyler through her scuffed fringe and then looked back down at it again, unimpressed. "Hey yourself."

"You new?"

"No." She snorted. "Don't make a habit of turning up, is all. School sucks."

"Right." Tyler nodded. He offered his open pack of cigarettes. "Smoke?"

She looked up at him, down at the pack, then up at him again. "Sure."

He fiddled getting the lighter from his pocket while she bent over to shield from any breeze. "Get caught?"

"No!" She puffed out some smoke, pouting. The very idea seemed to offend her. "Been called in, is why."

She spoke with a kind of mid-Atlantic accent but there was something about her speech pattern, and the way she used certain phrases, that made Tyler think she might be American - or, at the very least, heavily influenced by American TV shows.

"Right."

They stood leaning against the school wall, out of sight from the Science block, smoking in silence. The girl seemed in no mood to talk, focussed on her phone.

"I'm Tyler." He offered, hopefully.

"I know."

He waited for her to elaborate but she didn't. "Do I know you?"

"Not yet." She said, bored, and then shoved her phone into a pocket and turned to face him. "Do you want to?"

"Want to what?"

"Know me."

"Yeah."

"Why?"

Tyler was flummoxed. She was asking him a direct question and that always annoyed him. He liked to remain cool and aloof - enigmatic is what he thought of himself - and you couldn't be enigmatic if someone asked you a clear question, point blank. At least, he couldn't see how you could. He had a choice: sulk, snap back or be honest. He quickly weighed up these options.

"You look kinda cool." He said, boyishly.

She smiled. More than a smile, it brought her face alive and almost lit up his own.

"Tracey." She shook her head, still smiling, and looked him in the eye. "Wanna fuck?"

They lay, spent, on the mattress in Tracey's room. Tyler blowing cigarette smoke up into the air, jiggling his jaw, trying to make smoke rings. He was desperate to impress her; aching to show her that he was a real man, older than his years, worldly-wise and someone to be admired. Not the young, adolescent scumbag that he actually was.

"How many times have you had sex?"

Tyler was instantly on his guard. He hadn't expected that he would need to conjure up an impressive sexual backstory. At least, not right now, having so recently done the deed for what - only the third time?

"Oh, loads." He shrugged, reckoning that, given the exact wording of her question, wanks should count.

"With how many girls?"

"Oh, we're just talking about girls are we?" Tyler

spontaneously threw this in and then immediately realised this might not play too well.

"What do you mean?" Her brow creased and she propped herself up on one elbow next to him to look into his eyes. Tyler panicked.

"Nothing. I'm only joking." He smiled apologetically, and his mind raced as he tried to find a way to answer her question without admitting his lack of sexual experience. On the one foreign school trip he had ever been on, he had got off with a girl from Rio de Janeiro who had been backpacking around Italy. He leapt at this recollection like a tramp on a ham & cheese toastie. "I've slept with a Brazilian!" Tyler boasted.

"OMFG!" Tracey shrieked in horror. "How many is a brazillion?"

They had settled on an M.O quickly and readily. Responsibilities divided naturally enough, since Tyler wanted to make sure everything went according to his meticulous plans, and didn't trust anyone else not to cock it up. And Tracey wanted to ride Tyler's bike.

For someone who had a motorbike, Tyler didn't seem to care much for it. It was almost as if he had got it because it was expected of him. A bike to make him look cool and hard and tough, but he didn't like it because it was noisy and fast and it freaked him out when he went round corners too fast.

And he hid it from his mother. How embarrassing was that? "She'd kill me if I had one!" he had almost whined, and Tracey had looked at him as if he had just admitted to watching Downton.

"Unlikely." Tracey had offered. "She's your mother."

"Well, ground me then."

"Ground you? What are you, ten?"

Tyler had sulked for a while after that. Until she had sucked his cock.

But he had a motorbike nonetheless and Tracey's eyes had lit up when she had seen it. He had stolen it from someone's backyard in Penicuik and it was neon orange and black, chrome and white and it shone and sparkled while he kept it clean and new. And it wasn't just the fact that he had stolen it which had added to its appeal - it was Tyler's approach to stuff which she found fascinating and strangely alluring. Partially because it was so alien to her: she was impulsive and wild - some would call her random and scatty; he was methodical and planned. He would construct a plan in his head, work out all the steps and then proceed to follow them one by one in order to achieve his goal.

Need a motorbike? Well, he couldn't buy one - he was still too young. And they would likely want to know where he'd got the money from. But he could steal one. But stealing a motorbike meant they'd be on the lookout for it, once it had been stolen. So you needed to steal it from somewhere far away - or at least far enough away so that it was in a different constabulary or county, somewhere the police who spotted you riding it wouldn't care too much about.

Biggar was in South Lanarkshire, near the western boundary with the Scottish Borders; Penicuik was in Midlothian, just beyond the northern boundary. The two towns were only twenty miles apart but not just in different counties, they were separated by a third. The long, smooth A702 was a smashing 30 minute thrill-ride from one to the other on a bike and it had been oh-so-simple for Tyler to catch a bus, scout out Penicuik, find a suitable target, steal himself some bolt-cutters and thus acquire a shiny new bike.

Tyler stashed it in The Cave, as he insisted on calling it. A large storage container which sat out back, behind the Brewery outbuildings, where the edge of the site met a largely unused paddock. The container had been abandoned and neglected for some years now, and so far Tyler had done nothing with it except use it to stash anything he had acquired that he wanted to hide from his mother.

Which was everything he had acquired. Including his bike.

Tracey loved the bike, and every chance she got to ride it. The feeling of power at her instant control, the way it reacted and moved with her, the slightest changes of balance allowing her to sway it, violently if need be, this way and that. It was like besting a wild animal with convenient domestic controls.

While Tyler was busy planning each job, she had busied herself buying accessories, riding attire and addressing herself to the interior decor of their, now shared, Cave. She had spent half a weekend mopping and cleaning it out before starting the process of turning it into a kind of teenage studio apartment. Tyler thought she was mad and looked at her with a disbelieving off-kilter squint, like a Scotsman being asked if he'd like another drink. She had blithely ridden out his indifference and later his ridicule, buying his-and-hers helmets *"What the fuck? Do you want us to get noticed?"*, matching leather jackets, *"How many places do we have to rob before we make this much back?"* and then moving onto soft furnishings and IKEA basics *"Make sure you pay cash. Avoiding traceability is key."*

Surprised, she had given herself a good talking to in case she was unknowingly overseeing a metamorphosis from hardened, rebellious wannabe rock-chick to mumsy-homemaker-in-waiting. Tracey reassured herself that, genetically, she didn't have it in her. This was simply the first time she had had anywhere she could call her own, the first time she had any money to speak of, and the first time she had *carte-blanche* to exercise some decision-making which resulted in actual material change. If their new *pied-a-terre* and all the *accoutrements* that went with it (Tracey idly wondered if perhaps she wasn't half-French) was a life of crime, Tracey loved it and wanted more of it. She would urge Tyler on with greater urgency, using her sex and her ideas to entice, persuade and upgrade Tyler's own self-limiting ambitions.

As for the M.O., Tracey had gazed longingly at his bike while Tyler had explained, at length, the why's and wherefore's behind his thinking.

During school holidays, he had ridden in his mother's delivery van every day as she made her deliveries for the Brewery. They would pull up at a pub, the time and date unvarying: each pub had a set delivery day of the week, and his mother always did the round in the same order so the times were reliable, traffic and weather permitting.

At first Tyler would wait in the cab, idling on his phone and listening to some frantic *um-tsch-um-tsch-um-tsch* in his earbuds while his mother usually walked through a rear access door, always open, docket in hand and would return a minute or so later with a member of staff who would help unload the kegs and crates. Occasionally he would be called on to help, perhaps hold a door open or move some empties to one side to allow better access to the cellar or storeroom. But over the weeks Tyler had started taking more of an interest in things.

There was always, *always*, a back door open. Sometimes it was to vent heat or let in some fresh air, sometimes it was so that the kitchen staff could pop outside for a smoke, sometimes it was to allow easy access for rubbish to be piled by the door for collection. Whatever the reason, there was always an open back door to each pub premises and it was only manned when some stray employee sneaked out for a quick drag.

All Tyler had to do was walk in. So, one day, he did. And the following week. And the week after that. Over the course of one summer holiday he walked into a dozen different pubs and clubs, each time venturing further into the dark corridors and empty rooms, kitchens or offices, wandering around until he found something of value. It could have been a till, or a safe, or a trophy cabinet. Whatever it was, Tyler made a mental note and had later drawn up a detailed sketch of the layout, location of important items, doorways, likely position of staff, etc.

During each of the forays he was always ready to stumble upon someone who would ask who he was and what he was doing there, and he had an answer ready which was *"My Mum's delivering beer from the Brewery and I needed a wee."* Which, he thought, would be fair enough and indeed, one time he had been startled to turn a corner and find two kitchen employees trying to wrestle each other's tongues out of their heads. They had jumped, he had jumped, extended his story and ended up in the lavatories, gaining access to more of the building's interior en route. Thereafter, he was quite hoping to be discovered as it would aid his study of each place.

He soon had schematics and details of these separate establishments and started trial runs - small stuff at first.

Stuff he could put into his pockets and return to his mother's cab with, undetected and unsuspected. By the end of the summer holidays he had an intimate knowledge of these twelve places, and a small treasure trove of stolen items ranging from expensive-looking kitchen knives, through some very smart pairs of workboots, to the contents of three separate petty cash boxes.

He felt like a Master of the Universe, able to come and go at will - the Macavity of Pub crimes. Never seen, never suspected, never caught. Now, the pair of them together could move on up the value chain and find something better to steal.

"What do you say, Trace?"

"Hmm? Yeah. Cool." Tracey tore her eyes from the beautiful bike and tried to zone back into whatever Tyler had been saying. "What's our next target then?"

"I just told you. The Lamb & Flag."

"Right. Yeah. Gotcha. Just checking. Yeah."

From the get-go, Tracey had seen Tyler and his methodical planning as the hallmarks of a criminal mastermind. His ability to think through situations, predict outcomes and allow for things going wrong. It was some kind of magic, watching him think and then listening to him outline the plan in glorious shining detail.

But perhaps, Tracey was starting to wonder, he was methodical to the extent of being predictable and boring. And while Tyler could be relied upon to plan, work out the details and the order of events and follow it through, he was easily derailed by the unexpected. It was as if he had to have time to assess whatever it was, process it, work out a series of responses, select the right one and then put it into action. This all took time. It was like watching an AI computer responding in slow-mo. He seemed to have no instincts, no ability to function on autopilot without having been pre-programmed. You could never picture him, for example, catching a ball. The time taken to inform him a ball was on its way, locate its position in the air, identify its trajectory, plot its final catchable position, work out how to arrange his body to be in the right place at the right time and in the right arrangement of arms, legs, weight distribution and hand placement... the ball would just hit him in the face.

No, with Tyler you needed to pre-announce well in advance, provide all the parameters and address all of his concerns. Once done, you could rely on him to be there and carry out all the necessary steps to complete the task. All the eventualities he had foreseen, all the mistakes that could happen, he would be prepared for. But if something unanticipated went wrong, you were fucked.

And things were starting to go wrong. A lot.

They'd hit three pubs and one Ex-servicemen's club and the returns had been less than glorious. In fact, they had nearly been caught at the club when a different delivery lorry had turned up at the same time and blocked Tracey's exit route. Tyler had come whizzing out of the side door, pulled up sharply to avoid the reversing lorry, cashbox flying open and spewing its contents everywhere. She had had to manually jiggle and hump the bike through the narrowest of gaps between the lorry and the wall, while the unwitting driver shouted at them to get out of the way. She had fishtailed down the road, Tyler clinging on for dear life, her own pulse pounding in her temple.

Learning curve, Tyler called it. Bollocks, more like.

So while Tracey relished to some extent the danger and

risk that these adrenalin-filled cock-ups provided, she was also concerned that while they represented to Tyler opportunities for improvement, honing the plan and building a more robust process, to her they represented an increasing probability of being caught.

And that wasn't in her plans, thank you very much.

But she knew that Tyler wouldn't just let her go if she left, wouldn't accept it as some kind of clean, sudden break. He'd be clingy, she bet. Whiny. Tyler was like a minefield: easy to lay, a nightmare to get rid of. He would beg for a second chance or become some kind of stalker. That was what she was afraid of - she really didn't like the thought of some black-eyed proto-killer creeping around after her, seeking reconciliation and, when that didn't materialise, revenge.

She needed a dumping strategy. Some kind of unequivocal descent of their relationship such that the final kiss-off would be clean and inevitable. Like knocking over a coke machine - you didn't do it all in one go. You had to rock it back and forwards a few times. Build momentum.

# TWO

The first thing Paul saw when he turned back to the waiting kegs was his reflection in the mirrored visor. The second thing he saw was the knife gleam as the figure in the black motorcycle helmet raised his left arm in this shadowed section of the cellar.

Instinctively, Paul dipped his right shoulder away so that any swing from his attacker would put him out of knife range. It was a large chef's knife, sharp as hell by the look of it and, if it had been swiped from the kitchen in The Lamb & Flag, Paul knew it would be razor keen - through lack of use. Davy's kitchen output would never be mistaken for *haute cuisine* and microwaving frozen stuff didn't require much in the way of knife skills from what passed as his kitchen staff. Not that Paul could criticise - his personal culinary repertoire ran a limited gamut from *Saucisson en croute avec sauce brun* to *Digits de poisson et sauce rouge*. He may not have known one end of a mandolin from another but, in his capacity as experienced joiner and cabinetmaker, he was well versed in handling tools which could inflict serious damage. He knew a dangerous knife when he saw one.

The pair stood frozen, spotlit by the shaft of bright daylight streaming down into the beer cellar through the open hatch above. Paul raised both hands and swivelled his eyes this way and that for any kind of assistance or exit strategy. Through the hatchway came the sound of Davy humping a barrel onto the van and shouting down for the next one.

"Come on, Beep!" Davy's disembodied cry rang down in the echoing cellar. "On the clock here. Let's be having you."

His attacker glanced up, startled at the sound of another voice, and Paul seized his chance. He grabbed the empty keg nearest his right hand and swung it round in front of him, just as the helmeted figure slashed in his direction. The knife glanced off the metal barrel with a clang and clattered to the floor. The biker, now unarmed, started to back away, the helmet now scanning left and right for the nearest exit. Paul hefted the keg easily in his giant grasp and launched it straight at his attacker. The slender figure took this solid weight full in the chest and fell backwards onto the concrete floor as the remaining momentum of the metal cylinder sent it rolling noisily to a stop in the shadows.

Paul stood, unsure to what to do next, as the figure scrambled quickly but shakily to his feet, took one last look at Paul and then fled through the swing doors into the kitchen corridor. Whilst Paul hadn't been able to see a bloody thing through that visor, he was nevertheless convinced that the masked figure had glared at him, squinting menace in his eyes, as if to say *I'll be back.*

It was now that Paul realised he had been holding his breath this whole time and he exhaled in a heavy stream and bent down, meaty palms resting on his thighs. He heard a sudden commotion coming from the kitchen and froze again, only to recognise the clatter and growl of the landlord as he hustled down the narrow space between the stainless steel countertops and out into the corridor which led to the cellar. The sweating, red face of an annoyed

Davy appeared through the swingdoors, barking at anyone within earshot which, right now, was only Paul.

"Ere! Who's had my best knife?"

So this was it. This was the official beginning of the end. The coke machine was on the move.

Tyler had come half-running, half-limping round the corner screaming at her through his motorcycle helmet - she couldn't make out a fucking word he was saying, but there was clear and definite urgency in his tone. Tracey had revved the engine and zoomed off almost before he had settled on the pillion behind her. The bike had lurched forward, threatening to wheelie alarmingly with the extra weight and her over-enthusiastic revving, and they had careered down the road with Tyler hanging onto her with one hand and banging her side with the other in a gesture she later found meant slowdown but, at the time, she had taken to mean speed up.

They had rowed as soon as they were safely out of town and tucked away up a dirt track in the forest. Tracey had pulled up at a passing place and turned off the ignition. Amid the summer heat, the woods suddenly felt cool and silent.

"What the fuck did you do that for?" Tyler had taken off his helmet, his hair dripping and plastered to his head, sweat from adrenalin, tension, fear. There were stains under his armpits and his T-shirt was sticking to his back as he pulled himself off the bike.

"Do what for?"

"Shoot off before I was safely on the back? I nearly fell off!"

"You came pelting out of the pub, bellowing and

waving your arms in the air. I took that to mean you needed a speedy getaway." Tracey leant forwards at the waist, hands on her hips, leaning into the argument in case she needed extra emphasis.

"Yeah, well I did. But I wanted to come away alive."

"Well." She splayed out both arms. "Here we are!"

Tyler harrumphed and contorted himself trying to wipe his sweaty head on the capped sleeves of his T-shirt.

"So. What did you get?" Tracey asked.

"My head caved in. Nearly." He sighed heavily and looked at her with his brow creased. She couldn't work out if he was annoyed, worried or both.

"And... the money?"

"No."

"What? Why not?"

"I took a wrong turn and ended up in the cellar in front of some big lump. He threw a keg at me and I legged it." Tyler looked suddenly rather pale.

"My hero."

"Well, what the fuck would you have done, hmm? Bloke was the size of a tanker and I was off-guard."

"The landlord?"

"No. The landlord's a wheezy, weedy guy. This bloke was big." He suddenly twisted away from her, and threw up over a stand of tulips growing by the side of the track. It wasn't annoyance or worry, she realised.

"You total chicken." She spat the words, amplifying her disdain.

"What?"

"You pathetic, cowardly little shit."

"Fuck you, Trace." Tyler wheeled round and his eyes flared black and bright, all evidence of fear now vanished. Tracey hesitated for an instant, suddenly scared, but stood her ground.

"Fuck me? No chance. I don't sleep with little girls." She sneered. Tyler glared at her but said nothing. *"He threw a keg at me and I legged it."* She piped in a toddler voice, mincing as she did so. "Pathetic."

"Yeah? Well what would you have done, huh?"

"I don't know. Maybe, you know, like... fight?"

"He was big."

"So? Was he armed?"

"No."

"Were you?"

"No." Tyler said, reddening.

"You fucking liar!" Tracey's eyes widened and her disgust pounced on her receding fear and beat it to a pulp. She moved in on Tyler, real pity on her face. "You were armed! And you fucking ran?"

"He threw a keg at me!" Tyler whined. "The knife fell-"

"You had a knife!"

"He had a keg."

*"He had a keg."* She mimicked again.

"What could I have done, hmm?"

"Ooh, I don't know. Maybe you could have thrown up on him."

"Ha fucking ha."

"It's not funny, Ty. It is seriously not funny." Tracey shook her head, half in sadness and half in recognition.

"Am I laughing? No." Tyler looked at her intently but she had lost interest.

"Me neither."

"Look." Tyler grabbed her by the shoulders, trying to get her to look at him. "What do we do? We go back. We hit them again. And if he's there again... I shank him!"

"You shank him?" She looked up all right. And laughed in his face.

"I shank him." Tyler insisted, his face steely. "You in?"

"No."

"What? Why not?"

"Something's come up."

"What?"

My standards, Tracey thought. But she just shook her head and said nothing.

Cullen sometimes felt as if he had been born to walk. Trails, woods, fields, hills - the simple act of putting one foot in front of the other gave him serenity and calm. Others chose meditation or yoga, knitted or did crosswords. Cullen walked. It helped slot his crowded thoughts snugly into place and brought perspective and order to his troubled mind. He could feel the cool air on his face, or the patter of rain on his faithful hat, as the steady drip of the miles and the hours passed beneath his battered boots. They'd need replacing soon.

So, perhaps, would his hips. It had been a long time, wandering. Searching but never finding, only the journey keeping him sane.

Over the years he had wandered, his path stretching across the country, spanning East and West, descending down to the very border with England and as far North as Nairn - where his wife had been born. Scotland offered immense beauty and intense landscapes: cold granite faces, stone crags softened with moss, heathered hillsides and boggy moorlands, deep green coniferous swathes hovering over lochs of cold, liquid slate. The air, the sky, were ever changing - the wind could carry signs of welcome or danger, smells of hearth or damp, sounds of beauty or fear. For those who knew where to look, and what to look for.

Cullen had learned this, and more, as he had walked. And across those years, whenever he could, he had sought out shelter amongst the trees. Woods, forests, glades, copses. They hid you, gave you warmth, provided resources and security. The smell of pine needles laid soft and thick beneath the trees, the way the sound of the air was deadened and hushed by the branches, the wind marshalled and subdued, the slightest movement or change amplified and instantly detected. These forests of fir were his preference - his sanctuary - and he sought out their density whenever he could.

He had been hiking for days, slowly and systemically - he was getting slower these days, he knew, and he wasn't at all happy about it. But his route had been methodical, even if it wouldn't have appeared so on any map. Methodical and reasoned, retracing old steps, re-examining long-forgotten thoughts, seeking an epiphany amidst the past. He had come up along the Annandale Way, passing through Lochmaben, onto Moffat, traversing the Devil's Beef Tub before crossing to the Southern Upland Way and heading northeast towards the forests around Traquair. Here he had changed direction again, almost doubling back and heading due west across the hills between Peebles and Stobo, and onto Drumelzier and Broughton. The miles had stolen his hours and his thoughts, his footsteps leading him trance-like over the hills.

Which is how he reached the former railway line, long dismantled, which led to Biggar, its abandoned path running unkempt and neglected alongside Biggar Water and the small brewery which nestled there. There was no tree cover here, no lee where contours hid you from sight. It was a late June afternoon, the sun had been warm and constant, it was a further flat five miles into town and the smell of brewing had hit him like an alien, acrid fist - an unwelcome assault which made him realise how dog-tired he was. He was dead on his feet, his feet had known it for a while, and Cullen reluctantly gave in to their demands.

The small footbridge over the burn brought him up right onto the brewery premises, outbuildings and trailers littering a large flat asphalt square which was fed by a tarmac ribbon to the main road. Behind the main buildings, amidst what there was around here passing for foliage and cover, was an old storage container - a dulled burgundy lego brick, edged and brushed with low trees and bushes. Cullen didn't pause to reconsider, he instinctively knew there was no-one around and he stole the moment while he had it. Reaching the container across the clear area of tarmac took less than thirty seconds and, once there, he was able to duck behind the far side, between the bushes and its warm metal wall, and sit down in the shade.

He nodded off and when he awoke he was initially confused to find himself staring at nettles and brambles close up. He picked a few blackberries and chewed them, their dark sweetness flooding his mouth and he realised he was thirsty and out of water. With a new sense of urgency, he pushed himself back to his feet and ventured around the side of the container to the back doors. All was quiet and still now around the brewery and the sun had a welcome evening warmth to it, but the back of the container was locked.

This rear-end of the storage unit entirely comprised

two double doors, held in place by four vertical rods which slotted into metal housings top and bottom. The horizontal levers which swivelled the housings open were secured inside a covered lockbox in the centre where the door panels met. Accessible only from beneath, this metal lockbox contained a heavy-duty padlock, shiny and new - unlike the steel rods and levers on the doors, which were weathered and rusted in places.

Cullen pondered for a moment, weighing up the different courses of action open to him, and then reached into his pack for his set of lock picks, the barest smile of resignation playing across his lips.

Twenty minutes later, what little humour he retained had evaporated and the padlock remained stubbornly oblivious. Maybe it was some new type of lock, more difficult to crack? But whilst it was clearly new there was nothing about it that said expensive or premium. It looked like any other bog standard padlock. That left the possibilities that he was out of practice or losing his touch. Or just plain bloody exhausted, he accepted. Irritated now, he manhandled his tools more roughly and felt the sweatband in his hat overloading, the salt trickles pooling in his eyebrows. His vision swam and then doubled as he tried, and failed, to make progress. The air grew muggy and he found himself wheezing, the effort in breathing making his ribs hurt.

He looked at his watch, realising he couldn't quite make out what time it was, and came wearily to a decision. Scrabbling back out of sight, he leant against the side of the sun-warmed container, and slid down onto the dry ground. With the heat of the ridged metal oozing into his back, Cullen pulled his hat down over his eyes and let sleep take him.

"Where's the rest?" Carl looked askance at the single crate of beer in the middle of the floor, then scouted around the echoing container - unfruitfully. A forty foot-long, all-metal box with no windows, the recent warm spell meant a furnace-blast sirocco flew out at you whenever you unlocked the rear doors - like a curse escaping Tutenkhamen's tomb. The only ventilation available when the doors were closed were a series of small vents set in regular intervals high up in the sidewalls. Not enough to make the container unseaworthy, just sufficient to allow a trickle of air in and out, so if you spent an hour sitting inside you emerged blinking, sweating and gulping for air like some exhausted turtle dragging itself up the beach after swimming the Atlantic.

Propped up against the bare left wall was a set of low chipboard shelves piled with cardboard boxes, some open. Inside one was a set of sweatshirts, still tagged and in polythene. Further down was an old mahogany wardrobe, locked, which also acted as some kind of room divider and behind it were two stacks of beer crates, some containing unopened bottles, and a pile of empties on the floor beside them. Over in the corner was an inflatable double mattress on top of a large rug, pillows and a uncovered duvet thrown casually across it. An open suitcase lay on the floor beside this bed, unfolded clothes topped with scattered make-up, toiletries and a hairbrush.

The right-hand side of this sectioned-off bedroom was a head-high wall of more boxes, all still sealed, forming a smaller enclosure. Inside this were more beer crates, empty this time, topped with a door acting as a rudimentary worksurface. This was littered with empty fastfood cartons, pizza boxes and opened tins of beans. A two-litre bottle of Irn-Bru brooded half-full over proceedings. Leaning against this set of boxes was a motorbike, with glistening chrome wheels and bright orange petrol tank, the grain on the black leather seats catching whatever light was played on it.

This was The Cave: Tyler and Tracey's home from home, their secret hideout. Out in the wider world they were Tyler and Tracey; here they were forging a new identity and living it out. Here they were Bonnie & Clyde. And Carl - when he turned up.

"'S all there is." Tyler grunted. "Stop your fucking complaining. It's free isn't it?"

"I'm not complaining, Ty." Carl backed off, palms up, at the flash in Tyler's eyes.

"Sounds like you are." Tyler's snarled. "It's fucking free is what it is. And you should be grateful. Don't see you ever bringing anything to the party."

"Don't have your gift, do I?" Carl said, a compliant half-smile on his face. Carl knew better than to rile his friend, knew his place in the order of things and, truth be told, was happy to not be top dog. Top dog meant getting into fights, putting your neck on the line, being a rebel. Carl wasn't big on rebellion. Rebellion for Carl was putting the immersion heater on when his parents went out. No, he was happy to be the tagalong helpmeet, combined bigger-upper and dogsbody. Duties: do as you're told, take jokes like a man, and sit back and benefit from the bounty that the top dog brought to the table.

He was a little taller than Tyler, with a head of shaggy blonde hair and a Roman nose proudly situated between two innocent blue-green eyes. All of which made him look like he'd been to a posh public school and smelled fantastic, though neither were the case. He was a little bit chunkier than Tyler and a little bit slower on the uptake and had somehow been sucked up in Tyler's vortex at High School and carried along like a confused cow in a tornado. That had been some time ago now, but each seemed to appreciate the other for reasons neither could fully understand, so the status quo had generally and smoothly persisted.

"This'll do me anyway!" Carl cheered, elbowing Tracey in the ribs. "What're the rest of you having?"

"I told you." Tyler growled. "This is ALL there is."

"Only joking, Ty." Carl smiled broadly in an attempt at mollification.

"Plus the emergency backup!" Tracey announced, coming out from behind the wardrobe with another full crate.

"Yay!" Carl rubbed his hands. "Game on."

"Forgotten we had that." Tyler nodded to Tracey, pleasantly surprised.

"Right, what have you got?" Said Carl, rubbing his hands.

"Let's see... we have *Hop To It, Don't Worry Be Hoppy, Hop Replacement Therapy* and... *Barley's Ghost.*"

"Barley's Ghost?" Carl wrinkled his nose, brow furrowed. "I don't get it."

"Hmm. Me neither." Tracey admitted, giving a thoughtful little moue.

"It's Dickens." Tyler sighed. "Marley's Ghost. A Christmas Carol?" He looked disappointed at the blank faces around him. "Scrooge?"

"Oh, Scrooge! Got it, yeah." Carl lied, smoothly flipping off the bottle cap and taking a sniff. "Smells like... beer!"

"As opposed to?"

"Just sayin'." Carl looked at the label. "A smooth, caramel-flavoured ale with dark-roasted malted barley and our own special hops to give a unique Christmassy feel!"

"In June." Tyler's lip curled.

"Hmmm." Carl took a sip and smiled. "Well, beauty is in the eye of the beer holder."

"Just drink it, would you?" Tyler ordered.

"Yessir!" Carl happily obliged. "And if someone asks why I'm drinking beer this early in the day I can say I was only obeying orders!" He saluted playfully and then necked the bottle.

"I'll have a Hop Replacement Therapy." Tyler nodded to Tracey who passed him a bottle over.

"Why do they all have punny names then, these beers?" Carl wondered aloud, placing his empty gently on the floor

"It's a thing." Tyler said.

"I can see that. Beer me!" Carl shouted to Tracey.

"The brewery likes it. Makes their stuff more distinctive."

"Huh." Carl nodded and broke the top off another bottle.

"I heard the Marketing Director talking about brand names the other day."

"Ooh, get you! Marketing Director, is it?"

"It's his job title." Tyler sneered. "Not mine."

"Right." Carl acknowledged. "Soz."

"There was some kind of argument about the name for a new beer. This marketing guy was having a strop."

"Strop? Is that a Czech beer?"

"Carl." Tyler glared. "Fuck. Off."

"Ok, ok." Carl sighed. "Funny's off the menu today is it? I get it."

"Funny is off the menu, yes. And the reason it is off the menu is because we nearly got caught."

"Again." Chimed in Tracey. Tyler glared at her and she cracked a weak smile.

"And it is also off the menu because we only have one crate left."

"Two!" Tracey chimed in, pointing at the emergency crate.

"Two." Tyler turned his head, slowly, towards Tracey and she obediently drew a line across her lips with her thumb and forefinger.

"Well, get some more then. Simples!" Carl shrugged, his eyebrows communicating the genius of his idea while he chugged on his beer.

"Simple is it?" Tyler stepped menacingly towards his friend. "And what about the security cameras, hmm?"

"What cameras?" Carl started to retreat, worry on his face.

"The fucking cameras they're putting in tomorrow next door, dickbrain. Do you want me to get caught?"

"Why are they putting cameras in?"

"Because someone has been stealing money and beer from the brewery." Tyler's sneer could not have been more withering.

"They're onto you!" Carl blurted.

"No. They are not."

"And you nearly got caught!"

"No. We did not." Tyler glared at Tracey willing her to contradict him. She held his gaze for a second before looking away.

"The net is closing in!"

"Will you stop squealing like a fucking baby." Tyler's face was now thrust right up into Carl's, his friend pinned against the wall of boxes.

"He's right, Ty." Tracey spoke up softly.

"No, he's fucking not!" Tyler spat, his glare switching from Carl to Tracey and back again.

"Maybe we should stop for a while?" She offered.

"Stop?" Tyler turned away from Carl and moved to the middle of the floor. "Stop? Are you scared?"

"Yeah, Trace." Carl curled his lip, his sympathies latching back onto his friend now that there was some physical distance between them once more. "Think about the beer. If you won't do it for yourself, at least do it for the beer!"

"I'm not scared." Tracey returned, defiant.

"Good. So, the cameras rule out the brewery? Fine. Doesn't mean we can't carry on with the pubs and clubs."

"Hear, hear!" Carl raised his bottle in sozzled salute.

"And I'm not standing for it." Tyler started to pace, weighing his own bottle in his hand. "I've told Trace - we're having a piece of that Lamb & Flag. If that fucking fat bastard thinks he can deny me, he's got another think coming."

"Hurray!" Carl said and then stopped suddenly, cocking his head to one side. "Did you hear something?"

"No." Tyler looked across at Tracey who shook her head.

"Listen." Carl shhh'ed them and they all listened for a moment.

Tyler peered out through the daylight crack between the open doors of the container and saw nothing, but his hackles rose nonetheless. "Carl? Go check."

Carl, recognising the time had come for him to do his share, dutifully rose. "Here, hold my beer." And he stepped out into the hazy evening heat.

Carl blinked hard to try and adjust to the bright daylight after the darkness of the stuffy container. He felt the warm breeze on his skin wicking away some of the sweat it had acquired and curled his head slightly at the pleasant sensation, like a cat being stroked. He peered down the side of the container and saw only a mash of brambles, nettles and bushes which dwindled to a stop at the edge of the concrete hardpad on which the storage unit stood. A few empty bottles, carrier bags and cans lay scattered along the foot of the high container walls.

"Anything?" Tyler's voice came from inside.

"No." Carl stage-whispered over his shoulder.

"Go round!" Came the hiss.

Carl listened, heard nothing, and started padding slowly down the side of the unit. As he neared the corner he heard a loud clink of bottles and stopped, his lead foot mid-air. He swallowed hard and realised he had no weapon on him. Torn between the possible danger ahead and the certain wrath of Tyler behind if he didn't complete his task, he took a deep breath and poked his head around the side of the container.

He saw the back a lime green waterproof coat disappear around the other corner, clinking through a large pile of discarded beer bottles as it did so. Carl sprang forward and shot towards the vacated corner. When he turned it, he saw Tyler facing him at the far end of the container, partially obscured by the figure in lime green. He was several inches taller and broader than Tyler and was wearing a battered leather cowboy hat.

"Who the fuck are you?" Tyler's face had slackened, his eyes hooded and black. He didn't seem at all concerned about the size difference between himself and this stranger.

"I'm me." The man spoke, his voice quiet but steady. Although Carl could only see his back, the stranger didn't seem particularly worried or concerned about being threatened in this way. "Who're you?"

Carl's eyes widened as he saw Tyler heft the beer bottle into his left hand so that he was holding it by the neck, the last dregs dribbling onto the ground, and smash it against the side of the trailer. Glass shards and splinters glittered in the light as they fell onto the grass and an evil smile played across Tyler's lips.

"Let me introduce myself. I'm the bad guy."

It might not be much right now, but Tyler was proud of this place and his booty. He might owe the decorative touches to Tracey but the contents of The Cave - the beer, the boxes, the bike - that was all his. His idea, his efforts, his reward. And if this fucking cowboy thought he was going to nick it, or dob them all in, he was very much mistaken. Tyler didn't know if this man had overheard them talking, but he wasn't about to take any chances. He held his beer bottle threateningly by the neck and glared at the intruder, daring him to respond or react.

Annoyingly the man did neither. He just stood there, silently, his eyes alert and his stance open, both hands palms-facing, spread to either side, his feet apart as if ready to bear his weight for a long time.

The man was tall, around six foot, Tyler reckoned, maybe more. It was difficult to tell with the stupid cowboy hat he was wearing. Taller than himself anyway, and whilst he wasn't bulky he looked athletic and fit. His eyes were grey, almost faded beneath the shade of his grizzled eyebrows, and his face was lined and weatherbeaten - the face of a man jaded by experience and disappointment. There were no laughter lines, no trace of a smile. This face spoke of sadness, resilience and steel. And he seemed not at all perturbed that Tyler was holding a jagged bottle on him. But Tyler was small and wiry, a whippet to this man's scruffy Irish setter. He could bite and he wasn't afraid to attack. He just wasn't sure whether this man cared.

"Talk, fucker." Tyler shoved his beer bottle front and centre, rising onto the balls of his feet. The man didn't move.

"Hello."

"What?" Tyler snorted.

"Hello." The man repeated, his voice quiet but distinct. Tyler frowned, disconcerted further.

"Hello? Fucking Hello? What the fuck is this? What the fuck are you doing here?"

"Looking for a place to sleep." A simple statement of fact. Tyler didn't like this at all. Tracey appeared behind him, suddenly interested, and pulled playfully on a string of her chewing gum.

"Well, tough shit, Granddad. This place is taken."

"I can see that."

The man remained motionless and Tyler turned to look at Tracey, as if to say, *You getting this? Is this guy for real?* Tracey draped an arm over Tyler's shoulder - part assurance, part decoration. She looked amusingly at the man in the hat.

"Cut him, Ty. Cut him." She purred into his ear, and Tyler felt himself getting hard at the thought of taking a slice out of this stranger and then celebrating with Tracey on the mattress in The Cave, a slick of his blood on the floor nearby.

Tyler smiled. "You just barged into the wrong place, Granddad."

"Well, in that case. I suppose I will be going." The man pulled one side of his mouth tight, in a sort of half-smile, eyes on the bottle, but kept both hands out at his sides.

"Oh, not now, Granddad. Too late now. You've heard too much."

"What have I heard?" The man raised his eyebrows. "Some kids having fun in an abandoned storage container?"

"You say that now."

"What else would I say? And who would I say it to?"

"You're not going to say anything. To anyone." Tyler smiled, mock-apologetically, and shrugged his shoulders. "You need something to remind you to keep your mouth shut, I reckon."

"Do I? You have a choice. There's always a choice."

"Choice? No choices here, Granddad." Tyler cocked his head as Tracey whispered in his ear. He switched his attention back to the man, a slick grin on his sneering face. The man looked down at the ground, seemingly lost in thought for a moment, and then looked up and held Tyler's stare.

"Do I know you?"

"I... don't think so." The question threw Tyler momentarily and he blinked, confused, then recovered his composure. "I think you'd remember me. Don't you?"

"Definitely."

Tyler screwed up his face into a ball of hate. "Fuck this. We're done here. You're done here." Tracey withdrew from his shoulder and Tyler lunged forwards, and in one smooth move found himself disarmed and folded up in pain on the grass, clutching his elbow. Somehow the man had side-stepped his thrust, grabbed his wrist and cracked his arm over his knee. The bottle had dropped into the nettles and Tyler's elbow throbbed like it had been removed, hit with a lump hammer, and then put on backwards.

Tracey's mouth fell open, gum-chewing momentarily suspended.

The man stooped slowly to pick up his hat which had fallen off in the brief attack, adjusted it carefully on his head and then strode calmly towards the corner of the container and the paddock beyond. Carl and Tracey watched him leave. Tyler still lay writhing on the ground, trying not to cry out.

The man paused briefly, peering in through the open rear doors to The Cave. "Nice bike." He said, and then was gone.

# THREE

"Chuffing bastard." Muttered Freddie, as soon as he was out of Arthur's earshot. He had avoided slamming the office door, but only just. He paced up and down the warehouse corridor, like a man who couldn't find his haemorrhoid cream: annoyed and pained in equal measure.

His loyalty to the brewery had once again got the better of his anger and frustration. That and Arthur's calm diplomacy and just-bloody-annoying reasonableness. God, he was such a sucker for letting himself get talked into these things. Par for the course, he told himself, for being such a chuffing team player. Yeah, the team benefitted - but what about him? It seemed as if his own personal needs or ambitions continually got put to the back of the queue.

Freddie'd been working here over twenty years, seen one marriage fail and another on the verge of failing. Been denied promotion to Brewery Manager when there had been a management buy-out a few years ago and the new ownership team - Arthur included - had divvied up the management roles nicely between them. He had more experience than any of them - and what did he have to show for it? Ever-bloody-reliable, doormat Freddie - everyone's dogsbody, willing to pitch in whenever and wherever needed to make sure the customers got their orders and the business made its numbers. Meanwhile, he was pulling down the same wage he'd been earning five years ago, had no promotion prospects in sight, and he wasn't getting any younger. That financial adviser bloke that Arthur had arrange to speak to all the staff after the last wave of pension fund changes had flipped through Freddie's figures and sucked his teeth. Sucked his chuffing teeth! Things carried on like this and Freddie'd have no teeth - and no retirement to enjoy them in neither.

"Driving the forklift!" he had exploded at Arthur's proposal. "Accidents are too chuffing easy as it is - that two-ton scuttleshit is an accident waiting to happen. And when it does, it won't just be miladdo who cops it - he could bring down the whole chuffing place, state it's in!"

Freddie was referring to the decaying and decrepit fabric of the brewery buildings that Arthur knew were rickety. The place was leased from the council and had been an abattoir before that. No-one had wanted to take it on when it was lying empty so the council had dropped the rent to peanuts and Arthur and his partners had jumped at the chance. But that had been years ago. And the place hadn't been in great shape even back then. Since the council received next to no money for the place, they weren't in a hurry to do it up; and since Arthur and his partners didn't own the building (and the council wouldn't sell it) they were unwilling to spend money on it without any return (plus the terms of the lease forbade them from doing so without council permission). So they were stuck in a negotiating stalemate which had been dragging on for years now. Meanwhile, the fabric of the buildings continued to deteriorate and the working conditions were gradually becoming more and more pathetic. One good storm would likely finish the place off. Arthur had smiled apologetically and raised his hands.

"Which is why I want you to train him, Freddie."

"Look, Arthur. If you want to give the little prick something to do, there's plenty of manual labour or simple stuff he could be doing. God knows. But the forklift? You need someone responsible doing that."

"He is responsible."

"Right. Whenever anything goes missing, he's responsible."

Arthur had bristled, gritted his teeth and then forced himself to stay calm. "Freddie. Sit down. Please." Freddie had been pacing the office, his agitation and unease clear from both his body language and his voice. He now reluctantly fell into a chair and Arthur leant back in his own and pressed his fingers together beneath his chin.

"Are you making a direct accusation, Freddie?"

"No." Freddie had almost curled up into a ball on the chair in front of him, a small child being asked a direct question by an adult.

"You are referring, no doubt, to the rumours circulating that the spate of petty thefts is all down to Tyler?"

"Yes."

"Do you have any evidence? Any? Of any kind, that could be used to corroborate your, or anyone else's, suspicions?"

Freddie paused for a moment. "No."

"Ok, then. So, let us persist with the old tradition of presuming innocence until guilt is proven, shall we? We will give Tyler - and all the other employees, yourself included - the benefit of the doubt until such time as irrefutable evidence emerges."

"Are you accusing me-"

"No, Freddie." Arthur raised his eyebrows, alarmed,

and rowed back. "I am not. Figure of speech. Just... for me, hmm? Show him the ropes? You're right we don't want accidents, which is why it's important - I think - to have an experienced operator like yourself train him up. How often are we short-handed here?"

"All the chuffing time." Freddie smiled, despite himself, shaking his head sadly.

"You know it. So, having an extra pair of hands - on tap - to pitch in. Valuable, huh?"

"Yeah." Freddie accepted. "It would be."

"And, if his hands are being kept busy working, they can't be busy elsewhere now, can they?"

"So you *do* think he-"

"No. I'm not saying that. But the devil finds work for idle hands, and all that. Let's not give him the opportunity, shall we?"

Freddie took a long, deep breath and exhaled slowly. "Ok. Where is the little arsehole?"

"Last time I saw him, he was having a fag leaning against the spent grain trailer." Arthur slid his fingers between the venetian blinds to squint out of the grimy window. "I can see a pair of feet there now. Guess it's him."

"Figures."

"Freddie? Go easy on him? He's just a kid."

"Kid my arse." And he shook his head sadly as he closed Arthur's office door.

Standing by the small packing desk at the far end of the warehouse, Freddie leant on it, pushing his full force through his arms into the desk and down onto the concrete floor. He looked at the flat-packed gift boxes leaning against the wall. Twelve bottles to a pack, the printed logo on the side: *The Biggar Little Brewery. Smaller batches for a Biggar taste.*

Jesus. So, Little Miss Perfect gets her runt trained up does she? And of course knight-in-shining-armour, ever-amorous, thinking-with-his-dick Arthur "Jurassic" Parke didn't want her to be disappointed in any way did he? Oh no. It was alright for the rest of the staff to be on chuffing piecework or zero-hour contracts but not her. Heaven forbid she got a ladder in her tights or snagged a chuffing nail. No, she had to be kept pampered and pristine until she got down on her knees and sucked Jurassic's dick dry.

And now he had the job of baby-sitting her insolent toerag son into the bargain.

"Oy, soft ollies!" Freddie barked over at the silhouetted figure of Tyler, skulking beyond the warehouse double-doors. "Get your arse in 'ere. There's work to be done."

Tyler shuffled over, his brewery baseball cap on backwards. Christ, look at him, he was walking with a pimp roll, like some kind of gangsta rapper who thought he was so chuffing cool.

"Right. Knocking off time just went back two hours, young 'un. Time to put your back into it."

"I do put my back into it." Tyler's resentment was palpable.

"I'm talking about your work ethic, not your sex life." Freddie sniped. "If you have one. Shaving yet?"

"Yes, thanks." Tyler sneered. "Do it every day. Shaving too."

"Yeah? Well, wanks don't count, sunshine. So get your hands off your cock and start paying attention. Boss says I'm to show you the ropes on the forklift and I'm a busy man, so I'm not going to repeat myself. With me?"

"Aye." Tyler responded, sullenly.

"Good. C'mon, then. Haven't got all day."

Arthur stood by the portable heater in his office and leant against the window, craning to see Freddie and Tyler by the forklift in the far corner. The warehouse was a draughty outbuilding separated from the main fermenting room by a large waterfall of heavy translucent plastic strips. On one side of this doorway were pallets loaded with six or eight kegs each, stacked in piles five layers high. The kegs were all coloured to indicate their contents, with one stack of pallets bearing a series of multi-coloured kegs, looking like the Jamaican flag. These were the special anniversary concoction - initially a brainchild of the head brewer, Damian, who was given licences to experiment and pursue his own ideas to both keep him sweet and, Arthur hoped, provide opportunity for serendipity to come calling and deliver a new, original flavour sensation that the marketing team could then go mad with to drum up a novelty name and label combination.

The last one had been *Hop To It* - a blend of chocolate malts that gave a darker, but sweeter taste, which they had marketed as an Easter special and given a cartoon bunny label with outsize ears. The current one was their *Hoppy Anniversary* special which they were pushing hard to create a closer tie with as many local pubs and hotels as they could before the big brewery chain from Glasgow and the West - rumoured to be eyeing Lanarkshire and the Borders for their next expansion - muscled in and stole the business from under their noses.

Freddie was now gesticulating with that permanently-aggrieved expression he assumed whenever he clocked on, and Tyler was standing with his hands in his pockets looking up, down and around - anywhere but where

Freddie was needing him to look. How could such a beautiful, bubbly, fantastic woman like Angela have a surly, sullen string-of-resentment son like Tyler? Arthur couldn't understand it.

He'd had always had his eye on Tyler, for different reasons at different ages.

To begin with he had almost been jealous of the baby and the adoration, and proximity to Angela's breasts, that the child could claim. The maternal softness and richness that enveloped Angela for that first year or so had driven Arthur to levels of wet dream which had led to bouts of self-medicated masturbation which, in turn, had left him with an unappealing skin outbreak on his penis. He had told his doctor that the soreness was an accidental exposure to some new enzyme liquid they were experimenting with at the brewery. His Doctor had simply said, "Of course it is" and given him a prescription for penicillin.

When the baby had become a toddler, Arthur had felt the need to keep an eye out all over the brewery. It was like being a new father, constantly assessing his living room for sharp edges or things which could be put into your mouth, but with the added problem of it being a work environment, with other people around, and limited control of room temperatures, dangerous substances, traffic and noise levels. Looking back he felt like he had been living on eggshells for a year while Tyler had got the measure of this environment and Arthur had stuck notices up all over the brewery reminding staff to take extra care because there was a small child around and to look out in case he escaped. It had been like working at Jurassic Park, worrying whether this precious creature would escape the confines of his carefully controlled paddock, the only difference being that rather than injure the other occupants this creature would harm himself. He had made reference to this to other staff, jokingly at the time, only to subsequently discover that this had become a nickname they used for him, behind his back.

Arthur had been so relieved once Tyler had started school, he felt that he had suffered disproportionate hair loss due to stress. But he returned during holidays, and even at an early age, Tyler had seemed to possess some kind of talent for schizophrenia. He could play happily and entertain himself. But if you took something from him, or denied him a request, it was like shadow passing over the sun. His face would darken in an instant, and then in a blink of an eye it would be gone. Arthur was never quite sure if it had ever been there but he saw it again and again - enough to be completely unnerved by it. But never enough to mention it to Angela who, it seemed to Arthur, had never seen it.

But over the years, it appeared that other staff witnessed this facial transformation too. Whispered conversations bearing Tyler's name would suddenly stop when Arthur walked into a room. Normally cheery staff would give Arthur anxious sideways glances in the tea room and, when he asked them if they were alright or wished them a cheery Good Afternoon, they would smile nervously and scurry back to their duties.

And, this past year, petty pilfering had become a thing. It had started with Patti on reception claiming that she had lost a pair of earrings, then Mike began checking the levels of petty cash and was convinced there were weekly discrepancies, and there was a steady disappearance of bottles and crates from the onsite shop. Arthur had posted notices around the place saying, PLEASE DON'T

LEAVE YOUR PERSONAL POSSESSIONS IN PLAIN SIGHT and someone had scrawled underneath one of them: CLEVER GIRL. Underneath another: CRIME, UH, FINDS A WAY. When a weekly stock take seemed to show that over 50 bottles had vanished and Freddie was convinced that two kegs had gone walkies from the warehouse over the Christmas period, Arthur had no choice but to step in.

He didn't mention this, or any of his concerns, to Angela. He had just arranged for some CCTV cameras to be installed and now he had asked Freddie to give Tyler something to engage him. Oh, but his mother, Angela. What a sensuous, gentle, loving soul she was! Eyes like liquid chocolate, hair like waving barley, a voice like heather honey, an intoxicating smile, an aroma of soft femininity. One glance from Angela could warm your heart and melt your brain. Angela was a heady brew indeed.

"Arthur?"

Arthur clutched at his heart involuntarily as he was jolted from his daydreaming and momentarily couldn't work out where he was or what had happened. He felt his face cold against the glass and pulled back from the window, turning towards the door.

Patti was standing there with her eyebrows raised. Arthur wasn't sure which of them was the more surprised or startled. "CCTV man's here."

"Right, you are." Arthur cleared his throat, and checked that the front of his trousers was decent enough for him to emerge from behind his chair.

"Where do you want all this, then?" The workman

brought his trolley piled with boxes to a stop, wiped his nose on a sleeve of his once-white overalls and sniffed loudly.

"Well, I was rather hoping you could tell me." Arthur smiled hopefully, waving his arm somewhat vaguely around the draughty warehouse area.

"Not my department, guv. Do as I'm told, that's me. You want er... advice. That's extra. Consultancy is that. Head Office."

"Consultancy?"

"Yep. Not my department."

"Yes. So you said." Arthur wrinkled up his nose and scratched his neck behind one ear. "Well, you see it all rather depends on the scope really."

"Scope?"

"Yes, well there are certain... hotspots I suppose. Places which I would like to be monitored."

"'Nuf said. Point me at 'em."

"Yes, but I need to know that having a camera mounted in a specific position will monitor the scene I need, well, monitoring."

"Ah, gotcha." The man wiped and sniffed again. "Well, you show me where you want monitoring and I'll tell you where I can mount 'em. See, it's not just a case of coverage - that's what we call it, in the trade. Coverage - it's also about where we can run power to 'em an' that."

"I see."

"Then there's the issue of where you position your server. 'Cos you'll need it connecting to your network."

"Network?" The tiny start of a bad feeling was germinating in Arthur's gut.

"Yeah. You want to be able to see the images on computer screens don'cha?"

"Well, yes."

"Well the cameras are connected to a server and the server needs to be connected to your network so that the other computers on your network can talk to the server and see the pictures."

Arthur was now moving sweatily outside his comfort zone. "But we don't have a network."

"Eh?" The workman frowned and pulled a pair of crumpled xerox'd sheets from the back pocket of his overalls. "Says here you got wifi."

"Oh yes, we have wifi." Arthur said, relieved.

"Well that's a network then, innit?" The workman smiled. "Mind you, also says here you've been quoted for a wired connection, not a wireless one."

"Is that a problem?"

"No. Not a problem. It's extra, though, if you want wireless."

"Do I want wireless?"

"Well, that depends where you put your server!" The man grinned broadly, in what Arthur considered a quite unnecessary display of good humour. Like someone who rolls down their window when you're trying to find a parking space and shouts happily "They're all taken!"

"Right. Well, perhaps we can come back to that? So, for instance, I'd like a camera to be able to cover this area here."

The workman cast his eyes around the space, with its scruffy whitewashed walls, the corrugated roof inlaid with ancient cobwebbed skylights. "You got your tall ceiling here. Rafters an' that. We can run the cables along them and down to a power socket somewhere. Is there a power socket somewhere?" He looked wildly round, rather optimistically Arthur thought.

"It's a brewery warehouse. An old brewery warehouse. Used to be an abattoir, actually. Place is a bit decrepit, if I'm being-"

"Yeah, but you got another office over there aint'cha?" The workman interrupted. "Got power in there do ya?"

"Well, the light's on."

"Means you got power. Doesn't mean you got a power socket." The workman smiled. "I can fit you a new one if you don't."

"Is that extra also?"

"Yep."

"Thought so." Arthur sighed.

"Arthur!" Patti's head appeared cheerily through the open door to the admin corridor. She raised her eyebrows, her voice a bright stage whisper. "The Police are here."

"What? Oh. Er." Arthur was flummoxed. He looked at the stupidly smiling workman waiting for further instruction. "Look, I'm afraid I'm quite busy at the moment. Perhaps if you could have a word with my Foreman over there?" He nodded over to the small packing station where Freddie was standing, flipping through a printout. "He could show you the best places for... coverage... and you could start putting the cameras up and do all the necessary... connection stuff. And then come and get me if there's a problem?"

The workman sniffed, unimpressed. "What about extras?"

"Yes, well. If any are needed, I'm sure Freddie can deal with that. Freddie!" Arthur shouted across the echoing space and Freddie looked over. "CCTV man's here!" And Arthur scurried away back to his office to see what the Police might want.

Freddie couldn't chuffing believe it. He only had one pair of eyes and he was using both of them right now: keeping one on miladdo currently trying to guide the forklift between two piles of empty pallets like he was being asked to check someone's prostate; and the other on the stock-take sheets which, again, were showing discrepancies. Now Arthur had wafted some chuffer towards him and scurried off, leaving muggins here to deal with this upselling arsehole wearing overalls and a chuffing perma-grin.

Their initial conversation had been brief and now the CCTV man sniffed, offended. "Top of the line stuff this, you know. We only stock the best."

"Yes, well I can tell it's chuffing top-of-the-line from the chuffing top-of-the-line price, can't I?" Freddie wasn't going to let the man's patter get through his own natural chumminess-shield. "Don't you have anything a little less thousand-y?"

"Well, you see, the problem is that this quote here." The man waved the two xeroxed sheets airily. "Been done by some eejit up at Head Office, clearly doesn't know what they're doing. I can see with my own two eyes that it's all wrong for what you need. You have been misled is all."

"That's as chuffing maybe, pal. But my boss - the arse who pushed you over here, him? He has approved this quote and, between you and me, getting *any* money spent on this place is a minor chuffing miracle. We're only a small outfit you know. Not made of money. So, what I'm looking for is something which will work for us that'll fit into this chuffing quote."

"No extras?" The man's face fell.

"No extras." Freddie folded his arms and waited.

"Right." The man sucked his teeth. "Give me a minute."

Arthur Parke was a good man, a kind man. A gentle man and a gentleman. Thoughtful, sensitive, honest, caring, cheery, who looked for the good in everyone and was optimistic about the future and the prospects for the human race.

In other words, a complete sucker.

From childhood to his current late middle-age, when he really should have known better and at least learnt from experience, he had fallen prey to the petty, the dishonest and the criminal. All who could take advantage of him seemed to do so, as if his openness and hope shone like some kind of beacon above his head, flashing the word "Victim" in all directions. And, like trick-or-treaters attracted by a doorstep filled with beautifully carved pumpkins, the chancers and the scammers came calling. They recognised a quality victim when they saw one. And Arthur was quality all the way down.

He was a middle-sized, middle-aged man, not too tall, not too short. Unremarkable features, where nothing was outrageous or distinctive, arranged in such a way to make him always look a little sunken and lop-sided - as if someone had taken a souffle out of the oven a fraction too early. He had a fleshy nose, slightly askew, bright blue eyes which could twinkle in delight or sink into empathetic sadness beneath his beetle brows, and thick lips which concealed a generous array of somewhat crooked teeth. His complexion was ever-so-slightly pockmarked, such that you were never quite sure if it wasn't just some trick of the light, and his soft voice had a tiny wobble to it which only served to lend him more sincerity and kindliness than he had any use for.

Arthur was losing his hair and gaining a waistline like many a businessman who took insufficient exercise, insufficient care of their health, partook of too many business lunches or drained minibars on expenses. He had always meant to watch his weight, take care of himself, and as the years had advanced, hoped against hope that he would attract a wife before his weight got out of hand. But the hope and the motivation were no match for his lack of willpower. Weekly, he would draw up a shopping list of fruit, pulses and herbal tea and head steadfastly to the supermarket, intent on sticking to a meal plan and a healthy diet, only to find himself stuffing Scotch Eggs and Haagen-Dazs into his bag at the checkout. He didn't know he had done it, somewhere between parking the car and entering the store, a blanket fell across his mind and he sleep-walked around the aisles and only woke up again when he had swiped his card.

Thus was a typical big shop for Arthur, and thus was his life.

He was a sucker for weepies and nostalgia, musicals and happy endings, sad songs and rom-coms. No Big Issue went unsold, no tin-shaker unpassed, no Oxfam bag unstuffed. The Little Biggar Brewery contributed regularly to the local football team, rugby team, weekly open-air market, annual town festival, fireworks and High Street Christmas lights. They donated crates of beer to raffles, tombolas, Rainbows, Brownie and Scout troops, harvest festivals and school fetes. Arthur's partners in the business had given up complaining about the effect on their bottom line and accepted that there was at least some value in the immense social capital and goodwill the brewery built up as a result of all this philanthropy.

As a result, Arthur represented all that was good and noble about the business and could be relied upon to be the happy, smiling, munificent face of grasping capitalism while behind him his fellow managers could smile thinly about corporate social responsibility while they counted the cold hard cash. Whenever there were layoffs, or slowdowns or any bad news to be borne, his partners would wheel Arthur out to do his stuff and explain in pained, genuine, caring tones why this was regrettably necessary and that it was an ugly but unavoidable fact.

Everyone loved Arthur - just no-one loved him enough to want to share their life with him. And he knew it.

God knows he'd looked hard enough.

Once it became abundantly clear that there were no willing and eligible matrons in the local area, he had scolded himself for being so unambitious and gone online in search of love. What he had found had delighted him: an unexpected procession of beautiful women, mostly considerably younger than himself and all impossibly glamorous. The female populace of the Biggar-Broughton-Skirling triangle couldn't hope to compete with the bounty available from his own computer keyboard.

Each lady in turn would express their undying affection for him and desire to meet him, love him and spend the rest of their life with him. If only they weren't so very far away. Or labouring under the supreme difficulty of obtaining a visa. Or unable to escape from their current undercover assignment without having to buy themselves out in some way.

Even sending them money to assist them out of their difficulties hadn't helped and Arthur had found that, one after another, either further insurmountable problems had resulted and they had sadly had to give up their dream of coming to the UK, or regrettably take their leave due to family bereavements. In one tragic case (he later found out from another woman) one of his earlier girlfriends, Mathilde, hadn't disappeared but had been murdered by a jealous ex-boyfriend.

Whatever the detail, the pattern was always the same - not a single one of these relationships had lasted or even transformed into a physical one. Each had started out as a promising opportunity, blossomed into a rich potential which had him floating daily on air, only for life to cruelly puncture his inflatable and leave him watching distraught from the shoreline as his potential partner sank out of sight, waving a tearful farewell.

Oh, all those poor, poor women. Although, many of them hadn't been poor at all. Not financially anyway. They had all been quite wealthy, just temporarily unable to access their money due to circumstances beyond their control. He hoped, with the exception of Mathilde, they were all now at least safe and healthy and had finally managed to gain possession of the riches that events had previously denied them.

Which reminded him: he hadn't heard back from that Nigerian Prince recently.

"Ok. This is just the job for you." The CCTV man had returned from his van with a brightly coloured box, still in shrink, and plonked it on the packing station.

"Yeah?" Freddie waited, not optimistically, to be impressed.

"The XC-1100." The man's smile had returned and he

started stripping away the shrink-wrap to open the box. "New on the market."

"How much?" Freddie wanted to nip this in the bud.

"Don't worry about the price right now. We can do this on appro."

"Appro?"

"Yeah. Look." The man lowered his voice and cast his eyes around the empty warehouse as if about to divulge a state secret. "You're trying to catch someone at it, right? But you don't know what they're going to half-inch next. And you can't afford to put cameras up left right and centre 'cos you're a small outfit. Correct?"

"Correct." Freddie nodded in agreement, despite himself.

"So, this little cutie, you can stick it anywhere see. Rechargeable battery, wifi connectivity, motion activated. Put it in one place, leave it. If nothing happens it'll just sit there. Won't come on. Move it somewhere else, wait and see. If it detects motion in its coverage field it'll automatically start recording. Battery'll give you a week of recording. Almost."

"A week! How much chuffing tape is that?"

"Doesn't use tape!" The man grinned. "This the twenty-first century mate. Straight to disk. On the server. All you need to do is check the camera schedule - you'll see if any video was recorded. Then you can just play it back on the monitor."

"What monitor?"

"The monitor on the server!" The man shook his head. "And if it hasn't done the job for you in, ooh, four weeks, you can give it back. No charge!"

"And if it has?"

The workman passed him a slip of paper and Freddie

pulled a face. "Chuffing hell. Any way we can knock the price down of summat else? Take the edge off this if we end up having to pay?"

"Well..." The man thoughtfully waggled his head from side to side. "We could save a fair bit if you put the server where there's already power and network connectivity. Shorter runs from the other cameras would help too."

"Such as?"

"Well, there." The man pointed to the small hutch of a room with the tiny lit window to one side of the warehouse door.

"I use that as my office."

"And?"

"Fine." Freddie sighed, resignedly.

From outside the open sliding warehouse doors there suddenly came the sound of a collision and many pallets crashing to the ground.

"Chuff's sake. Stick it in there. For now. I'll come and look at it when you're done." He wheeled and charged out of the warehouse, already yelling at the still invisible Tyler.

"Just in here, officers."

Arthur breezed in to the small cabin which Freddie called his office, followed by two policemen in uniform, their caps in their hands. Along with Freddie's desk newly-crammed with a large computer screen, a big beige box humming beneath it and the still partially unwrapped XC-1100 in front of him, the office was now officially overcrowded.

"S'alright Arthur. No need to knock." Freddie sniped.

"Sorry, Freddie." Arthur smiled apologetically and then noticed the new equipment on Freddie's desk. "Wasn't this stuff supposed to go in my office?"

Freddie returned the smile. "Extras."

"Ah, right. Ok." Arthur nodded. "Well, officers, this is it. Newly installed today as you can see."

The lead officer leant over and scanned the screen layout in front of Freddie, running his eyes across what he saw quite expertly. Freddie watched him and his partner, curiously: two young policemen looking like they had only just acquired their newly-minted uniforms. The other officer still stood on the threshold, gazing idly over his shoulder at something of interest in the warehouse.

"What's this all about?" Freddie resented the intrusion. It wasn't officially his office - wasn't officially anything other than a storeroom which he had acquired by stealth over the years, until it had become his *defacto* office. If he couldn't have the post of Brewery Manager, Freddie figured, at least he could acquire some of the trappings.

"Standard visit, Mr...?"

"Hughes."

The officer in the doorway suddenly woke up and scribbled in his notebook.

"I asked for security advice, Freddie. After the last time." Arthur said to Freddie, as if in cahoots.

"Always happy to assist when the public want advice on security." The lead officer smiled. "Perhaps, Mr Hughes, Mr Parke. Whilst you're both here, you could just help us with something else we're pursuing?"

"Oh aye?" Freddie looked up at Arthur who shrugged and raised his eyebrows.

"Yes. We're investigating a series of thefts at pubs in the surrounding area. All customers of yours, as it happens." The policeman flipped open his notebook. "The thefts - perhaps I should say, attempted thefts - all took place at the time of a delivery from this brewery."

Arthur's eyes widened and before he could stop himself he had blurted out "I hope you're not suggesting Angela could have anything to do with-?"

"Who's Angela?"

"Angela McKenna. Our delivery driver."

"I'm sure it's just a coincidence." He made a note in his book. "But we would like to speak to her - as a potential witness. If you could let us have her home address?"

Arthur nodded. "Yes. Of course."

Freddie stifled a laugh. "Wouldn't be too sure about it being a chuffing coincidence myself."

"Freddie!" Arthur bristled.

"Why do you say that, Mr Hughes?" The officer was immediately alert.

"Her chuffing son, Tyler. Sent him home early not long ago. Useless chuffing-"

"Freddie." Arthur attempted a gentle scolding. "Just because he doesn't know the ropes yet, doesn't mean-"

"Arthur, you may think the sun shines out of her arse, but I wouldn't let that little shite out of my sight, personally." Arthur's eyes bulged and he glared at Freddie, but Freddie ignored him. "And there's plenty others here who'd say the same."

"Is that right?"

"Aye, chuffing right. He'd be the first name in my notebook if I was you." Freddie stuck his chin out by way of emphasis. Arthur gritted his teeth and silently shook his head in denial.

"Mr Hughes. You wouldn't happen to know if Tyler McKenna owns a motorcycle, by any chance would you?"

"Wouldn't chuffing think so!" Snorted Freddie.

"May I ask why you're so sure?"

Freddie laughed. "Little toerag couldn't steer his dick into his trousers, never mind a motorbike. Not if the way he handles that chuffing forklift is anything to go by."

# FOUR

Cullen stopped halfway up the climb over the pass in the hills to Stobo, sat on a pile of felled timber just off the trail, and looked back over the valley. The brewery lay peacefully in the soft evening light, the last of the day's warmth slowly rising towards the sky. But Cullen wasn't seeing it.

He was seeing a pair of dead, implacable eyes. Eyes that looked clean through you, like you were an invisible piece of shit, not worth wasting photons on. The kid had looked like he'd seen it all and couldn't give a fuck anymore. Cullen didn't believe in reincarnation. The idea bothered him. *He* didn't want to come back - not to this life. But he didn't think anyone could have eyes like that and not have lived a long vicious life of evil.

But, though this bothered him, something else disturbed him much, much more. Something less reachable, sitting out there just beyond the grasp of his recall. Cullen closed his eyes and reached for it.

He had seen eyes like that once before.

A young man had come to the door, back when Cullen had still been on the Force. A small, dingy council flat, several floors up in a dismal block. Graffiti and the smell of urine decorating the stairwells and the landings. He had opened the door, wearing a vest and jeans and an evil smile beneath that black mirror stare. Cullen had caught a glimpse of a heavily pregnant girl, even younger than the man, lurking in the background over his shoulder, calling out to ask who was at the door. But his eyes were dragged back to this man's face, a sullen dead-eyed look of casual, dismissive malevolence - a conviction that nothing could touch him and nothing mattered.

Cullen had later shown him how wrong he was.

Angela was always tired, often exhausted. When she managed to find a moment to sit quietly and think, it would only take one little thing to send her off down some dark, depressing rabbit-hole where she questioned everything and came up with no answers other than that she felt a failure. Working two jobs and caring for Tyler - and even now he was on the edge of manhood, make no mistake, he still needed caring for. Cleaning, cooking, laundry. She would work tirelessly to provide and maintain, looking for some sign from him that he appreciated it, or even noticed it. The most she got was the occasional tight smile or merest nod of the head. It was as if her son had decided that communicating with the world outside his head was a waste of energy - energy he could better husband and expend on worthwhile things like… well, she had to admit to herself during these moments of sad reflection, that she didn't really seem to know her son at all.

It hadn't always been like that, so her first inclination was always that she had somehow screwed up. The one job she had in life, her role as a mother, was what defined her. What she lived and breathed for. And yet the sole product of all that love and effort and care and hope was an unresponsive, some would say sullen, teenager who showed his mother as little affection or attention as possible. She tried to remember when he was smaller, more active, curious. Had he been a lively little boy, hungry for knowledge and fun and love, and somehow she had missed it?

She couldn't seem to conjure up images of Tyler as a child, now. Instead this same daydream sequence kept returning to her, blocking out everything else. She was on a windy, empty platform waiting on a train. A small child (perhaps Tyler, perhaps not) clutching her hand tightly, saying "Mummy, Mummy! Look, look!" He wanted her attention, her praise, her love. But she was focussing all her attention on the horizon, searching for that train. "Not now" She says. "Once we get on the train."

And every time she looks down, the child is a little older, a little more withdrawn. And she stands on that platform, wondering. Worrying but not doing anything. Thinking: What if, by the time the train comes, the child is a teenager and doesn't want to show me love anymore? What if, next time I look down, the child has grown up and left? What if, maybe... just maybe, that train never turns up at all? What if, I end my days on that platform all alone, wishing I'd spent more time in the here and now with the child at my side, instead of looking down that track for the train that never came?

And then the oven timer would sound and Angela would sleepwalk into the kitchen and take the pie out.

Tyler's father, Iain, had been a wrong'un, and Angela had known it from the first. She just couldn't help herself. Maybe it had been teenage rebellion, maybe it had been hormones and his chiselled features and his insouciant manner, maybe it had just been an attempt to kick back at her smothering parents and say "fuck it." Which she did, and thus Tyler was conceived.

Her relationship with Iain was never smooth - if it was smooth she was after she would have chased after Michael Ainsworth instead. He was Headboy, smart, suave and everything a girl's mother would have wanted in her daughter's boyfriend. But Michael was too neat, too nice, too... vacant. There was more in an Easter Egg. He had no rough edges, no cool remarks. Kissing him, she imagined, would have been like being nuzzled by Tim Brooke-Taylor's spaniel. She wanted danger and adventure and drama and risk - she wanted to feel alive - and Iain ticked all those boxes

He was a teenage dream: experienced, knowledgeable, tough. He could protect her - he had been the cool, hard kid at school that bullies stayed away from and who wouldn't go looking for trouble, but could handle himself if it found him. And he could pay for her - he was an apprentice plasterer and was bringing in a decent wage, cash in hand, every week. Iain was almost twenty, accessible adulthood made flesh. He was all hers and she fell for him. Hard.

But not as hard as he would hit her.

Oh, he had apologised and bought her chocolates, sworn he'd never do it again and said he knew it was his fault. And Angela forgave him and told herself it was a solitary moment of madness, he'd been drunk, tired, unaware of what he was doing. Until he did it again. This time he had meant business. Not some off-hand slap which had stung mentally and physically - this had been a beating. In anger. They had rowed about the coming baby and the costs that were starting to mount up - eating into Iain's weekly wage. He made a tidy sum but he had never been a saver and Angela was still at school. Once her parents had thrown her out and disowned her, they were suddenly on their own. A flat was needed, food, bills, all that was enough. But then infant paraphernalia, more furniture, sterilising stuff and bottles and nappies and wipes and on and on and on. Iain took to going to the pub to avoid coming home to more requests for stuff. And the more he drank, the more resentful he became and the more easily he found a way to justify his bitterness so that it easily twisted and festered into anger at the slightest provocation. And Angela found it so, so easy to unconsciously provoke him: asking him about his day, cooking him dinner, snuggling in on the sofa. It was all too much for him. Too smothering. He was choking and needed air.

And then one day a police detective came to the door looking for him, and away he went. Angela never saw or heard from Iain again. She had no idea what happened to him. She contacted the police but they claimed not to know anything about him. She asked his friends, checked with his work, his parents. He had disappeared off the map and no-one knew when, or if, he was coming back.

So, eight months pregnant and just about to turn eighteen, Angela was alone, expelled from school, parentless, homeless and about to become a single mum.

She built a life for herself and her son. Slowly, painstakingly and tenaciously. Working whenever she could, night and day, falling back on the kindness of friends and neighbours to look after Tyler, living on the knock-off supermarket shelves and charity shops, carboot and rummage sales. She had housing benefit, maternity benefit, child benefit and income support. She managed. It was grim and it was tough and she felt that she was ageing at an astonishing rate. The idea, and memory, of getting dressed up and having a night out some vague, foggy dream of someone else's life - certainly no longer hers.

By the time she was twenty she was at least keeping her head above water, even if it was falling into the sink every time she got home. Tyler's cries and cuddles were sustenance enough and she survived on that. Just.

Mostly because she had an unlikely guardian angel, in the shape of Arthur Parke. She had started working at the Brewery as an admin/receptionist/dogsbody and, as the business had been slowly but discernibly declining, she had increasingly taken on other's tasks when staff left the company, all in search of a little extra money or a little more overtime. Nothing strenuous, but she had stood in for the delivery driver, Eric, when he had been unwell, and Renee who did payroll, after she had retired.

With the management buyout there had been an influx of new owners, a more professional approach to running a business, and a changing of the management guard. One of the new bosses' wives was trained in Accounts, another was a marketing and branding expert who wasn't afraid to man the sparsely visited reception desk and answer the phones. That left Angela without portfolio, until Arthur had suggested she take on the mantle as the sole, permanent delivery driver. She had protested due to the fact that it wasn't guaranteed five-days-a-week and it also meant she couldn't have Tyler by her side. She couldn't afford childcare and working in the nice warm office had allowed her to have a wee playpen and cot for him where she could keep an eye on him and know he was safe.

Never mind, Arthur had said. You can have him in your cab and they had rigged up a child's carseat and installed a special harness to ensure it met all necessary safety regulations. But what about five-days-a-week? Ah, Arthur had said, Yes we can't guarantee that, but we are moving ahead with ambitious plans to develop new product lines, new customers and targetting larger upscale clients who will give us a more predictable and healthy pipeline of orders. Angela had been dubious and concerned, but Arthur was one of the few, kindly honest men you could trust. He didn't have a mean bone in his body. How anyone could ever mistrust him or fail to confide in him, she simply never knew.

But there was much Angela never knew.

She never knew how much Arthur had had to fight and negotiate and argue for those little kindnesses and gestures and commitments for her which had made it possible for her to stay. She would never know how much Arthur watched her from his office window as she carried Tyler on her hip to the cab and hoisted him up into his car seat, her short jacket riding up and exposing her smooth, snapped-back-into-shape midriff. The way she tucked a persistently stray strand of hair behind one ear when she was trying to fasten the seatbelt, the way she licked her top lip with the tip of her tongue when she was checking the delivery manifest, the way she pulled funny faces in the rear-view mirror when she was putting on lipstick before setting off.

She never knew how close she had become to being laid off when the new orders didn't materialise, or how much of her "overtime" pay went unrecorded on the payroll records because it came out of Arthur's own pocket.

But one thing she did know. She had grown to love, love, love her job as delivery driver. As she bounced down country roads, her son burbling happily in the seat beside her, the sun shining and a whole day of driving through bonny Borders' scenery, she would think of Iain, sometimes with gratitude, sometimes with remorse, but mostly with a bitter-sweet combination of joy and sadness when she looked at her son's face. He had his father's eyes and mouth, her nose and chin, and there was something in the liveliness of his gaze when he looked up at her in the cab that made her heart shoot through her ribcage. Those huge, round, inky eyes which seemed liquid and rich and fiercely intelligent. Even before Tyler could speak she knew he was going to be smart. A winner. A son to be proud of.

And he would be her son. Only hers. Iain had forfeited the right to be associated with Tyler the moment he had buggered off. She would sometimes have nightmares, when she could manage to sleep at all, where he reappeared one day on her doorstep and Tyler would fly down the hall, arms outstretched, crying "Daddy! Daddy!" and Iain would scoop him up into his arms, swirl him round high in the air and then the pair would stride off while Angela stood, chained to the spot, unable to call out or make a sound, and struggling to do anything while her son and his father disappeared down the end of the street and turned the corner for ever.

She would wake, crying, her nose streaming, her breath ragged in great heaving gulps. It always felt so real and it would take a few days of telling herself that this was just a nightmare: Iain had gone, years ago. Tyler was hers, and she was his. And that was all there was to it.

And she told herself this every day, as she looked at her son, her chest bursting with love and pride. She didn't need to worry. Her son would never leave her, never not love her. Never hurt her the way Iain had.

Never.

"What were you doing humping barrels in the first place?" Cullen asked.

"Davy's short-handed. I'm a regular. On a Tuesday." Paul waved an arm loftily around the pub as if he had part-ownership.

Paul, also known as Big Paul, sometimes abbreviated to BP and then further to Beep, was not a small man. Broad, stocky, massive, huge. These were adjectives which meant little when you stood them up next to the man and saw how they paled against his frame and heft. He was 6'5", a little more with the wind behind him, and whilst his weight had varied wildly in the past - once even ballooning past the twenty-one stone mark - with the advent of his relationship with Shirley it had gradually settled into a healthier eighteen-nineteen stone bracket. Shirley called this health-management: keeping her man fitter and his lifestyle more compatible with her ambition of seeing out a ripe old age together; Paul called it mithering - albeit not to her face. His strategy for coping with imposed fried-food deprivation and processed-meat portion control was to smile lovingly and resolve to bolt a couple of pasties down at the next petrol station forecourt.

So this man-mountain's stature may have screamed "Beware!" but when you looked into his face and beheld the broad, beaming smile and big brown eyes which glistened in his smooth olive-skinned face, your senses translated this as "Big Ted" and you instantly relaxed into the company of a man whose hands were rough and hard from the carpenter's trade but whose heart was gentle, honest and kind.

And who often had a raging thirst on him.

Cullen pulled an incredulous face. "Only Tuesdays?"

"Alright, Wednesdays, Thursdays and Fridays an' all." Paul relented. "But Tuesday's delivery day."

Cullen smirked. "Busy Mondays then?"

"Smartarse." Paul sneered. "I'm a mate, as well as a good customer. One hand washes the other." Paul swigged down the last half of his drink and wiped his mouth extravagantly on his sleeve.

"With beer?" Cullen questioned, arching one eyebrow.

"Cash as well. He needs some odd jobs doing - maintenance, running repairs, whitewashing. Like that."

"Branching out from joinery then?"

"Not really. My battery's on its arse."

"Battery?"

"In the van. Fecker won't start. Need a new one." Paul gave a tight smile. "Bit short, right now."

"You don't say."

"Aye, well. Can't reliably get anywhere so wanted something handy, earn a few quid, replace my battery."

"And a few free pints." Cullen smiled in understanding.

"It's good stuff, this. Centenary brew. *Hoppy Anniversary* it says, look!" He swivelled the bottle round so that Cullen could see the label, as proud as if he'd brewed it himself. "Glad I helped Davy bring it in. It's on special you know."

"Hmm." Cullen could not have appeared less interested. Paul didn't let that trouble him. The last thing you did with Cullen was go by appearances. It wasn't what he said, or how he looked - it was what he didn't say and what he did that you had to watch out for. Reading between the lines might just get you to Point A, but typically by then Cullen was already at Point D, heading for Point G with a secret plan to get to Point P.

You would end up there too, in the end, and just as you were working out how it had all happened, Cullen would be off and gone and you wouldn't see him again until the next time. Whenever that would be. You had to go all-in, play your cards blind and trust that Cullen knew what was best. Fortunately, this was fine by Paul. He was not the demanding type. *Trust the soup* was Paul's attitude: everything will be alright in the end so, if it's not alright, it's not yet the end. His role was to be ever-reliable, ever-trustworthy, ever-ready. If you needed someone to step up to the plate, Paul was your man - as long as the plate had some bacon on it.

And Cullen was here now, looking for Paul. Which meant he had a plan. Which meant... well, Paul wasn't sure what it meant - other than it was an opportunity to get some free beer.

"Special as in specially-brewed and labelled. Just for Davy." Paul wished to impress upon his friend just how honoured he was to be drinking this particular concoction - partially to show Cullen how clued-in he was with the goings-on around him (not something Paul could usually brag about, or indeed even comment on) and also in the vain hope that Cullen might indulge him with another free drink.

He didn't.

"Oh aye." Cullen said, summoning all the interest of someone being asked to select their favourite dog shit.

"Aye. Well, not just for Davy you understand. That would be a bit much, wouldn't it? No, I mean it's the brewery's centenary. Or summat. You know, anniversary of the first time they... did summat. Whatever. Detail. Point is, they have created this one-off blend and only pubs that are long-standing customers in the local-"

"I'll stick to this."

Paul pulled a face. "What IS that?"

"Water."

"Man, you can do better than that."

"It's water, Beep. Water. Healthy, simple, pure."

"From Davy's tap?" Paul winced. "Plus, you do realise that 100% of people who drink water end up dead."

"Seriously?"

"Straight up. Water is the silent killer." Paul nodded, case closed. "Never touch it."

"Right. Just beer for you then?"

"Don't look at me like that. Beer's one of your five a day."

"Along with...?"

"Well, bacon. Obv." Paul tapped meaningfully on his glass and gave the matter some thought. "Erm..."

"Ok, I'll buy you another. If you explain how beer is one of your five a day."

"Easy! Beer is made from hops. And barley. Barley and hops are plants. QED." Paul beamed. "Beer is basically liquid salad."

Cullen sighed. "QED, huh?"

"Never mind that." Paul waggled his empty bottle in Cullen's direction. "Same again."

When Cullen returned with another drink, Paul gratefully swallowed most of it and then began regaling him with a significantly embellished version of the events from the other day.

Cullen interrupted. "A leftie you say?"

"Aye. Although I can't speak for his politics." Paul replayed the scene in his mind's eye now, to confirm that the biker had indeed held the knife aloft in their left hand.

Satisfied he had it correct, he nodded to himself and made to finish the rest of his beer.

"Did he have dead eyes?" Cullen interjected.

"What?"

"You know, dead eyes. Eyes that kind of looked through you and didn't give a shit."

"Who?"

"Your leftie with the knife."

"I don't know! He had a helmet on." Paul was irritated that he had now lost his train of thought.

"Anyone else see him?"

"No-one else round was there, first thing?"

"First thing meaning...?"

"Well, ten I guess."

"Can't you be precise? Be better than guesswork."

"It's precision guesswork!" Paul cast his mind back. "It was just gone ten. Pub wasn't even open!"

"Hmm."

"Why does it matter anyway?"

"Dead eyes. Left-handed. Motorbike helmet." Cullen intoned, ticking off some mental list.

"I just said, I didn't see his eyes!" Paul sighed, getting as close to exasperation as he could, which was usually a long way away. Paul was not the exasperated type, more the type to generate exasperation in others, and it was unusual for Cullen to be so... unusual. "What's with all this dead eye stuff?"

"Maybe nothing."

"Maybe nothing?"

"Aye."

Paul screwed his face up, but Cullen ignored him, his pupils zigzagging as he wandered alone in his thoughts.

"Build?"

"Uh. Skinny." Then, remembering his embellished story, Paul corrected himself. "I mean, athletic. Wiry. Plenty of speed and agility."

"Fast?"

"And strong. He was very strong. Surprisingly so."

"For one so slight?" Cullen's arched eyebrow could have been indicating scepticism or intrigue. Paul plumped for the latter.

"Aye. He leapt up, despite me throwing that keg at him, and shot away like nobody's business. Fit and athletic, I'd say." Paul considered. "Maybe he's a pro-wrestler?"

"Or young."

"Oh." Paul's face dropped. "Aye, may be more likely that."

When Tyler came home it was almost dark. Angela had tried distracting herself by making an over-elaborate meal, fussing and preparing in the kitchen, all bustle and purpose. Then she had sat trance-like in the living room, watching the light fade while the dinner slowly burnt in the oven.

"Where have you been?" She rose, her agitation zipping from a simmer to a rolling boil at his nonchalant entrance. Tyler could do that to people, she knew, like he was some kind of catalyst. She loved him, totally and completely, but she was under no illusions that her son had some innate ability to ignite fear or loathing in other people merely by his physical presence. She had often wondered whether it was pheremonal or something - an odour which was undetectable but that people unconsciously picked up and had them instantly on their guard.

"Work." Tyler droned. It was difficult to get an

enthusiastic or even multi-syllabic response from her son at the best of times, teenagers being what they were. Boys especially. Expecting a cheery wave and an engaging smile from a seventeen year-old male was like hoping to wake up next to an Infinity Stone.

"The police were here today."

"What?" Suddenly there was fire in her son's eyes, as if someone had just plugged him in. Angela gawped at the transformation and a sharp memory flashed through her head, leaving her momentarily breathless. In the space she left, Tyler prodded: "What did you tell them?"

"What do you mean? What is there to tell?"

"Nothing."

"Tyler?" Angela looked askew at her son. "What do you think they were here for?"

"Nothing."

This wasn't what she had expected. Their interest in Tyler had been confined to a few questions tagged on to the end of their conversation with her. Angela had assumed they were innocent, an afterthought, and that her son would be as bemused as she was by their interest in her and him. Apparently she was dead wrong. "Why? What's this all about?"

"Nothing."

"Nothing? The police come here and clearly there is some reason for it that you - and they - aren't telling me. What the hell is going on, Tyler?"

"Nothing, Mum." Her son was still animated and visibly alert. She was going to get to the bottom of this.

"Don't *nothing* me, Tyler McKenna. What have you done?"

"I haven't done anything!" He was actually gesticulating now and raising his voice, his jet black eyes flashing angrily. "Why do you assume I've done anything? Why is it always me?"

"What do you mean, always you? When have I ever accused you of anything? Always you. What are you on about? And I think, when you are wanted by the police, it is a fair assumption that you have done something. Something wrong!"

"I haven't done anything." He repeated, gritting his teeth, his face hard and menacing. Tyler turned and headed for the stairs.

"Don't you go anywhere without giving me an explanation, young man!" Angela was caught between being furious and bursting into tears. Where was her sweet, placid son? Who had replaced him with this evasive and petulant grunt?

"I'm going to my room"

"You are not. Not until you have told me what you've been up to."

"I told you." He wheeled and his face was a mask of cold hatred. Hatred! Angela recoiled from this face, one she had never seen. Her eyes widened in horror as he glared at her, his voice suddenly slick and menacing. "I haven't done anything."

Angela swallowed hard but stood her ground. "Don't you DARE talk to me in that tone! I'm your mother!"

She was up close to him now, right in his face and his eyes flicked this way and that, focussing first on her left eye and then her right. She held his gaze and waited for a response - one which he seemed to be weighing up. In the end he thought better of it and turned away without saying anything, disgust clear on his face. He headed towards the stairs once more and Angela launched herself forward and grabbed at his left arm.

"Don't you EVER turn your back on me when-"

Tyler wheeled and time slowed to a trickle. Angela watched in shock and disbelief, as his snarling profile twisted towards her over his right shoulder as he pivoted, followed by his arm, extended and swinging in a heavy arc in her direction. She started to lean back, instinctively distancing herself, but her movements were glacial and his arm turned into a hand that loomed towards her. She saw the veins and hairs on it, the bitten nails on his splayed fingers as it filled her vision. And before the pain struck, before the impact made itself felt, Angela watched her lifelong dreams shatter in the back of her son's hand.

"Well, what does Shirley think?" Cullen asked.

"She thinks I shouldn't wash my whites with my colours."

"What?"

"I should wash my whites and colours separately. Apparently." Paul looked bemused. "Some kind of laundry apartheid."

"And you don't think that's a good idea?"

"Nah. Stick 'em all in together. Sink or swim, I say, see what survives. Survival of the fittest innit? Darwin."

Cullen waggled a finger in his ear, trying to dislodge Paul's logic before it took root. "Can we get back to working? I meant what does Shirley think about -"

"Look." Paul leant back, folded his arms and exhaled loudly. "I may not be the sharpest coat in the fridge..."

"Granted."

"But it's like the laundry innit? Darwinian."

"Not for the first time, you have lost me."

"Striving for this, struggling for that. It's like a big

contest, right? And in any contest - EVERY contest - there are winners and losers, yeah?"

"Hence the term *contest.*"

"Exactly! And that's why they call it the rat race. Race, contest, same thing." Paul was gratified to find Cullen was starting to see things his way. "But there are always many more losers than winners. There's usually only one winner, but there's hundreds - thousands, millions - of losers."

"And your point is?"

"Well, statistically speaking then, I am much more likely to be a loser than a winner, aren't I?"

"Perhaps." Cullen said, cagily, reluctant to endorse his friend's fast-approaching conclusion.

"So, why fight it?" Paul shrugged. "Accept your fate with good grace and enjoy what you have. Life's not all bad. Something will turn up. We can't all be Head of the BBC."

"Trust the soup, you mean?"

"Correct." Paul nodded with a smile, his case concluded.

"Drift towards your destiny like... krill." Paul objected to this metaphor but couldn't find a suitable response. Cullen persisted. "Or, take the opposite tack. Throw yourself into your work."

"What?" Paul snorted.

"Work harder. Build a career."

"A career?"

"Alright. Baby steps. But hard work pays off. You could meet your bills, save for a pension-"

Paul cut him off. "Hard work pays off... eventually. In the long run."

"So?"

"Laziness pays off right now! It's a no-brainer."

"Ok, Mr No Brain. If you're not going to work, how are you going to pay your bills?"

Paul scrunched up his features, as if pondering the origins of the universe for the first time. "Well..."

"You're not intending to sponge off Shirley are you?"

"Fuck no!" Paul glared menacingly at Cullen, the very suggestion a wound.

"So...?"

Paul carried on thinking, the silence heavy in the air, until he gave up. "Nope. Got nothing. You?"

"Well, generally if someone needs money they earn it-"

"Next!"

"Or take an income from any savings they have built up."

"Sadly, that train has sailed."

"Or they dispose of any assets they may have."

"Assets?"

"You know. Items of monetary worth."

"Sell something, you mean?"

"It's an idea."

"Would be, if I had anything to sell."

"What about your van?"

"My van? Haven't you been paying attention? My van is knackered. Battery, arse, et cetera. No, wait!" Paul's face lit up, a startling epiphany revealed to him. "It's the soup! Telling me to sell my van."

"The soup?"

"Absolutely!" Paul was triumphant. "How much would you give me for it?"

"Your van?"

"Yeah." Paul prodded. "A grand?"

"I don't want a van."

"£800?"

"You just said it needs a new battery."

"Alright, £750."

"I don't need a van."

"£700?"

Cullen squinted across at Paul and sighed. "Has it got a full service history and a valid MOT?"

"Oh, forget it." Paul stood up, annoyed. "I need a waz." And he disappeared off in the direction of the Gents.

When he came back, Cullen was waiting for him with a strange look on his face.

"What?" Paul asked, senses suddenly alert.

"It's Tuesday tomorrow isn't it?"

"So?"

"So be ready."

"For what?"

"Just be ready." Cullen finished up his glass of water. "How about I give you a tenner to borrow your van for a bit?"

Paul's eyebrows shot up. "How about twenty?"

"How about ten and I'll put a bit of petrol in it."

"It's a diesel."

"And another pint."

Paul ruminated for barely a moment. "You'll need a push to get it going."

# FIVE

The padlock was easy this time. Cullen didn't understand it but sometimes that was just how it went. What was it Paul said: *Trust the soup?*

A warm summer breeze whispered over the paddock and brushed his face as he opened the container doors. Despite the fact that it was almost eleven pm, it was barely twilight and perfectly bright enough for him to double-check the instructions on the leaflet from the box. The XC-1100 was simplicity itself, it seemed. Back on the desk where he had found it, Cullen had keenly read the blurb, installed the battery, checked it had some initial charge, and registered it on the wireless network. It was all too straightforward.

Even finding the stuff had been easy.

He had slipped into the warehouse at the rear of the building, parking Paul's van up next to the brewery's own delivery Nissan. In the dusty, tired interior the shiny new camera sitting high in the creaking rafters above the loading bay had winked at him like a co-conspirator. Tracing the wires back from the camera to the server in the small office, he had found the portable camera fresh in its box on the desk, an unopened Christmas present in June.

The soup again.

He stood on a couple of empty crates and planted the camera in the top corner of the container, above the doors, where it would catch any movement inside. He flicked the switch on the back and waved his hand in front of it, watching the light wink on and off again. Satisfied, he locked the container back up and strode back to the van. When Tyler and his crew returned here tomorrow with their haul from The Lamb & Flag, the police would have all the evidence they'd need.

It was only when he was all done and found he couldn't start Paul's van that he was rudely awakened from his soup slumber. But wait a minute. Maybe the delivery van's battery would be compatible.

Just how trustworthy was this soup anyway?

"I'm sorry." Angela's voice was a plaintive, hushed apology. Arthur could barely hear it over the thrum from the photocopier next door.

"Hey, hey hey." He soothed, adopting a hushed tone of his own, and leant forward in his chair. "You've no need to apologise. You've done nothing wrong."

She lifted her head, the heavy veil of hair falling to one side of her face with the tiniest of head movements - unconsciously keen to look good even in her distress - and he could see a huge red weal across her cheek.

"It's happening again." She sobbed and dropped her head, hiding her face once more.

"What is?" Arthur stood up from his chair, newly concerned, and walked around the desk. He sat on the edge next to her forlorn figure and reached out to touch her hands, only to pause and retract. He dug into a pocket instead and offered her his hankie. "Has Tyler hit you before?"

"No!" She hissed, the tears coming again. "Never. I...

I..." She shook her head and broke out crying once more.

Arthur stood aghast at his own inability to do anything apart from show concern while his heart thumped out his anguish as he helplessly looked on. Angela was sitting in his guest chair, her knees clasped together, hands wringing in her lap, head down, sobbing and trying to hide the angry mark on her face from him. From everyone. Like Angela, he was trying his hardest to hold back his own tears. He needed to do something.

Arthur got up, walked round the other side of his desk and knelt down next to her chair. Without further thought, he put his arms round her and rested his head on her shoulder. He didn't know if this made her feel better, but it immediately did wonders for him. "Come on, now." He murmured, trying his best to reassure. "Let's not have tears, hmm?" He looked anxiously up and through his office window, suddenly worried that someone might see them and get the wrong idea.

Or report him to HR.

Wait a minute, he was HR.

Nevertheless, in these post-Weinstein days anything could be taken the wrong way. By an outside observer, for instance. Or by Angela herself. Arthur hastily recollected himself and stiffened, a change in his posture that Angela detected through his hug.

"Is everything ok?" She whispered, softening in his embrace while he tried to hug her tenderly and maintain a rigid formality.

"Yes." He said, honestly. Something about this felt so natural, so lovely, so close. "Don't worry about me. You've had a terrible shock. It's okay to be upset. Normal. Look, take the rest of the day off. Go home. No - don't go home!" He corrected himself, realising that some distance from her son was called for here. "Stay here. You can sit in here. Or lie on the treatment couch in Sick Bay. I can get Patti to bring you a cup of tea." Suddenly he was full of ideas.

"But what about the deliveries? I can't Arthur, I've got a full round to do."

"Shhh. Don't worry about it. I'll ask Freddie to cover. You just take it easy, try and stay calm. You're in shock. We don't want you driving around like this!"

"But-"

"No, but's. That's an order." Arthur pulled his head back from her shoulder and nodded at her mock-sternly. "Ok?"

Angela peeped at him through the tear-damped strands of hair plastered to her forehead. She smiled tearfully. "Ok. Thank you."

"Good." Arthur stood up, instantly all business again. "So, here or Sick Bay - which'll it be?"

She took a deep breath and exhaled loudly and slowly. Arthur wondered if perhaps he had lifted a bigger weight from her than he had realised. "Here, please."

She smiled again, and with that sad face, her eyes all swollen and full, Arthur thought she was the most beautiful, precious thing he'd ever seen. His heart ached in his chest and he swallowed with difficulty. "Right. I'll speak to Freddie and organise some tea for you. You stay right here." He pointed a finger downwards, mustering a gentle authority, then stood to leave.

"Arthur?" Angela lifted her face, revealing the angry mark blooming on her perfect cheek. "Don't say anything to anyone. About this? Please?"

"No. Of course." Arthur took her hand and patted it, revelling in its warmth and softness, and the way her slender fingers looked safely ensconced in his own pudgy palm. And all the time thinking, *what the fuck am I going to tell Freddie?*

"You'll never chuffing guess!" Freddie exploded the moment Arthur walked into his office. "Our light-fingered visitor's only gone and nicked the security camera!"

"What?"

"Left it here last night - on my desk! Come in this morning - there it isn't. Chuff's sake."

"Yes. Ah. Right. Yes. I see." Arthur seemed to be lost in his own thoughts, not taking in the severity of Freddie's news.

"Did you hear what I said, Arthur?"

"Yes, Freddie." Arthur smiled embarrassedly. "Yes, It's just that, well something's... come up. Angela's not well. Nothing serious, you understand. But I need someone to make the deliveries today."

"Nothing serious?"

"No. She's fine. Really."

"So why can't she make the deliveries herself?"

"Because..." Freddie watched Arthur's eyebrows strain upwards. Either they were searching for a convincing explanation to pluck from the ether and insert rudely into this transparent fiction that Arthur was pushing, or they were trying to get as far away as possible from the bullshit he was shovelling out of his mouth. "Because she can't." Arthur pursed his mouth. "It's a confidential Personnel matter, Freddie."

"It's a bollocks matter, is what it is." It was seldom difficult to read Freddie's mind and not often that anyone could mistake him for a cheery soul. This was not one of those times.

"Can you help me out here, Freddie? Please. Just this once."

"Just this once? What do you mean, just this once? I've been wet-nursing her chuffing nipper for a week - her maternal duties, as his Mother. And now you want me to do her chuffing actual duties an' all?"

"Please?"

"Why me?" Freddie crossed his arms and stood his ground. He knew full well how this was going to end, but he was damned if he was going to let Jurassic here walk all over him without due notice that this was not the way of things. He was the Foreman! He had seniority - in fact, come to think about it, he'd been here longer than Arthur! He should outrank this pallid Pilsbury Doughboy, by rights.

"Because I can rely upon you." Arthur smiled again.

"Because you can rely on me!" Freddie repeated, shaking his head. "Of course you can rely on me, I'm your chuffing Foreman! I think that's probably high up on the list of job requirements isn't it? Reliability."

"Freddie. Look." Arthur tried to put two friendly hands on Freddie's shoulders but Freddie stiffened and Arthur stopped midway, presumably thinking better of it. *Point chuffing taken*, thought Freddie. "I wouldn't ask if it wasn't urgent. And important. I can't ask just anybody. It needs someone I can trust. Hmm?"

Freddie snorted. This was bollocks of the highest order and, like a new Rolf Harris album, no-one in their right mind would buy it. But it wasn't so much that Arthur couldn't really trust anyone else to do it, it was more the case that Freddie *knew* that no-one else could be trusted to do it. If it wasn't for him, cracking his Foreman's whip left, right and centre, the whole place would grind to a halt. There'd be salt in the beer and chuffing sand in the barrels and everything would go to shit the minute your back was turned. If Arthur's wet dream was indisposed, for whatever reason, then who else was going to drive the chuffing van? Freddie knew all this, and knew that Arthur knew it and he glared at Arthur, simultaneously suspicious and resentful - like a muddy dog being tricked into having a bath.

"Well?" Arthur prodded.

Freddie exhaled sharply. "Give me the chuffing keys."

He stormed out the back of the warehouse to the loading area where the van was parked, muttering to himself. Chuffing Jurassic, blindly following his dick around, tagging along behind it hoping it would lead him to the promised land. In the meantime he would fall for any sob story - Freddie had heard *all* the rumours, and believed all of them - any Moomin-faced menopausal minger who fluttered their eyelashes or shed a tear or showed a bit of cleavage. Jurassic'd be on them like a randy dog on the nearest leg, panting and jiggling until a cold dose of reality threw him off.

He blipped the alarm off and climbed into the cab.

Now this one, the blessed Angela, who could do no wrong and who Arthur seemed to worship - fair enough, she was a decent looker, Freddie wouldn't kick her out of bed for farting - and she had scrubbed up marvellous for the last Christmas party - but the fact that she went in and out in all the right places and was easy on the eye was no reason to go all doolally, give her a cushy number, and give her chuffing tealeaf scumbag of a son a job as well. Bugger me!

He adjusted the mirrors, checked the manifest sitting

on the passenger seat and punched in the first postcode on the satnav.

And what was wrong now, then? Did she have the painters and decorators in or something? Was that it? Arsenal were playing at home so Muggins here had to man the pumps and drop everything to make sure the customers got their orders? Christ on a bike! One day - one day - he'd be in charge. Then we'd see. Management? Pah! Just tell people what to do, shout at them if they didn't do it quickly enough and fire 'em if they didn't turn up. The rest of your time, just sit on your arse watching it get fat, and count the money as the tills rang. Piece of piss.

Freddie turned the keys in the ignition and for a long moment nothing happened. Then the van coughed, coughed again a little more reluctantly, made an effort to turn over, then gave up.

"You're chuffing kidding me!" He thumped the steering wheel with both hands.

"She's late." Tyler had been checking his watch every fifteen seconds for what seemed like ages already and Tracey sighed impatiently as he did it again. "Definitely late."

"And?"

"And she's never late."

"Never?" Tracey made a face as if to say *she may be your mother but she's not infallible.* Then realised he was sitting behind her so couldn't see it.

"I used to ride with her all the time, remember? She had a sheet with the deliveries on it, in order, and she would pencil times against them all. Made it a kind of game - something to keep me engaged or entertained. See if I could pay attention and challenge her to make it on time."

"Huh" Tracey swizzled her lips and cheeks, trying to scratch her nose without taking her helmet off.

They were both sitting astride the bike, engine off, at the end of the street from The Lamb & Flag. The pub was set back from the road in a small courtyard laid out, optimistically, with tables, chairs and parasols for customers who might want to sit and drink while absorbing the sun's rays for the nanosecond between it rising over the towering rooftops of the solicitor's office on the third floor opposite, and setting behind the church clock tower which clanged out every fifteen minutes and represented the only external sound which could drown out the traffic as it hurtled down the street and out of town.

They were parked at the far end of a row of cars, just before a set of commercial blue waste bins, and had a clear view of the whole road, including the junction with the High Street from which any delivery van would emerge, the road being a one-way street. Opposite the pub was a small row of shops: a newsagent, a florist, a chippie, an estate agents and a bookies. Most of the daily traffic was small cars which would briefly pull up outside the shops, leave their indicators on, while their occupant bought a paper, put a bet on or ordered a quick fish supper, only to depart to the general honking of horns and semi-audible "away with ya" which accompanied any attempt to flout local parking restrictions by other motorists attempting to do the very same thing.

The morning was warm already and Tracey was uncomfortable behind her visor, sweat from her forehead and cheeks soaking gently into the enveloping helmet padding. She lifted her visor and turned round on the bike to half-face Tyler.

"Go in anyway." She urged. "There's no reason to wait for the van."

"There is." Tyler hissed. "It's the plan. The delivery is a distraction. Staff busy loading and unloading, moving crates and barrels. Easier for me to nip in and out."

"Like last time?" She couldn't resist a dig and could almost feel him bristle on the pillion behind her. He flipped his own visor up angrily.

"Last time was... unfortunate."

"Maybe he'll be there again."

"Good." Tyler shrugged, defiantly. "I see no reason why he would be, but if he is - I'll be ready for him." He patted one zipped chest pocket with his left hand and smiled, a devil's smile. Tracey's heart leapt.

"Go on." She whispered, her voice dropping a register to what she hoped was insistent and sexy at the same time. "Why wait? You're good enough. Your plan's good enough." She reached around with her right hand and stroked his thigh, rising up towards his crotch. "No need for any... distraction is there?"

Tyler swallowed audibly, suddenly uncomfortable, and checked his watch again seeming to ignore her caress. He squinted as he surveyed the largely empty street with still no sign of an approaching van.

"Go on!" Tracey's eyes glistened, her hand continuing its wandering, and she bobbed her head slightly upwards in encouragement. "I dare you."

Tyler locked eyes with her for the briefest moment and she saw the blackness in them flare. He flipped his visor decisively down, swung his leg off the bike and strode over the road towards the pub.

"Are you sure you don't need my help?" Paul's voice was almost an uncomprehending whine as he called to Davy through the open cellar door.

"Be fine!" Davy yelled back. "She's late, any road. Maybe she's not coming. Better that you focus on the job in hand right now, mate." He left the rest of the sentence *"And let me keep my kegs undamaged this time."* unsaid.

Paul sighed, disappointed, and bent once more to dip the large brush into the bucket of whitewash. True, he was a bit fed up with joinery; true, he was happy to do a bit of mindless manual labour in exchange for a few pints and a few quid towards a new battery; true, he was never happier than when he was in The Lamb & Flag - except when he was with Shirley, natch. Wouldn't want Shirl to think she came second to the pub. Perish the very thought.

But whitewashing? He couldn't get worked up about it. It had been fine at the start, transforming the dirty, dusty walls to a bright and new white, if not brilliant-white then at least new-improved-off-white-with-a-hint-of-cobweb-white. But the novelty had worn off, mostly because this bending down and dipping his brush then straightening up and painting the walls was playing hell with his back and physical flexibility was not Paul's long suit. Shirley had once asked him what his long suit was and Paul had just grunted evasively and then gone to look it up. Turned out it was something to do with Bridge, the card game, which didn't help. About the only thing Paul knew about Bridge was that it was like sex - if you didn't have a good partner, you needed a good hand.

He smiled at the thought of Shirley, his partner, and their last tangle in the sheets. Temporarily revived by this memory, he looked down at the half-empty bucket and the last wall, only two-thirds done and then sighed again. Maybe if he could finish this off before lunchtime, nip home and catch Shirley on her lunchbreak? Paul smiled at the idea, almost attempting a cheery whistle, and then decided he would crack on and do just that.

After he'd had a quick waz.

Tracey was on high alert the minute Tyler disappeared from view. She started the bike and kept nervously revving the engine, reminding herself she was set to fly the moment he flung himself onto the seat behind her. Her pulse was racing and she felt hot and anxious and excited and horny, all at the same time. This was the high she sought - the excitement and danger and adrenalin of this moment and the one soon to come when Tyler would fly out across the road, she would flip her visor down and, racing with him clinging onto her for dear life, shoot the tight bend at the end of the street and vanish from sight. They would scream and shout with relief and excitement, inaudible inside their helmets, as they rocketed out of town and made their way back to The Cave, where they would hungrily tear at each other's clothes, wrestle themselves half-naked onto the mattress and have hot, thrashing, noisy sex.

Then, when she came down from the high, she'd remember the coke machine and the need to be shut of him.

She flicked her eyes between the open side door to the pub that Tyler had slid in through, and the end of the street for signs of the overdue delivery van. Back and forth, like a metronome, she started to lose herself to the rhythm and began counting the beats as a way of keeping her heart rate under control: pub-one-two-three, van-one-two-three, pub-one-two-three, van-one-two-three.

Hypnotised, it took her a second or two to actually notice that the motorbike engine beneath her had cut out.

Paul was zipping his fly when his phone pinged in his pocket. He took it out and swiped the screen.

INCOMING.

That was all the message said. It was from Cullen.

Christ, what was it with the man? Plans and cryptic messages and shit. Just talk to me, man. Fill me in. I'll understand. He opened the door and stepped out into the corridor, stabbing grumpily at his phone.

Incoming what?

Like a freight train on a collision course, Tyler sprinted around the corner of the corridor as if he was on rails, and then ploughed straight into a large mass moving towards him. His momentum carried him partially over the object, which had collapsed into a pile below him, but still represented a hurdle sufficiently high that he was unable to leap over it. Tyler went down at the second time of asking, the cashbox spraying its contents of silver and notes all across the slippery tiled floor.

When he got to his feet, he still had the knife in his hand and the hurdle had revealed itself to be the crumpled shape of the big bastard who had twatted him with a keg last time. This time he was unarmed and there were no kegs, or anything else for that matter, within reach. Tyler held the knife out threateningly, its blade gleaming in the overhead strip light, and the large man held both his hands up and started backing away towards the double swing-doors.

"Don't do it, kid." The man pleaded. "Not going to end well."

"Oh yeah?" Tyler sneered, pushing forward still as the man continued to retreat. "Why's that then, porky?"

The man was up against the doors now and he backed through them into the cellar and Tyler's hackles rose, the musty memory of this room fresh in his nostrils. The voice of an insistent Tracey rose in his mind to address him:

*Get the bastard!*

We don't want anything within reach that he can use as a weapon!

*Then strike now and get out!*

But the clock is ticking - and the cash is gone.

*Yeah, again! And this is the guy who denied you. Twice!*

But the plan!

*The plan's toast. Shank him!*

Maybe I can just shut him in and grab some notes off the floor?

*It's a swing-door dummy. Cut him - now! And let's go.*

The dialogue ricocheted back and forth in his head as he forced the man further into the cellar, his options narrowing with every step. Tyler was just about to win out when his vision suddenly went completely white.

"What the-?" Tracey had looked down at the bike to restart the engine, noticed the key was suddenly missing, and then looked up again. Her outrage was simultaneously extinguished by four things:

1. The delivery van had just appeared at the top of the street.

2. Her ignition key was dangling brightly from a large thumb and forefinger, right in her eyeline.

3. The thumb and forefinger belonged to the man in the cowboy hat they had threatened at The Cave.

4. He was smiling at her.

"Hello again." He said, brightly. "Revving and idling?" He tutted, shaking his head. "Think of the pollution."

"Give me my key back, dickbrain." She said through a clenched jaw, her eyes narrowing.

Neither of these things seemed to make any impression on the tramp. He screwed up his nose and waggled his head from side to side, as if in thought.

"Nah." He said, obviously having arrived at a decision.

Then he launched the key overarm, sending it arcing through the clear blue sky and plopping gaily into the brightly burbling stream which ran along a ditch beyond the edge of the road.

Paul looked on with some satisfaction as the idiot in the motorcycle helmet careered off the cellar walls like a demented pinball. It had obviously dawned on the punk that the thing to do was lift his visor, freshly daubed as it was now with whitewash, but presumably he was reluctant to do this as he realised Paul would then be able to identify him. Whatever, his loss. Paul stood amused at the Keystone Cops effect of this blinded buffoon trying to grapple his way to the exit through the use of touch and memory alone.

Paul reached to dip his brush into the whitewash bucket for a second coat but when he looked up again, somehow the kid had found the exit and was rebounding off the corridor walls following the scent of the outdoors like an injured homing pigeon with a faulty compass.

Chuffing technology, thought Freddie. Chuffing hate it. What's wrong with pen and chuffing paper? Was good enough a few years back. Now they've got to reinvent everything. Can't have a pencil, have to have a stylus. That doesn't work as well as a pencil. Can't have paper, have to have a touchscreen. Which doesn't work as well as paper, can't be seen in the sunlight and needs a chuffing battery!

He stabbed at the now useless satnav, wanting to kill the current job and type in the postcode for the next delivery. Sure, he should probably wait until he'd actually made this delivery, but he was chuffing late! This piece-of-shit van needed three Hail Mary's and a pushstart before it would go and he'd taken to leaving it idling at the last two jobs, hoping it didn't conk out on him while he left it running. And, now he was low on diesel! Bugger me - what else could go wrong?

He grabbed for the manifest with one hand as he steered down the narrow car-lined street with the other. Someone somewhere honked and he hoped for their sake it wasn't at him, or they would get what was coming to them. Just as soon as he'd dropped these chuffing crates off at the... what was it? The Lamb & Flag. At least it was a proper pub name. There was another thing they couldn't bloody leave alone - pub names. Days gone by it was The George, The Prince Of Wales, The Red Lion. Now it was all Three Cockles On The Nightstand, or The Kipper In Short Trousers, or some other chuffing bollocks.

Oh, just wait until he got back to the Brewery and gave Arthur a piece of his mind. He'd think twice about sending him out to do the job his bit of skirt should be doing, by

Christ. It was one chuffing thing after-.

In a heartbeat, Freddie's fuming turned to cold, cold shock as he slammed on the brakes.

It soon occurred to Tyler that, if he was going to escape at all, he had better address his vision problem. This he did by wiping a sleeve across his visor, thereby succeeding in smearing the white mess further and bouncing off the wall again. It was like trying to see out of dirty bathroom porthole while sitting in a one-man bobsleigh.

He lifted his visor which granted some blinkered but clear visibility and took a sharp left towards the bright daylight broadsiding through the open fire-door. As he emerged blinking into the fresh air, clattering through the empty tables and chairs littering the forecourt, his visor slithered stupidly shut again, the whitewash acting as some kind of infuriatingly effective lubricant. He grappled with it, trying to wrestle it free as he half-hurdled, half-ran towards the road and he hoped - because he certainly could no longer see - a waiting Tracey.

Inside his helmet that he swore he would never, ever wear again, Tyler was incandescence itself - a sulphurous flame ignited by a failure to retrieve the money, fuelled by a second defeat at the hands of a bludgeoning loaf and the realisation that he had dropped his knife (again), and fired by a shame that, for all his planning and calculations, he was failing to live up to his own expectations (and, he knew, Tracey's). Only this flame didn't burn with a cool, liquid blue; it burnt with an angry, livid black. As black as his heart, as black his fury, as black as his eyes.

And as black as the radiator grill on the approaching delivery van as Tyler stepped wildly into its path.

## SIX

The good weather broke the following week, the June rain returned and the chairs and tables on The Lamb & Flag forecourt stood neglected while inside Paul gulped thirstily at his pint.

"Not bad." Paul, seeing Cullen's expression, slowed his pace and took a sip, trying to nod as appreciatively as a connoisseur - which, in the realm of beer, he supposed, he probably was. "Nutty. Some caramel in there. Aye. Not bad."

"It's called *Pulling Out All The Hops*." Cullen gave a wry smile. "It's alcohol-free."

Paul spat out his mouthful, splattering Ant & Dec at his feet. They barely looked up. "What d'ya give me that for?"

"You said you liked it."

"That was before I knew it wasn't beer."

"It is beer. Alcohol-free beer."

"Contradiction in terms." Paul stated, wiping his mouth with one grubby sleeve, trying to remove the remnants of the taste. "Like vegan sausages. Or American chocolate."

"It's a very popular range, the guy at the bar said."

"With women."

"With non-drinkers."

"Same thing." Sniffed Paul, sitting back, arms folded defiantly at the pint in front of him. "I'm supposed to be celebrating and you give me cat's piss."

"It's alcohol-free beer." Cullen reiterated, as calmly as he could manage. "And what, exactly, are you celebrating?"

"Vanquishing the miscreant." Paul raised an eyebrow proudly.

"Vanquishing the miscreant? You been reading a book again?"

"'Swhat I did."

"By miscreant you mean Tyler McKenna?"

"The very same. Who I twice foiled in his attempts to steal Davy's valuables"

"Does Davy have any valuables?"

"Obv!" Snorted Paul. "Or why would Tyler have been robbing the place? Twice?"

Cullen ignored this circular logic. "And by vanquishing you mean chasing away, so that he fled into the path of an oncoming vehicle?"

"No. I mean obscuring his vision with whitewash from my bucket so that he could be apprehended by the authorities."

"You *have* been reading a book."

Paul ignored him. "Whilst being assaulted."

"You or him?"

"Me! He was going to assault me - again! With a knife - again!"

"Right." Cullen sighed. "Well, beats my plan I suppose."

"Yeah, about that. You could try sharing you know - I'm not a complete bell-end. Incoming." Paul snorted.

"No. You're not."

"So what was the plan then?

"That was my backup plan."

"I was your backup plan?"

"Backup plan to keep you safe." Cullen gave a thin smile.

"Ah, Cullen's got a plan so we're all safe are we? I didn't feel safe with a knife pointing at me."

"Would you have felt safe if you'd known it was part of a plan?"

"Part of a backup plan? That didn't work, you mean?" Paul sniped.

"My first plan was better."

"And what was that?"

"Doesn't matter now, does it?"

"Doesn't it?" Paul was aggrieved. "So you had two plans and you didn't share either of them with me. If I want life to tell me '*bite the pillow, I'm going in dry*' I'll let you know. Maybe next time, a bit more lubrication-"

"That's quite a disturbing mental picture."

"It's a metaphor. Lubrication in this instance is-"

"I get it."

"Yeah, well. You want a plan to succeed, maybe sharing increases its chances - all I'm saying."

Cullen sighed again. "Quite the pub philosopher, aren't you? What with this and the soup."

"Well, its the soup what won it!"

"Hmm." Cullen pondered this for a while. "Tell me more about this soup then."

"You wouldn't understand." Paul smirked. "It's a metaphor."

"Another one."

"What do you want to know about it?"

"Never mind. Cheers." Cullen raised his glass. "To vanquishing the miscreant."

"Aye." Paul scowled at him, not wanting to raise his

own. "And to the magical transformation of my van, now a smoothly-starting miracle machine."

"Really?" Cullen remained impassive.

"Straight up. Since you brought it back, starts like a dream." Paul leaned in close. "What did you do to it?"

"Nothing." Cullen lied. "Must be the soup."

"Eh?"

"The soup that was telling you to sell your van, is now telling you your battery's fine. Get back in the joinery saddle."

"The joinery saddle?"

"It's a metaphor."

"Huh." Paul thoughtfully took a swig from his pint, then put it down swiftly, remembering the contents.

# POSTSCRIPT

**Tyler McKenna** was charged with assaulting his mother, **Angela McKenna**, two counts of attempted armed robbery from The Lamb & Flag, and four other robbery and attempted robbery offences. Tyler did not make a statement, declined to testify at his trial and is now currently in detention at HM Young Offenders Institute Polmont, near Falkirk. As a result of the injuries he received in the road accident he is no longer able to ride a motorbike.

**Tracey Marshall** was never arrested, since Tyler never made any statements regarding his crimes, and was able to return to The Cave and squirrel away Tyler's motorbike and all other incriminating evidence. She has been spending every evening since the summer searching a ditch for the ignition key.

**Angela McKenna** fell headlong into the arms of **Arthur Parke** and has barely come up for air since. Finding a man incapable of abusing her made her feel like a new woman and, in the process, released many pent-up desires. Their relationship was consummated on a mattress they found in an abandoned storage container at the rear of the brewery.

**Freddie Hughes** was subsequently promoted to Brewery

Manager after he diplomatically confronted Arthur with video evidence of his and Angela's liaison in the container. He was, and remains, chuffing delighted.

**Arthur "Jurassic" Parke** returned the XC-1100 security camera within the agreed four week approval period, free of charge. He has cancelled all memberships of internet-dating sites and has since focussed his romantic attentions on Angela McKenna. He is still waiting on a response from that Nigerian Prince.

**"Big" Paul McInnes** continues to embellish the story of how he saved The Lamb & Flag. Davy is getting quite sick of hearing it, especially now that Paul finishes it with a lame joke about how Tyler was done for assault but Paul got the battery.

**Mungo James Cullen** went back to Biggar to scavenge what he could from what was left in The Cave. Amongst his finds were three cans of orange spray paint that he believed he might be able to find a use for, one day.

# AUTHOR'S NOTE

My thanks to Broughton Ales Brewery and David McGowan who gave me twelve free bottles of beer. Sorry, I mean a tour of the brewery. For research purposes. Hopefully the punny names I came up with for some of their beers will be useful in any future marketing ventures (perhaps in at least ruling them out as ideas to follow up!) and help offset the fact that I changed the name of the brewery and made up Arthur, Freddie, Angela et al. They bear no resemblance to employees of the brewery, past or present.

I apologise for not featuring other brewery-specific aspects more prominently in the plot, but the delivery van/rider angle was enough I felt. One of the problems with novellas - at least the way I write them - is that they are too short to allow for an intricate comeuppance for the bad guys. In a novel there is room to build a plan and resolve it, taking multiple strands and weaving them tightly together to form a satisfying conclusion to the narrative. In a novella, it's: "Ach, I'm out of pages!"

Thank you to my Beta readers Deidre M, Lynn H, Pete B and John K and Jane - their comments and typo-catching facilities have greatly improved the book you've just finished reading.

Biggest thanks must go, again, to Claire who gave me heaps of constructive feedback and comment on the tone and plot when I foolishly thought it might be finished. The changes I made as a result have hugely improved the final story. You, dear reader, will never know how embarrassed I would be if I had to send each book out in its "alpha" form for you to buy.

Finally, a shout out to the soup. This book is dedicated to it and you, too, could learn to trust the soup.

Or not. It's up to you.

I'm not bothered.

mjf
23.3.2019

## Join the Cullen & Big Paul Fan Club!

If you enjoyed the adventures of Cullen and Big Paul, why not join their fan club? You'll get early notice of new books, special offers, a monthly newsletter from the author, unique free content, invitations for discounts and more!

JOIN at **download.markfarrer.com/signup**

## Tell others what you thought...

If you enjoyed this book, please leave a review on Amazon

## About the Author

You can learn more about Mark Farrer at **www.markfarrer.com** or follow him on Twitter **@mark_farrer.**

Printed in Great Britain
by Amazon

78876685R00203